David Ashton was born in Greenock in 1941. He studied at Central Drama School, London from 1964 to 1967, and most recently appeared in *The Last King of Scotland*. David started writing in 1984 and has seen many of his plays and TV adaptations broadcast — he wrote early episodes of *EastEnders* and *Casualty*, as well as the *McLevy* series for Radio 4.

You can visit the *McLevy* website at www.inspectormclevy.com

and discover more about the author at www.david-ashton.co.uk

SHADOW OF THE SERPENT

1880, Edinburgh: Election fever grips the city. But while the rich and educated argue about politics, in the dank wynds of the docks it's a struggle just to stay alive. When a prostitute is brutally murdered, disturbing memories from thirty years ago are stirred in Inspector McLevy, who is soon lured into a murky world of politics, perversion and deception — and the shadow of the serpent.

DAVID ASHTON

◆

SHADOW OF THE SERPENT

An Inspector McLevy Mystery

Complete and Unabridged

CHARNWOOD
Leicester

First published in Great Britain in 2006 by
Polygon
an imprint of Birlinn Ltd
London

First Charnwood Edition
published 2017
by arrangement with
Two Roads
an imprint of Hodder & Stoughton
London

A catalogue record for this book is available
from the British Library.

ISBN 978–1–4448–3458–1

Published by
F. A. Thorpe (Publishing)
Anstey, Leicestershire

Set by Words & Graphics Ltd.
Anstey, Leicestershire
Printed and bound in Great Britain by
T. J. International Ltd., Padstow, Cornwall

This book is printed on acid-free paper

TO
TOM CHISHOLM
a straight driver

1

The Diary of James McLevy

There is a legend that after Lucifer had been cast into hell, God granted him the one wish to make up for what must have been a severe disappointment.

Satan thought long and hard, then averred that he would wish to grant mankind the gift of desiring power.

God could see no harm in that: He Himself had possessed supreme omnipotence for all eternity and see the good job He'd made of it.

So, God granted the wish.

And Satan has been laughing ever since.

I have reached my third coffee. The cup has left a yellow ring at the top of the page where I write but nothing is perfect. Not even myself.

I am James McLevy, inspector of police. I record in this wee book what the French call my 'pensées', or what the Scots would term 'whatever passes through a body's mind'.

My existence is a struggle between personal human frailty and the desire to serve justice. An exactitude forever compromised by the very people who framed the laws they now wish to bend.

I look back to see the anguish and pain I

have caused for others and caused to myself by the unyielding pursuit of justice. I look ahead and see much the same prospect. So be it.

Break the law, high or low, I'll bring ye down. Suffer injury, high or low, I will avenge ye. To the best of my compromised ability.

I'm down to the dregs now. Coffee is like blood in my veins.

Out of my attic window, I can see a thousand torches flickering in the sky from the direction of Waverley Market.

They light the way to power. Politics. The dunghill upon which many a cock has crowed.

I turn the other way and look out over my kingdom.

2

Who finds the heifer dead and bleeding fresh
And sees fast by a butcher with an axe
But will suspect 'twas he that made the
   slaughter?

WILLIAM SHAKESPEARE,
Henry VI, Part 2, 3, 2

Leith, March 1880
Sadie Gorman shivered as the cold east
Edinburgh wind bit into her bones. No place to
hide. She looked down at her dress, dirty yellow
like the lamplight and thin as a winding sheet.
What kind of life was this? She should have
decent drawers, keep her old bones warm and
cosy, but no, she had to be accessible to all
comers. Shed her shanks to liberal or conservative. All comers.

She laughed suddenly and the sound echoed
in the silence of Vinegar Close. It was late, past
midnight, other folk in bed, ten to a room, drunk
men snoring, children clenching knees to keep
the contents of their wee bladders at bay, and the
women?

Well, whatever they were, at least they were
spared standing on a corner in Leith on a dank
March night, hoping for some mortal old
fornicator fuddled with drink on his way home
from the big meeting. On his way home, but,
Christ Jesus this wind was cold, just enough

3

blood in his veins to prove that a standing cock has nae conscience.

The gaslight flickered and she caught sight of her image on the other side of the street, reflected in the oily glass of one of the half-uncles, the wee pawn shops, dotted round the closes. A shop she'd been in many a time herself, the door well locked, window empty save for this daft soul in a yellow dress slavering back at her.

Look at the sight. The woman was ancient, for God's sake, if she was a day. A single white feather stuck in the back of her wispy hair added a gay touch to the shipwreck.

What year was it now? Soon she'd be coming up to fifty. Sadie shared a birthday with Queen Victoria, May the 24th. That day Her Gracious Majesty would be a sight older but better preserved. People would kiss her hand, kiss her backside if they could find such under all those skirts and petticoats and God knows what else. Aye they'd get lost in there, choke on all that flannel guarding the Queen's private parts, choke, kiss her backside and sing the National Anthem. All at the same time. On their knees.

She walked across the street and looked closely at herself in the glass. By God, she was a treat to behold. Face white with powder and chalk, eyes black as pitch, cheeks rouged up like a paper doll and her mouth a big red gash. Not exactly a shrinking violet but what's a shop without a sign? She opened her lips, and pouted comically at herself. A big mouth. Her speciality.

In the silence, faintly, the sound of a child

4

whimpering from one of the black, grim, warren of houses in the close, then it was quiet.

Set out with high hopes this night, high hopes. Some palaver-merchant had been blowing up a storm at Waverley Market, big crowds, men getting demented over politics. That was good, good for business; they would spill down the hill to Leith, lash out their money and their love-drops; that baby's howling again, must be her teeth coming through, poor wee soul. Born tae suffer.

None of that for her, no cuckoos in the nest, she sheathed the custom up, and if not, a sponge-and-vinegar girl. Not a seed born of man survived that barrier. A sponge-and-vinegar girl. In Vinegar Close.

Sadie's face went slack for a moment and her eyes, looking deep the other in the glass, seemed like a child's, full of pain and vexation. Her white plume moved in the cold wind as if waving goodbye.

What was it McLevy had said to her? All these years ago, all these years.

She'd dipped a mark in the Tolbooth Wynd, while the man was standing to attention, him being an officer of the guards, and slid the wallet over to her then fancy boy, wee Dougie Gray.

Dougie had taken off round the corner while she gripped the mark fast in pretended passion. The man discovered his loss but she gave gracious pardon, it must have fallen from his pocket or perhaps it was at home with the wife, never mind settle up the next time, eh?

He cursed her something fierce as a rancid

5

wee whore, but the smile froze on her face when Dougie marched back round the corner, arm in arm with Jamie McLevy, prime thieftaker of the parish of Leith, in the city of Edinburgh.

The policeman was limping though, puffing for breath; wee Dougie must have kicked the clouds but the ploy had not worked. Not well enough.

God bless wee Dougie, took it right on the chin, said he'd delved in regardless, nothing to do with her, no proof, she was free of scath. But, even though, even though, McLevy turned those slate-grey eyes on her, wolf eyes in that big white face that looked like it never saw the light of day. He smiled and her bowels lurched, then he reached out and gently flicked the feather which even then she wore as her proud emblem.

'One day, Sadie Gorman,' he said, and his voice pierced in deep. 'One day, your wings will be broken and you shall fall to earth at my feet.'

Well, he could kiss the devil's arse because here she was alive and kicking. But still. His voice echoed in her mind. All these years.

And wee Dougie had died in the Perth Penitentiary, defending his honour against some brute from Aberdeen. He did not deserve that. Nae justice.

The east wind nagged her back to the present. She turned and looked at the dead street. Not a hunker-slider in sight. That bloody wind must have frozen the randy boys where they lay.

Sadie shivered and glanced around again. This dark time, the evil hour, played tricks upon your mind. Satan might be watching, long black nails and big red eyes. She had felt him on her trail these past nights.

She dare not go home empty-handed. Her pounce, Frank Brennan, was a big Irish lump with hands like a navvy's shovel, genial enough save in drink but, by this time of night, he'd be steaming like a horse dollop and looking for his due reward. Her face was safe but God help her belly from his fist.

For a moment she felt a sense of panic, desperation, as if she was sliding away from what she knew into the darkness, some pit where only monsters waited. She'd seen a drawing once, a woman drowned at sea, a great big octopus dragging her under, the mouth open, screaming, hair wrapped round her face, breasts naked, dress ripped from her by the slimy tentacles. Of course it was to ginger up the clients in the Holy Land the bawdy-hoose where she'd first been on the bones. Should have stayed there, Jean Brash would have seen her right, but no, she was too young, too restless, she liked it free and easy. Free and easy. Look at her now.

A hard shake went through her whole body. It was cruel and cold. No mercy. She'd have to go home. Take her licks.

She could stand the panic now. It was like a dull ache but a thing she knew.

But then the fear charged in again, like a black mist. She heard something in the shadows, a rat chittering; what if the beast scuttled right up her leg? She detested rodents. Now wait. What was that? God's mercy on a cold night maybe?

Footsteps, coming towards her, through the

7

narrow wynd, heel and sole on the cobbles, a fine firm masculine step.

Aye, there he was now, oh definitely on the prowl, ye could tell. Under the tile hat, a furze of white hair shone in the gaslight, a patriarch, even better, might settle for a wee flutter of the fingers, gentleman's relish, but see the light grey frock-coat — that's quality, that's good money, that's more than promising.

Sadie licked her lips and pulled a touch back into the shadows, distance lends enchantment. She laughed softly, the man's head turned, slow, ponderous.

'Well, my braw gallant,' Sadie spoke low, inviting, she had a fine organ for that, whisky tonsils. 'Is it company ye're searching for? I'll wager you could tremble me, I can tell just looking. I know a strong man when he comes a-calling.'

She laughed, kept in the shadows, extended a white arm; her arms were her best point these days, elegant, long, supple fingers waggled saucily.

He also kept out of the light, but she could see, straining her eyes, that he was a fair age and height, white sideburns, eyes deep set below craggy brows, shaded by the brim of the hat. The mouth worried her, it was not a kind cut. And there was an odd smell in the air. A hospital smell. Coal tar.

This might be slow fruit and it would help if the auld bugger might think to say something. Now, wait. She knew that face surely, she'd seen it before but not in a serving capacity, no, that

8

mouth the downward set of it, in the newspapers maybe? Not that she could read but the photos, or was it somewhere else? The man fumbled inside his jacket; if he brought out his wallet then to hell with what she knew or didn't know, business was business.

She pitched her voice soft and throaty. 'I can see a man of substance, a man of style, a man whose wishes must be met. I can satisfy you, sir, satisfaction is my aim, tell me your heart's desire.'

She risked coming forward a touch more, threw back her head, thrust out her chest, maybe her titties would take his eyes off the state of her teeth.

'Tell me your heart's desire.'

Sadie's first lover had been a flesher's assistant; he would present her the odd mutton chop when chance arrived.

She loved to watch him at work, a butcher's boy; his big meaty hands wielded the cleaver with surprising delicacy. He had a delicate touch with many things. The flash of the blade through the air always excited her as the edge bit into the lamb's neck. A flash of steel.

The axe blade hewed straight through her collarbone, crashed through the ribs and only stopped when it reached the heart. Sadie fell like a stone. The man, with gloved hand, carefully wiped the sharp edge of the weapon clean on her yellow dress and put it neatly back inside his coat.

The plume still clung to her hair like a last vestige of life, though the top had snapped off.

He picked up the fragment, placed it into a side pocket then walked off with measured tread.

Above her sightless eyes where she lay was a motto carved on one of the doors. *In Thee, O Lord, is all my trust.*

Her blood flowed out in a hot gush. A rat scuttled in the shadows but Sadie didn't mind. It was the first time she'd been warm all night.

The white feather had been broken. The east wind blew it from her hair, and cast it out into the darkness.

3

Death is the cure of all diseases.

SIR THOMAS BROWNE,
Religio Medici

McLevy stood in the cold room, watching Dr Jarvis plucking away at the dead body on the slab as if it were a chicken carcass. The police surgeon was a tall cadaverous man, with small watery eyes and long skinny fingers that poked and prodded while he whistled through his teeth.

The surgeon was, not to mince words, an overweening tangle of vanity, a veritable struntie who was passable at his job but not as masterly as his self-esteem would have folk believe.

Once, through his carelessness, he had caused a man's death. A good man. A bad death. Of course Jarvis would deny it. Medical men, since the beginning of time, have known how to cover their own backsides.

'Now see here, inspector,' with his forceps he held a glistening shard up to the light, 'I have a bone to pick with you.'

The surgeon whinnied at his own wit but it faded like a shaft of sun in Stornoway.

For many years he'd tried to get under McLevy's skin, but the fellow was impervious. Jarvis sneaked a look from the corner of his eye at the solid immovable presence, bulky body, legs on the short side, hands surprisingly small and

11

delicate at the end of the stubby arms. But the belly, now that was a market pudding.

Cut into that belly with his best slicer, pull out the entrails, and spread them like a deck of cards!

The doctor stopped, a little mortified at his speculations and, truth to tell, the blankness of McLevy's gaze unnerved him somewhat. Surely he couldn't know the thoughts, the wicked pulsing thoughts that went through a medical mind?

'Well,' he said primly, 'we have a dead body here. The bones splintered, the force considerable, the instrument a keen blade with a heft of weight to it.'

'Such as?'

The door behind them opened and the lanky figure of Constable Mulholland, McLevy's right-hand man, slipped in and stood, unobtrusively as he could, at the back.

Even taller than Jarvis he loomed over the scene, with the same watchful deliberation as the inspector. The two of them were enough, as the common herd would put it, to give you the sulphur jaundies.

'How should I know? You're the great detective McLevy, the criminal classes of Leith wake in a cold sweat each morning at the thought of you bestriding what remains of their dirty squalid streets like a Colossus. What do you think?'

'I think you might wish to answer my question.'

The surgeon gave vent to an elaborate sigh

and tapped one of the exposed ribs as if cracking open a boiled egg.

'Possibly an axe or cleaver; you might pursue the flesher shops, search out blood on the butcher's block and arrest the fellow immediately.'

Another dry laugh met with no response; really the fellow was dead to badinage.

'Right-handed, I would surmise.' The surgeon pursed his lips to indicate a keen intelligence at work.

'My thought also. Above average height?'

'From the direction of the blow, possible, possible, hmmm . . . a strong right hand.'

Jarvis glanced down at the gaping wound in the body and his watery eyes became momentarily thoughtful. Then he struck a pose and smiled annoyingly at the inspector.

Thy strong right hand, Lord, make it bare
Upon their heads.
Lord, weigh it doon and dinnae spare
For their misdeeds.

'Robert Burns, as I am sure a man of letters like yourself will recognise, McLevy.'

Jarvis, as McLevy well knew, regarded him just above a Hottentot in terms of erudition, so he let the quote sail past and contented himself with dry observation.

' 'Holy Willie's Prayer', but I don't think the poet was advocating carnage of womankind, was he?'

'Only God's vengeance on the unworthy.'

13

'I believe that was meant in satire.'

'I know how it was meant!'

Mulholland shifted uneasily; there was a sudden edge to the exchange.

'Do you have anything further to lay before us?'

'Not a blind bit.'

With that flat statement, the doctor dropped the shard from his forceps to join other fragments of bone and tissue he'd collected in an evidence bag, pulled the sheet over the body, took off his surgeon's apron, flipped away the forceps and commenced to wash his hands with great vigour.

The cold room was a study in light and shade, the darkness of the police tunics contrasting with the white bare walls. The granite colour of the slab matched the fashionable hue of the doctor's trousers; he fancied himself as a bit of a dandy, cream shirt, sleeves rolled up to the elbows. A necessary precaution for the prudent when sticking their hands into someone else's exposed and messy guts.

Jarvis wrung out his fingers, dried them on a soft piece of cloth and affected to turn his wedding ring so that it gleamed in the harsh light.

'When was she found?' he asked.

'Two o'clock in the morning.'

'From the state of her, died not long before; nothing much in the stomach, no evidence of congress, just another wreck washed up on the shoreline.'

The corpse's arm had fallen down when Jarvis

14

had pulled at the sheet and McLevy carefully placed it back under the covering, the hand, held in his, fingers rigid, still an elegant shape, as he tucked it out of sight.

'Nothing under the nails?'

'Dirt. What she trafficked in. Dirt,' the surgeon pronounced this word with some satisfaction.

'But the woman deserves justice,' McLevy said softly.

'Does she? A common whore from the looks. They come and go; their lives, I am afraid, are worthless.'

'They provide a service to the community at large.'

'*At large?* You mean the desperate cases.'

'I mean respectable men who find the married bed a damp prospect and their breeks round their knees in a deep wynd at midnight. Surely you would agree with that, Dr Jarvis?'

Damn the man! Jarvis turned away to hide a sudden flush. Two years previous he'd had the misfortune to be caught with a young magpie just off the Royal Mile by a passing night patrol, some what *in flagrante*. A gold coin had solved the matter and no law had been broken, but surely McLevy couldn't know of this? The Royal Mile was not his parish, they wouldn't let him cross over the bridges.

McLevy noted the shaft had gone home and repeated with no particular emphasis, 'She deserves justice.'

'You find it for her. One of her own kind would do this, molassed with drink, and not even recall such in the morning. You find it. I have better to accomplish!'

Jarvis, reaching jerkily for his topcoat, knocked his bag of instruments to the floor and had to scrabble around in retrieval. An obscure sense of humiliation caught hold of him and he ached to stick one of his sharp blades right up the man's anus; see now, here he was frenzied inside his head, damn the man, damn him!

An icy silence. Jarvis searched for the last word, a word that would redeem all.

McLevy watched him. The inspector had perfected a small secret smile which always daunted his superiors. As if some defect of theirs had amused him but his contemplation was too perfect to share.

He smiled it now. The silence grew.

Constable Mulholland reached into his pocket.

'You were right, sir,' he said. 'Took a deal of finding, but found it was, in the guttering at the other end of Vinegar Close. The wind blew it, I expect. It was a hands-and-knees job, muck to the elbow. A deal of finding.'

In fact a few stale buns had bribed a pack of street children to swarm over the close like wasps at a cowpat to search out the God-forsaken thing otherwise he, Mulholland, would have been on his knees for the foreseeable future, running the risk that folks might mistake him for a Papist.

With his soft country accent and guileless Irish-blue eyes, Mulholland might well have been mistaken for many things.

A fool, however, was not one of them, not by McLevy at any road. The inspector squinted at the suspiciously clean fingers offering forth . . . a

16

bedraggled white feather.

He took it from Mulholland and peered close. 'The top is lacking,' he said.

'Not recovered, sir. But it was a correct assumption. The plume was on the scene.'

'It had to be somewhere,' he muttered. 'She never was without one.'

'You know the woman then?' asked Jarvis.

'Sadie Gorman. These many years. She used to be a pretty wee girl.'

'She's left that far behind. A broken doll.'

McLevy looked down at the waxy face of the corpse, powder-caked, red mouth open as if to laugh.

'She had spirit,' he said. 'She deserves justice.'

'You sound like a parrot, McLevy. Ye'll end up in a cage, chewing betel nuts and defecating all over the floor!'

Jarvis, considering this enough of a *bon mot* to be leaving on, sprang the door with a flourish and cast a last disparaging look at the corpse. 'I'm away to my club, a glass of claret will restore my faith in the beauty of women and the delicacy of their intentions. I'd invite you along, inspector, but it's medical men only.'

The door shut behind him then it suddenly opened again and the doctor stuck his head back inside.

'What is it you often call these creatures, by the way? It has slipped my mind.'

'Nymphs of the *pavé*,' was the sardonic response.

'Nymphs! What a treasure you are to me, inspector, that'll keep me going all through the roast. Nymphs! Oh, and by the way, she doesn't have the pox so you won't get cuntbitten.'

The door closed. There was a long silence. McLevy put his five fingers to his nose, pursed his lips, then made a loud farting noise through them. It was aimed at the door and would seem to indicate his opinion of the departed medical man. Mulholland did not bat an eye.

Having released this salvo, the inspector returned to the slab, twitched back the sheet again and looked at the gashed body, ribcage broken, bones sticking out like the spars of a ship.

'You noted that the good doctor was about to say something when he looked into this . . . desecration?'

'I did indeed, sir. But then he thought better. What could it have been, I wonder?'

'These pillars of genteelity, they need their whores but they despise and hate themselves for it. And some of them hate the whores even worse.'

'That's very profound, sir.'

McLevy looked sharply at his constable but the face before him seemed smooth and untroubled by irony. The inspector pushed out his lips and took on the air of a child playing at being a portentous adult.

'He may have been about to say, *'I might have done this, I might have chopped the sin out of her body.''*

'Just as well he kept it to himself, then. Otherwise he could end up suspect,' said the constable.

18

'I'm sure he has an alibi.'

Mulholland nodded solemnly. 'Mrs Jarvis. They'd be locked in matrimonial embrace all night.'

'Indeed. *Shackled* thegither.'

A glint of mischief between the two. The younger man had walked the conglomerates of Leith these many years now with McLevy. He knew the humours and most especially the rages which burned in the inspector's breast. Not that it didn't stop him having a wee provocation now and again, but he tried always to follow his Aunt Katie's advice. *'If you're going to poke the anointed pig, make sure you're well behind the fence.'*

'One more thing.' McLevy pointed at a smear of blood on the side of the dress, separated from the dark red river which stained the rest of the material. 'What do you make of that?'

'Her hand perhaps? Clutched at her wounds and then — ' Mulholland stopped. The pained look on the inspector's face did not encourage further speculation.

'Look at the line of blood. Straight. As if, perhaps, something was wiped clean.'

'The murder weapon? A cool customer.'

'Or someone . . . detached. Who looks down on humanity as if it were just so many insects, crawling under his feet.'

There was a mystical intuitive side to the inspector which Mulholland found more than a little worrying. An ability to empathise with the criminal mind which one day, if the wind was in the wrong quarter, might lead to demonic possession.

Don't turn your hinder parts on the black bull, leave that to the cows.

One of Aunt Katie's more cryptic sayings. God knows why it should come into his head at this moment.

He watched McLevy replace the sheet up to the neck of the corpse and then carefully pack away the broken feather in the top pocket of his tunic. How would he describe the man, now? Average height, heavy set, dainty little trotters, the comical thing being if the inspector ever had to run, which he hated with a vengeance, only the arms and legs moved, the rest of the body was perfectly still, as if in protest.

The features now, would suet come to mind? But behind that fleshy casing was a substance the like of which you might see down by the Leith shoreline where the east wind over time had stripped the rocks back to their very essence.

The face at times was that of a pouting child and then again something carved out from the Old Testament.

Pepper-and-salt hair stood up like a wire brush. And yet the whole, and this irked Mulholland profoundly him not having the physicality for it himself, could become easy invisible. You might pass this by in a crowd. Unless you caught sight of the unguarded eyes, then were you a woolly animal you'd be heading back to the fold praying not to feel the hot breath of the wolf upon your neck.

The white skin on that big face; if Mulholland was out in the wind for five minutes his cheeks were of the damask rose, but the inspector's never changed. Like parchment. He might have been Ancient Egyptian.

'What're you grinning at?'

'Not a thing. It's a serious business, sir.'

'It is indeed. A *ferocious* business. Enough force behind that blow to split the Scott Monument. A savage hatred that never leaves the streets.'

Something in the tone alerted the constable but he contented himself with watching as the inspector shook out a reasonably clean handkerchief, which he laid gently over Sadie's face.

'She has fallen at my feet. She will have justice, Mulholland.'

'I'm sure she will. Is there . . . perhaps something you yourself are not revealing at this point in time, sir?'

'Me?' McLevy spread his hands, his face a parody of hurt innocence. 'I am an open book, constable. As you well know. An open book.'

4

As you pass from the tender years of youth into harsh embittered manhood, make sure you take with you on your journey all the human emotions. Don't leave them on the road.

NIKOLAI GOGOL,
Dead Souls

Leith, 14 April 1850
George Cameron watched in grim amusement as the young constable spewed his guts all over the baker's shop doorway. A nice filling for the cakes.

That's the bother with these Lowlanders, no ballast. He glanced over to where the girl's body lay slumped against the wall; ye could not blame the boy, I suppose, first night on patrol with his big Highland sergeant, excuses himself to go up a back street then finds he's near relieved himself upon a corpse.

The constable had nothing else to offer but his shoulders still heaved. Dearie me. The dry boke. Few things are worse.

Unless you've had your brisket mangled. He turned away from the grovelling young buckie, took a deep breath and delicately pulled away the girl's dress. My God, she'd been split apart.

Cameron took some eyeglasses out of his pocket, perched them on his nose and looked to his heart's content.

His father had worked as a gillie on the laird's estate; he remembered the first time he saw the auld man gralloch a deer, the gush of entrails followed by a ritual smearing of blood on the son's forehead. Most unwelcome. Some had dribbled right down his nose. Cameron sniffed. But that was just a drop in the bucket compared to this, a drop in the bucket.

He gingerly lifted the head of the corpse which had fallen face down on to the ravaged breast. Cameron did not recognise the features, but the clothes proclaimed her profession. A young face, mouth parted, sweet lips, nae scabby gums. She'd be new at the whoring . . . come from nowhere, gone to the same place.

A noise by his side, the constable had returned dabbing at his mouth with a big white hankie.

'Now, don't you be spewing up again,' said the sergeant. 'Not over me, not over the corpus. We do not want our evidence obscured by vomit.'

The young man swallowed hard. He wouldn't give this big Inverness teuchter the satisfaction. He forced himself to look at the terrible gash in the girl's body.

'Not be the last cadaver ye see on these streets. I've witnessed twelve murders in ten glorious years,' announced the sergeant. 'But I have to confess, this one's a sight all on its own, son. All on its own.'

The constable nodded. He noticed something in the hand of the corpse and gently teased it out. It was a fragment of thin black cloth which the sergeant took from him and held close to his

23

thick eyeglasses, then sniffed.

'Fine quality, new bought, but torn from what? A cravat, stocking, glove?' He looked at the constable who made no answer. 'Are you in the huff because I watched ye cast up?'

Shake of the head. Cameron was amused, vomit or no, this boy might have the makings. 'Away tae the station, son, get me the hand cart and we'll fetch this lassie home, well as near home as she'll ever find this night.'

As the young man started off Cameron called after.

'And as ye make your way, review the events of the night. In case something comes to mind. It's always a good idea. To review events.'

'I'll do just that,' said James McLevy.

5

I slept, and dreamed that life was beauty;
I woke, and found that life was duty.

ELLEN STURGIS HOOPER,
American poet

'Are you listening to me, inspector?'

McLevy was hauled back into the present by the querulous tones of Lieutenant Roach, his mandated superior at Leith station.

Roach was a more or less permanently disappointed man, with the saving grace of a waspish humour some of which he even, at times, directed against himself.

His disappointment lay in the fact that, despite being vice-president of the golf club and rolling up his trouser leg on a regular basis at the best connected of Masonic lodges, he was stuck to Leith like a fly in a dung pile till retirement laid its fell hand upon his shoulder.

His predecessor, Lieutenant Moxey, had left somewhat under a cloud and Roach had been swiftly drafted in from Haymarket to fill the gap after almost giving up hope of such promotion.

He remembered the trembling excitement when he had first viewed the drab exterior of Leith station; never mind, he would change it into a stepping-stone towards greater achievements.

Now fifteen years later the station was still the

same and he could well understand what had driven Moxey to such base acts of deliverance. Understand but not imitate. The Good Lord and Mrs Roach would see to that.

Why the powers-that-be could not discern the true gold that lay under his careworn exterior and raise him out of this creeping decrepitude to the lofty reaches of a sublime incumbency was a mystery which taxed him into many a shank on the fifth hole.

His humour was a direct result of having to deal with McLevy for almost a decade and a necessary bulwark against the potential bedlam it involved.

'A murder is the last thing we need.' Roach shook his head at the injustice of it all. 'It is most inconvenient.'

'Especially for the corpse, sir.'

'What?' Roach shot a look at Mulholland but the candid face seemed innocent enough. 'Yes, of course there is that to consider but . . . aghh!'

The lieutenant stood up, flexed his skinny arms and swiped an imaginary ball two hundred odd yards, splitting the middle of the fairway, only to see it disappear down a rabbit burrow.

'We have an election on hand, the streets are infested with liberal incitement and the few decent conservatives left are huddled together in doorways. There is a meeting at the lodge tonight and Chief Constable Grant will be there.'

In his mind's eye Roach could see a smooth green and a white ball rolling eternally towards the hole. Never quite getting there. Never quite.

'I had hoped to impress him with the changing

face of Leith and how we discharge our onerous duties to keep the streets clean as a whistle; what with the eyes of the country focused on Edinburgh, what with Gladstone landing his great fundament upon Midlothian — '

Roach came to a sudden halt. He had made the mistake of looking into the blank, incurious eyes of his inspector and, as a result, had completely lost track of what he was saying.

'What with? Gladstone was landing his fundament?' prompted McLevy.

'Yes. That is correct. Of course. To impress, and thence to discuss with the chief constable the gravity of the political situation and, despite the fact we both distrust the machinations of Disraeli, nevertheless he is a Conservative and so are we. A parity of belief!'

This 'we' obviously did not include Mulholland and McLevy who sat there, in Roach's view, like dangerous radicals waiting to sprout. He took another deep breath.

'But instead, Sandy Grant will shake this murder in my face and demand it be solved at once. I shall be reduced from one of equal standing to that of a plague carrier!'

'I'm sure if the woman knew what a nuisance she was going to be, she'd have arranged to be murdered in another parish, sir,' said McLevy.

'There is no call for impertinence, James.'

But the interjection did the trick. Roach, who had been winding himself into a whirligig of indignation, sat quietly back at his desk.

'What about her pounce, could he be our man?'

27

'Frank Brennan? In anger he might crack her rib but not hack her to pieces. He's a Dublin man, the only blood they like is in their sausage.'

The inspector shook his head and gazed at the portrait of Queen Victoria which glowered down from the lieutenant's wall. Her Sovereign Majesty. Putting on the beef.

'Besides, why kill the goose that lays the golden egg?' he added.

'*Raddled* egg from all accounts. She may have been holding money back on him, you know what these people are like.' Roach shook his head in Christian sorrow.

'I know what they're like,' said McLevy.

Roach waited for more but the inspector had his *broody* look on, might as well converse with a wooden Indian.

'Anything from the scene?'

'One decapitated white feather, property of the deceased,' offered Mulholland.

'That's helpful,' said Roach sourly. 'Witnesses?'

'Had it been one of the big new streets we might have been in business, sir. But it's the wynds. In these alleys, every eye is closed to crime, every door is shut to probity,' sighed the constable, his eyes radiating a holy rectitude. 'More's the pity, sir. A lost tribe.'

The hypocritical, unco guid quality in Mulholland's tone made McLevy want to spit. Sookin' up. The constable was sookin' up to the lieutenant. The bugger was after something. And McLevy knew exactly what it was, the sleekit lang dreep.

He stood suddenly, moved to the door and turned the handle.

'I'll go shake Frank Brennan till his teeth rattle, though I doubt we're wasting our time. Sadie lived hard but she survived. She knew the streets and could look after herself in her chosen profession. The strike was from close by. It would be trade. She wouldnae let rough that near. It would be trade. Respectable. A *clean* blow.'

Then he was gone. Roach sighed.

'Why is it Inspector McLevy, given the choice in matters of heinous crime, will always seek out culprits from amongst the respectable classes?'

Mulholland, to whom this appeal was directed, made the following response.

'I have sometime asked the inspector that, and he has given me always the one word in answer, sir.'

Roach waited.

'Experience,' said Mulholland. He nodded politely and followed his inspector out of the door.

6

I have fought for Queen and Faith like a valiant
man and true.
I have only done my duty as a man is bound to
do.

ALFRED, LORD TENNYSON,
'The Revenge'

Benjamin Disraeli followed the erect form of Sir
Henry Ponsonby, the Queen's private secretary,
down a long corridor of Buckingham Palace
towards the Royal reception chamber.

They walked in silence. Disraeli measured the
man's military back and wondered how many
daggers he could safely plunge in. Quite a few. It
was a broad back.

He did not trust Ponsonby. The secretary
belonged to the other camp and who knows how
many were the keyholes against which he pressed
his Liberal ear?

One of Disraeli's many talents was insidious
character assassination, an invaluable weapon in
politics, and he had no scruples about using this
talent to poison Victoria's mind against the man.
To a certain extent he had succeeded:
Ponsonby's influence had waned and Disraeli
gloried in the fact, but not enough, not enough
by a long chalk, the fellow was still too close to
the Queen.

Close enough, for instance, to look over her

shoulder and slide the resultant information of her communications with Disraeli towards the enemy.

Ponsonby stopped at a door and turned.

'Her Majesty is most anxious to see you, prime minister,' he said in his usual bluff direct fashion, not that it fooled Disraeli. It was an honest open face and therefore all the more to be suspected.

'Dear me. And what has caused this anxiety, I wonder?' murmured Disraeli, eyes veiled in apparent thought.

'I am sure she will tell you, sir.'

But then as Ponsonby lifted his hand to knock softly upon the door, Disraeli slid in the knife.

'The election, Sir Henry, how do you think it will result?'

'I am sure I do not know,' was the careful reply.

Disraeli laughed suddenly, eyes creased in amusement, charm personified.

'But you are of the Liberal faith, Sir Henry. You must wish William Gladstone to prevail, trample us Tories to the ground like so many snakes!'

He laughed again. A high-pitched sound, like steel on stone, and his eyelids batted together in a strangely feminine fashion.

All terribly pleasant. Ponsonby's back stiffened a notch.

'My politics have never interfered with my function, sir. I merely wish what is best for the country.'

'And your Queen, surely?' responded the

31

prime minister with devious, toxic humour.

'And my Queen,' came the stolid reply.

Sir Henry always seemed to play with a straight bat. That was even less to be trusted.

'Then let us hope,' said Disraeli with a winning smile, 'that both are satisfied. Queen and country.'

For a moment the two looked at each other, then Ponsonby nodded somewhat jerkily, tapped upon the door and opened it slowly.

'The prime minister, Your Majesty,' he announced.

Disraeli slid through the aperture and the door closed behind, shutting off Ponsonby, his abhorrent Liberal tendencies and the rest of the known world.

Now, for as long as this lasted, Disraeli was safe. The door was thick and there was a large key stuck in the lock to this side. No eavesdropping from the enemy.

In the middle of the room, stood a small, dark-clad figure. His Queen. He resisted the impulse to fall upon his knees, it would be the devil's own job getting up again.

She extended her arm. Benjamin Disraeli took the plump little hand in both of his, bowed deep, kissed it and murmured as always, 'In loving loyalty and faith.'

He straightened up with some difficulty, and looked into the worried eyes of his Faerie Queen.

'That dreadful man, you will defeat him, Mr Disraeli. Anything less shall not be counte-nanced.'

Queen Victoria waved her arms in the air as if

pursued by Highland midges and motioned her prime minister towards a chair which she herself had set, precisely in the middle of the reception room.

Disraeli sat down gratefully although he had, of late, been experiencing some severe pains in the region of his back passage, and the chair, like so much of Buckingham Palace, seemed to have been constructed with the utmost discomfort in mind.

'I shall do my best, Your Majesty,' he replied a trifle wearily, 'but I am afraid the final decision will be that of the populace, an unfortunate disadvantage for our small measure of democracy.'

She adored his sly humour but took a stern part in the dance between them.

'Shame on you, sir, to doubt the people of this country. They have more sense than to vote for someone of such . . . questionable temperament.'

'Many things about Mr Gladstone are questionable, save the one. He has stamina. Mark you, so does the hybrid mule.'

Victoria smiled and Disraeli put up a languid hand to touch the one dyed black curl which dangled down the centre of the mighty dome of his forehead. His dry skin and hooded eyes brought to mind the appearance of some exotic reptile.

In 1874, these six years past, his Conservative party had swept in with a healthy majority over the crumbling Liberal government of William Gladstone. Disraeli himself had been prime minister in 1868, before being leapfrogged by the

People's William, and, having triumphed once more, teetered back towards his Queen like a slightly mildewed second bridegroom.

From that very moment they were in accord. She had not enjoyed her sojourn with Gladstone who had treated her like a public department. Disraeli treated her like a woman and would defend the empire to the last drop of blood. He had very lofty views.

Victoria watched him where he sat and nodded silent approval. He was her prime minister and for these six happy years they had mourned together, she for her husband Prince Albert, he for his wife Mary, though Victoria always thought the woman a bit of a flibbertigibbet while pleasant enough.

Nevertheless, Disraeli, like herself, grieved *constantly*. The black border round their letters had not diminished in thickness by one iota during all that time.

And within these black borders, he had courted her assiduously, a delicate chivalrous courtship which, of course, would never speak its name. A conduct most becoming.

She was Victoria Regina after all, the Empress of India, the imperial bond between them reinforced each year he stayed atop the greasy pole of politics. She felt at home with this strange creature, this Jew who had taken the Church of England as his guide and buckler. But now . . . ?

The Queen moved away restlessly and Disraeli watched with a certain detached amusement as she glided around the room like an anxious little

34

pigeon looking for berries.

'I received your letter in thanks for the snowdrops, it was most . . . welcome,' she said distractedly, fussing with a particularly hideous brocaded cushion which was not worth the fussing over. Indeed, were that all to Othello's hand in the play when he sought to smother Desdemona, the poor creature might yet have lived. Even the Moor in the height of his jealous passion would not have deigned to touch such a gruesome object.

Disraeli roused himself from this meditation.

'As were the flowers themselves, ma'am. Faerie gifts from Queen Titania.'

'From Osborne House to be precise,' she replied dryly. 'Primroses will follow.'

'Your Majesty's sceptre has touched the enchanted isle.'

He opened his arms in an extravagant gesture as if receiving an onslaught of flowers and her lips twitched in response. He did lay on the flattery with a trowel but she bathed delightedly in the wash of words.

'Indeed the Isle of Wight can be enchanted and so *before* the rest of the country.'

'In climatic terms, most definitely,' was his dry response.

Disraeli had, from time to time, visited her island retreat at Osborne and found little there to occupy him, except the avoidance of seagull droppings.

She sensed the cynicism and bridled a little.

'I am aware, Mr Disraeli, that you do not hold Nature in great affection.'

35

He put his head to one side, like a curious tropical bird.

'Dear madam,' he murmured, 'if you but command me, I shall cover myself in woad and spend the rest of my life in woodland contemplation.'

The image was so ridiculous that she burst out in laughter. He followed suit and, for a moment, the two of them guffawed like a pair of old wives at the market. Then there was silence.

'I am reminded,' her eyes were glinting in mischief and there was a glimpse of a younger self, 'for a reason I cannot bring to mind, of the time my dear mother walked out of the dining room holding a fork, which she had mistaken for her fan.'

She let out another roar of laughter then put a hand up to cover her mouth as if to contain the life force.

He did the same in perfect mimicry and they looked at each other like two Wise Monkeys.

When she removed her hand, the face was once more the solemn, heavy visage which the world knew as Victoria Regina.

She turned away, went swiftly to the window and gazed out into the Mall where her subjects moved and jostled in an incessant stream, the carriages clattering, pedestrians swarming like ants, all going about their business, all with their secret thoughts. All, well at least those who were franchised, soon about to vote.

Disraeli, meantime, was in a quandary. It was a great honour to be allowed a seated audience, in fact he knew of no other person granted this privilege, and he would take care, as always, to conceal the chair behind a screen before leaving so no one might ever discern the fact. But for now he was rather *incarcerated*.

Like Macbeth. *Cabined, cribbed, confined . . .* and what was the rest of the quote? . . . *bound in to saucy doubts and fears*. Quite so. Quite so.

He may as well be wedged in a chamber pot. His buttocks were chafing on the stuffing of the chair, which seemed to be composed entirely of granite chips. Yet, he could not rise without Her Majesty's permission. He was a victim of her uniquely granted privilege and favour.

The phrase amused him and his long upper lip twitched like a horse's as he gazed around the room.

Disraeli disdained Buckingham Palace, so much of the decor seemed like some sort of vulgar wedding cake.

Above his head, a garish chandelier hung like the sword of Damocles. That phrase did not amuse, so he fixed his eyes upon the broad back of his beloved Faerie Queen.

She had assumed the throne at the age of eighteen and they thought she would come in like a lamb, but, by God, they quickly changed their tune. Forty-three years on, and she still had the heart of a lion. What nerve. What muscle. What energy. Some Faerie.

And indeed, he did love her. She was the only person left in the world that he could love. He remembered a moment not long after his wife had died when he to his Queen, quite out of the blue, a surprise even to himself, had said

. . . 'Every night, when I return home, I find another empty room.'

Victoria had looked at him with such feeling in her eyes. She understood the emptiness within. It was a moment of rare simplicity. They both treasured such moments.

'Did you know,' she still gazed out of the window, 'that when I was very young, they used to pin a sprig of holly to the front of my dress?'

'The Ancient Romans,' Disraeli shifted uneasily, 'considered the holly sprig a symbol of health and well-being, Your Majesty, and of course at Christmas time we are *festooned* from top to bottom with that particular evergreen.'

'It was not for that.' She turned back from the window. 'It was to keep my chin up.'

'A somewhat unnecessary precaution, I would have thought.' He shifted buttocks again. Damn the thing.

'You may stand, Mr Disraeli.'

He uncoiled from the chair with as much grace as his ageing bones would allow, stuck out his right leg and assumed a posture which suggested that of an actor about to deliver a long speech.

'As Your Majesty commands.'

Disraeli took out a scented handkerchief and dabbed at his lips, the rings on his fingers glittering as he took care not to stray to where the rouge delicately enhanced the pallor of his cheeks.

'I am told,' Victoria said abruptly, 'that your friends call you . . . Dizzy. Is that so?'

'A derivation more than a description, my dear

madam,' he drawled, the ghost of a smile on his lips.

There was a churning in the royal stomach. She did not want to lose this man. She had been bereaved of her beloved Albert and it near broke her heart. She was unsure if the same organ could stand the prospect of losing another dear friend. It could not be.

'You must win this election, Dizzy. You must remain my prime minister. I will not have the barbarian at my gate.'

'The portents are promising, Your Majesty.'

Yet somewhere, despite the recent fervour created through the opening of Parliament by the Queen in her new glass coach, the Royal visage being seen from every angle, despite the recent by-election results, results so favourable they had seduced him into going to the polls in the first place, despite publicly flaying Gladstone's Liberals as a party of appeasement who would muzzle the British bulldog, despite all this, Disraeli sensed the people might possibly alter course.

The imperial dream had spawned some puny detractors and then there was the recent fiasco of the Zulu War where the Queen's great favourite Lord Chelmsford, a vainglorious idiot in command of the British forces, had caused the death of nearly fourteen hundred men at Isandhlwana.

Disraeli had protected the lying numbskull because Victoria doted upon the fellow, but it had cost the prime minister in public and political opinion.

It had been a pre-emptive war, an invasion under the guise of freeing the land from a despot, King Cetshwayo. Of course the fellow was a tyrant but he hardly presented a threat to the Western world, which was the other fictional reason for the offensive action. To invade another country at this juncture was not a good idea.

Not with the Russian bear growling in Afghanistan, which was another pretty kettle of fish. The Forward Policy to defend India's borders by extending them as far as the Hindu Kush and bring a large part of the country under imperial rule had ended in military victory.

But defeating the tribesmen did not necessarily mean controlling them, as the First Afghan War had so painfully proved. Now there was a second, and once more the threat of local uprisings against the occupying army which presented an easy target to those who wore no uniform, struck from the shadows and then melted back into a sympathetic populace.

The cost of the conflict and, from Gladstone's entrenched moral probity of opinion, the doubtful ethics involved, had unleashed some of the most excoriating oratory from the great Midlothian tree-feller.

'Remember that the sanctity of life in the hill villages of Afghanistan, among the winter snows, is as inviolable in the eye of Almighty God as that of your own!'

Gladstone had thundered thus in Dalkeith.

Indeed the man was thundering everywhere like an American stumping orator.

Also there was the small matter of six bad

harvests in a row. Disraeli had not personally arranged the weather but politicians get blamed for everything.

The Queen did not seem totally convinced by his reading of the oracle, so he tried a recent witticism which had its roots in a dark wish.

'Does Her Majesty know the difference between a misfortune and a calamity?'

'I have had both in my life,' was the response.

Oh dear. Not promising, never mind, press on regardless.

'If Gladstone fell into the Thames, it would be a misfortune. But if someone dragged him out again, that would be a calamity.'

A small smile. No more than that. Then, for the first time of that meeting, they looked squarely into each other's eyes. A rare simplicity.

Victoria drew herself up in queenly stance to match his actor's pose.

'We must put our trust in God, Mr Disraeli,' she asserted somewhat throatily. 'He will command the field.'

'He will indeed, madam.'

But Disraeli did not say what form this God might take. Or where He might strike. Like a serpent.

Certain words had been dropped in a certain quarter, as regards the Queen's deep disquietude. Certain events might have been set in motion and, if need arose and these events assume an ominous turn, what would he know of it all?

His hands were clean. Especially under the nails.

7

I met a lady in the meads
Full beautiful, a faery's child
Her hair was long, her foot was light
And her eyes were wild.

JOHN KEATS,
'La belle dame sans merci'

McLevy on the saunter, Mulholland loping along at his side like an Irish setter.

This had once been the inspector's favourite pursuit, a gentle perambulation through the streets of Leith to observe his charges, most of them doing their level best to avoid his eye.

The delvers, the nymphs and their pounces, the low and high thieves, the bolters, the pleaders, the sneaks, the climbers, the thimblers, the cardsharps, the young keelies with their shooting jackets, caps and fancy girls, the dollymops, shopgirls and maids who slipped out from their place of work to sell their favours, then last but not least, the lost causes.

This was McLevy's private appellation for the unfortunate carriers of the pox who gave many a man his Canongate breeks, so called because that particular quarter, despite the nearby sanctuary of Holyrood, had become a hotbed of venereal splendour.

He knew them all. They *belonged* to him. The bolder fraternity stood proud and cheeked but inside, in the gut, they recognised he was their master.

Once he had heard an exasperated mother threaten her snottery son with the words, 'If ye don't do what ye're tell't to, I'll get McLevy to come and throw ye in the jail, like he did yer father!' He had become the bogey man, a myth in his own lifetime.

Recollection brought a smile to his face but it faded as he regarded the changing scene.

Constitution Street, down which he and the constable were wending their way towards the Old Docks where, with a bit of luck they would find Frank Brennan, was a handsome wide thoroughfare, thronged with carriages and, despite the present election fever, sober-suited and pious-minded pedestrians.

An example of the new respectable parish and there was more to come. The Leith Improvement Scheme was shortly to be enacted, a swathe from Great Junction Street would be cut through all the closes, narrow lanes and courts, ending at the Tolbooth Wynd.

His own subjects were being herded like animals farther and farther back into their lairs, cleansed from the main promenades, and he mourned their passing.

'What joy can be found in a stiff collar and tight whalebone?' he announced suddenly.

Mulholland had been casting a wary Protestant eye at the sole representative of Romanism in Leith, the Catholic chapel of Maris Stella, cruciformed, high-roofed, fetid, he was certain, with incense.

43

A black-clad priest emerged blinking into the light of day and waved over. McLevy waved back.

'Father Callan. A decent enough soul,' he opined.

'You know him well, then?'

'Sufficient. He keeps his own counsel. More's the pity.'

There was a cryptic quality to that remark which hinted of past encounters but Mulholland let it lie. He was unsure of the inspector's religious bent. The man did not worship at any known designation.

There was a rumour that his mother might have been Catholic, but, in that case, it would have been a miracle for McLevy to attain the rank of inspector. Mark you, come to think of it, miracles were exactly what the Pope sold to all and sundry. And what of indulgences? Plenary, partial, temporal or perpetual, all sold to the highest bidder.

Martin Luther had the right idea, nail rebellion on the chapel door and foreswear the Diet of Worms.

'*So?*' said the inspector fiercely. 'What joy?'

The constable was lost. 'Ye'd have to come at me again with that, sir.'

'Come at ye, I'll come at ye all right.' McLevy took a deep breath and changed tack. 'Sookin' up!'

'I beg your pardon?'

The inspector glared at Mulholland in a sudden fury. 'Ye were sookin' up!'

'I was not!' came the injured response.

44

'Ye were. To the lieutenant. Sook, sook!'

Mulholland indeed was plotting to ask for some time off in order to attend his Aunt Katie's third marriage in Kerry, she was a terror for the altar that woman. He had no scruples about buttering up Roach to that end, but hadn't thought to be caught out at it. He tried the dignified card.

'It appears to me that, for once in your life, sir, you run the chance of mistaking polite agreement for — '

'Sookin' up! Kiss my arse, I'll bring ye parsley.'

My God, see the man scowling up at him like a frog with the mange. Mulholland wished to be a heron looming over that foul-tempered amphibian. A heron with a long sharp beak. Stab through the belly. Out come the guts.

McLevy smiled thinly. 'You're thinking something nasty about me, constable, because I caught ye blowing in his ear. Something nasty.'

'Farthest thing from my mind, sir.'

McLevy could not explain whence came these fierce squalls of rage which shook him like the aspen tree, but he enjoyed them anyway. Good for the blood.

'You'll go far, Mulholland,' he said ambiguously.

'That is my intention.'

The inspector took a step back and appraised his constable.

Mulholland stood his ground. He knew that squinty-eyed look and had seen many quail before it, but he was sterner stuff.

45

The two of them remained like statues as the people brushed past and who knows how long they would have been frozen there had not a woman's voice interrupted.

'James McLevy,' the tone was low, husky; a liking for strong coffee and the best champagne had moulded the melody of her laughter. 'Can you not pick on someone your own size?'

A splendid private carriage had stopped, and leaning out of the window was a female McLevy knew only too well and for far too long. Jean Brash. Her full lips curved in a smile, hair red as the deepest sin.

Despite her forty-some years, like porcelain was her complexion. Her sea-green eyes with their deep mocking inner light sparkled in the weak rays of the Leith sun. He had almost drowned in these eyes a few times but fear, a dark primitive fear of losing his very soul, had hauled him back from the edge. Just as well. He could not swim.

In sport, she extended a dainty, gloved hand, which he took in his paw and bowed over in equal mockery.

Twenty years ago they'd walked the same streets, whore and constable, then, by various crimes and misdemeanours, Jean raised enough money to emulate the vigorous activity she witnessed below and above her person. She became half-owner in a low dive of a bawdy-hoose, the Happy Land, a place of sliding panels and slippery licentious women where a watch and wallet might disappear in the blink of an eye.

Her partner, Henry Preger, a notorious desperado, died of accumulative poison in mysterious circumstances, and with sorrowful heart she moved up a notch to her next bawdy-hoose, the Holy Land.

Many years passed. She and her girls grasped the staff of righteousness. The place burnt down. It had been insured as a lodging house and the head of the company was a regular client, so with that money and what she had garnered from the sweat of the two-backed beast, Jean moved right up the hill to inhabit a stately mansion that she named the Just Land. She was now the premiere madam in Edinburgh.

Men of the cloth, men of justice, medical men, fellows of the university, all respectable, all with the same itch to scratch, slipped in at the back door.

Safe in the knowledge that the sheets were clean, the champagne decent, the magpies raring to go, wallets and confidentiality guaranteed, they indulged their libidinous, maritally marginalised passions up to the very hilt.

Some of them even brought their own wife's clothing for the lassies to don.

Some of them even wore it themselves, corsets, drawers and all.

Jean Brash provided a cornucopia of depravity with the one proviso that no violence was visited upon her girls.

On the other hand, the said girls were not averse to dishing it out.

She had invested in a Berkley Horse precisely for that purpose, a device upon which the gentleman might be stretched and flogged from any angle. A particular favourite for those captains of industry who spent their days ruling others with a rod of iron.

Jean had, moreover, within easy reach, a selection of whips, birches, canes and battledores.

Thistles were also very popular. In season. Jean even grew them in her garden. *Onopordon acanthium*, she knew the Latin name for many plants. The tap root of the thistle was one foot long. She'd found a use for that as well.

There was a time McLevy's desire had been to see her on a transportation ship but that chance had gone.

Now, she was protected by a bullet-proof decorum, and if not legalised most certainly tolerated, since a sizeable proportion of the city council found their way to her abode for various non-municipal satisfactions.

Still, there was always the hope that one day he might view her fair visage through the bars of a cell. Crime had brought Jean to this pretty pass, crime might yet be her undoing. There's always hope.

She knew what he thought. And he knew that she knew. It was a perfect circle.

They observed each other with a certain bruised affection, like two pugilists who had hammered for many rounds, in many bouts, at each other and found respect in the adversary's punching power.

'I haven't seen you for a while, James. It's not the same without you . . . indulging yourself in my wee bower.'

48

She made the best coffee in Edinburgh. Like her, he was a fiend for coffee. They would sit in her rose-filled garden, sip the brew, and gossip together like a pair of old sweetie-wives.

'I've been busy,' said he.

'Aye. Persecuting the innocent,' rasped a voice from behind and an older woman leaned out from the shelter of Jean's fashionable back.

Snub-nosed, pug-faced. Hannah Semple, keeper of the keys of the Just Land and Jean's right hand. A squat tough old bird.

McLevy had personally sent her twice to Perth Penitentiary, once for common assault and the other for a cut-throat razor held under the nose of a recipient of her dubious charms who had been reluctant to pay the piper. The fellow flinched convulsively and had a chunk cut out of his neb. Serve him right in McLevy's opinion but unfortunately he was a magistrate's son.

Hannah's life had been on a downward course, a third conviction would have seen her die in prison, but Jean Brash had redeemed the fallen soul; all that practice in the Holy Land had not been in vain. The older woman loved her mistress as well as her caustic nature would allow and would happily kill to keep Jean safe.

'Poor auld Sadie Gorman,' Hannah sucked at her teeth and resisted the temptation to spit out of the carriage window, 'didnae deserve that, eh?'

'The wages of sin, Hannah,' was his solemn reply.

'Stick them up your backside, McLevy. If it wasnae for sin you policemen would have bugger all to do with your life.'

49

This time she did spit, accurately past Jean out of the carriage window and close enough to McLevy's foot that he jumped back a little.

'Now, now, Hannah,' murmured Jean. 'The inspector is merely being provocative.'

Her face became grave, the green eyes thoughtful as she thus addressed him. 'I liked Sadie. She was a wild wee devil. She might have remained in my company but she would go her own way.'

Then her eyes creased up. 'Though even when I saw her of late, old as the hills, plying her trade, she still could make me laugh.'

'Aye, she had humour. By the bucket!'

McLevy suddenly let out a harsh whoop of laughter, a strange sound which caused some decent folk in the street to turn and others to avoid the group quite altogether.

'In Meikle John's Close, she emptied a full chamber pot from high above, aimed at my poor head. Gardyloo!'

'Did she hit the mark?' Hannah asked hopefully.

'She did not,' said Mulholland. 'He jumped sideways and out. I got the full deluge.'

'He knows better now.'

McLevy made the remark with a serious air and both women could not resist laughter. Mulholland, calculating he was being paid back for sucking up to the lieutenant, cut his losses and played a part.

'Like the urine of the wild boar,' he announced.

More laughter. Then silence. Jean leant out farther so that she looked McLevy straight in the eye.

'They say she was cut to pieces. Is that true?'

'She more or less held together,' he replied cheerfully. 'One blow. I don't think she saw it coming.'

'Otherwise she would have got the hell out of the way,' said Jean, nettled by his apparent insouciance.

'I have to agree with you there,' McLevy replied.

He glanced up at the coachman. Angus Dalrymple, a massive figure. Once he'd been a respectable tradesman, a blacksmith, but now he sat behind the horses and his twin daughters worked tandem in the Just Land.

'Keep it in the family, eh Angus?' McLevy said happily.

The man stared straight ahead. The inspector turned his attention back to Jean.

'Sadie was a wily old cove. But she never saw it coming.'

'Then it was trade,' she asserted.

'That's possible.' His face gave little away.

'If I hear anything on the streets,' she had a network of spies, 'you'll be informed.'

McLevy said nothing. Mulholland hastened to fill the silence. 'Any information will be welcome, ma'am.'

Jean withdrew into the carriage. 'Take us onwards, Angus,' she commanded, then in the same tone, as the driver clicked at the horses, 'You will find this man, McLevy.'

He stiffened at the arrogant tenor of her words. 'I'll do my job,' he muttered.

'Sadie Gorman did not merit such a death.'

'That's what happens when you live outside

51

the law. One minute you're safe, the next, the axe falls.'

A cold look passed between them.

'If I ever lived outside the law,' she replied, 'it was from necessity. Now, I have no need.'

'Crime is a bad habit,' said McLevy. 'Ye never lose it.'

She smiled suddenly and leant out again so that their faces were almost touching.

'When you find this murdering bastard,' she whispered softly, 'I'll have the coffee waiting.'

The carriage departed and one of the horses left a large mound of dung behind as a parting gift.

McLevy marched off abruptly down the street with Mulholland lengthening his stride to keep pace.

The inspector sounded like he was chanting something under his breath; the constable caught a few notes and recognised the old Jacobite air, *'Charlie is my darling, the young chevalier'*, usually heard when McLevy was in the extremities of good or bad humour. Which held sway was difficult to fathom from that exchange.

By now they had reached the bottom of Constitution Street. Mulholland swung left automatically heading for the Old Docks, but McLevy halted to point the other way.

'That new building which stands so proudly in Salamander Street there, what is its function, constable?'

'It's the slaughterhouse, sir.'

'So it is,' said McLevy. 'So it is.'

8

But keep the wolf far thence that's foe to men,
For with his nails he'll dig them up again.
                              JOHN WEBSTER,
                              The White Devil

Frank Brennan gasped for breath as he lumbered up the steep brae of the Coalhill. The hounds of hell, oh Jesus, and he innocent as a newborn babe, had stalked him all the way along the Old Docks. He could hear them howling still.

Thank the Living Saviour that bastard Mulholland was such a height. His helmet stuck out like a pea on top of a mountain through the dusty windows of Docherty's Tavern and Frank had seen it miles away, above the crowd.

Just time enough for him to dive out the window, kick the scabby hens out from under his feet in the backyard, and be about to prise open the rearwards door when some instinct caused hesitation. He looked through a crack in the wood and what did he see but nothing more than a much worse bastard, that vindictive evil snaffler, McLevy.

Waiting to sink his claw.

Frank had managed to clamber over a couple of walls to the side and come out at a back alley on to the docks; he'd crossed over the wee bridge which led to the shore and then he'd run for his life, leaving the warm cosy tavern behind.

53

He'd been revelling in the sorrow of Sadie's death and the drinks bought in sympathy, him pleading the broken heart and the whisky going down nicely; mind you he'd bought them all enough the night before, only his due, money to burn the night before, money to burn. Blood money.

Don't think on that, Frank, don't think on that.

Then an old bitch, Agnes Stein, one of the wrinkled crones Sadie used to sit with in the corner, had walked straight up and given him the evil eye. Evil.

'I never did a thing wrong,' said he.

She picked up a whisky glass and threw the contents straight in his face, the waste of it as well, and her voice rang out through the place.

'Ye were her man. Ye should have been on the qui vive, on the streets with her, watchin' her survival. Ye're not even a half-decent pimp!'

The black mist came down and he raised his hand. The landlord grabbed it. She was just an old woman, let it be, Frank.

No matter how old, he'd break her neck, no one insulted him like that.

Then the mist cleared, he looked out the window and saw the constable from afar, tall as a gallows tree.

These thoughts in his head as he got to the top of the brae, nearly safe now. Duck into the wynds down the other side, ye could lose the devil himself in there. Behind him a police whistle sounded, oh Jesus, it sounded close.

He took a deep breath and hurtled himself

over the break of the hill.

Up above, in the cold blue sky, a flock of ravens wheeled in circles, attention fixed on something in the distance below.

Their harsh cries broke out like a complaint against the dirty tricks of Fate.

9

Asperges me, Domine, hysoppo, et munabor.
Sprinkle me with hyssop, O Lord,
and I shall be cleansed.
Book of Common Prayer

In Vinegar Close, one of the ragged children, egged on by his companions, their feral white faces alive with unaccustomed glee, pissed copiously upon a red patch on the cobbles. He sent a proud jet of urine high up into the air to spatter down while the girls shrieked encouragement.

The boy, Billy Johnstone, shook his wee tassel in their direction to provoke more shrieks, then tucked it away inside his torn, dirty trousers. They gathered all together and looked down at the rust-red patch. It had not altered one jot. Soaked in deep.

Footsteps. A man ran into the close. His brow was sweaty, a big beefy man, purple-faced and pursy. He had a wild look, knuckle-handed, a clout from one of these big fists might break your jaw. But worth a try.

'Hey, mister,' called Billy. 'D'ye want tae see where she was split? The auld whoory woman?'

The man stopped dead, his face looked like someone had just kicked him in the testicles.

'It'll cost ye,' said the bold Billy. 'She bled like a pig.'

Jesus, Mary and Joseph. Not true. He'd only heard where it happened, not come to see. Only heard. But there was the name, high on the narrow wall. Frank could read, he was a good reader, his mammy had taught him, it put him a class above. He read it now. Vinegar Close.

'She died where you look, Frank,' said a voice. 'Did your guilty conscience bring you down here?'

A shadow had appeared like a bird of ill omen in the entrance of the close. McLevy. The light streamed in behind his shrouded figure.

As Brennan desperately tried to wrench himself away, it was as if his feet were stuck in mud, like a dream where the odds are stacked against you; a feeling not helped when Mulholland stepped past his inspector and clipped Frank a judicious blow with his truncheon, just at the back-hinge of the knee.

The constable had varnished and decorated this instrument himself. It was made of hornbeam and delivered a blow like a hammer. The big man collapsed, howling in pain, to the ground. He sat there, blubbering like a baby, till they hauled him up and pinned him against the wall.

The various crumpled, poverty-stricken inhabitants of the close who had been sitting on the steps, stupefied in the pale sunshine, vanished in an instant. Only Billy and a couple of girls were left. The boy recognised Mulholland.

'Are ye goin' tae buy us any more buns, sir?'

The constable tossed over a small coin before

the Godforsaken wee devil let the cat out the bag.

'Now, get to hell out of it,' he said sharply.

They did. So it was just the two policemen and Frank Brennan in the empty court.

'You broke my poor leg,' the big man whined.

McLevy smiled but the wolf's eyes were without pity.

'That's only the beginning, Frank.'

The inspector puffed out his cheeks. He had not enjoyed the pursuit, anything above a brisk walking pace was, in his opinion, indecorous.

As Mulholland put the restrainers on and hauled the man off, McLevy added more salt to the wound.

'Wait till we get you to the station. Wait till the door closes. Wait till we send out for the bucket and the mop.'

The three men disappeared through the opening of the close and then it was empty. Only the red patch remained, a last little patch of urine steaming faintly beside it in the wan sunlight.

The mist spiralled up then disappeared like a departing spirit.

10

When the sun sets, shadows, that showed
   at noon
But small, appear most long and terrible.
                                    NATHANIEL LEE,
                                              Oedipus

McLevy's method of interrogation was simple.
He tailored it to type. With Frank Brennan it was
fear. The looser his bowels, the greater chance of
truth.

Although the man seemed an abject coward
and easy mark, he possessed, nevertheless,
bovine strength and an animal cunning which
had to be taken into consideration.

Fear was a science. McLevy was a great
student of scientific invention. See what it had
given humanity in recent years, barbed wire and
dynamite for a start.

They brought Brennan into the interrogation
room, a bare functional space with mysterious
stains of varying colours on the walls. In one
corner might be seen a large gouge in the bare
plaster as if a bear had swiped its claws along the
surface.

There was a small table with two rickety
chairs, one on each side, in the centre of the
room, They sat him down and then both the
inspector and Mulholland fell into what seemed
like a trance.

59

The silence stretched. Brennan licked his dry lips. He looked down at the table surface. It, too, had stains, some faded yellow, some pale red which had soaked into the naked grain. There was also a deep scratch which had been scored the length of the wood in a diagonal slash. That appeared more recent. Perhaps yesterday. Ten minutes ago, even.

Sweat poured down his face. Still the policemen said nothing.

A young constable came in with a bucket and a mop. Brennan's eyes bulged as the items were left in a prominent position. The constable departed. McLevy turned a large key in order to lock the door, put the key in his trouser pocket, then leaned back against the panels of the wood.

Mulholland was standing quietly behind the man so that Brennan's head was near jerked off his shoulders trying to keep an eye on both these evil bastards at the same time.

Finally, McLevy moved to sit opposite the big man at the table. The inspector laid his hands upon it like a minister about to deliver a sermon. Brennan flinched slightly as if too near the hot flame.

A big flashy-dressed fellow, certain women might find him attractive; he possessed a false gallantry which fooled them time and time again.

McLevy adjudged it the moment to begin. There was a rancid odour from the man's mouth, either he had some gum disease or he lived on carrion flesh.

'So ye killed her, Frank,' he said. 'Was there

any particular reason?'

Delivered in such tones as would suggest a pleasant choice between two fine whiskies set upon the bar, it inveigled Brennan into a nodding agreement before self-preservation set in and he howled denial.

'I did no such thing! Why would I do that, now?'

'She wasnae bringing in the coin. Ye like your drink. Ye saw her on the corner, not a penny had she earned.'

Mulholland chimed in. 'Justifiable anger, Frank. Ye've a terrible temper, everyone knows that. It just swept over you. A righteous wrath, then the sword was lifted.'

'I don't possess such weapon as a sword.'

'But you have the anger, no denyin' that,' said the constable, closing one of his blue eyes in a wink of complicity. 'The wrath.'

'Righteous,' agreed McLevy. 'A man needs his money.'

'I'd *plenty* of money for drink that night. I bought for the whole place.' Brennan affected a haughty air to cover his desperation. 'I had people at my beck and call, they kissed my hand. Late into the night, we drank.'

'How late?' Mulholland took over, he had noticed the inspector go very still all of a sudden.

'It was past three in the morning when I spent the last penny. I bought for all, a roaring boy. The landlord was of the company, he'll tell you.'

'The changeful wing of an alibi.' Mulholland quoted a dictum of his yet silent inspector.

Brennan had got some of his nerve back. 'John

61

Docherty is an honest man. An upstanding host!'

'How so?' McLevy sprang into life.

'What?'

'You said plenty of money. Bought for all. How so?'

Brennan's eyes shifted sideways. 'I won it in a game of chance.'

'Ye're a liar.'

Mulholland backed off; this was the inspector's show.

McLevy's eyes bored into Brennan, the big Irishman tried for bravado. A mistake.

'No one names Frank Brennan a liar, no one living on this earth — '

The inspector's hands moved so fast, Mulholland missed it entirely. Brennan did not because he found himself grabbed by the shirt front, pulled bodily out of his chair and spun round like a child's top till he slammed up against the wall with an impact that near jolted the malodorous teeth from out his head.

Then he was off again, another circle, and then another, round and round, a bizarre dance of controlled violence, till the big man was deposited back into the very chair from which he had been plucked.

Slack-jawed, eyes glazed, he watched as McLevy deliberately unbuttoned the hooks and eyes of his tunic, slid it off and laid it neatly on his own chair. His shirt followed to reveal a long-sleeved red semmit, over which he hitched his braces again in two straight lines to contain his little mound of a belly. A comical sight if you discounted the coal-black fury in his eyes.

'Is there any water in that bucket?' he asked.

Mulholland craned his long neck. 'Full to the brim, sir.'

'I will ask you once more, Frank Brennan.' The inspector might have been carved out of stone. 'How so?'

The big man's mouth opened and closed. No words emerged. McLevy, now standing over him, reached forward slowly and took hold of the front of Brennan's throat. He cocked the other hand and sighted down it as if about to release an arrow.

Brennan was paralysed. The fingers of the hand on his thrapple were digging into the soft tissue. Jesus, Mary and Joseph, the man would rip out the whole works; where is the mercy of God here?

'How so?' There was no mercy. Not in these eyes.

An awful smell arose as Brennan lost touch with his bowel movements and emitted a long fearful fart. Mulholland wrinkled his nose but the inspector didn't seem to notice.

'Where did you get the money, Frank?'

'I was paid. Services rendered.'

'*What* service?'

'I — I — ' Brennan's eyes filled with water and he shook his head. McLevy's hand tightened as the truth and one more fart were squeezed out. 'It was gentry. See, this fellow hailed me outside the tavern. I was on my way to find poor Sadie, descry how the wee soul was faring — '

'Ye were off to skim the cream like many a pimp before you. So?'

63

'He offered me a payment. He had a friend he said, liked the cut of Sadie's jib. He would pay me in advance. I was to go back in the tavern. Enjoy myself. Services rendered.'

McLevy let go of the neck and wiped his hand on his semmit. Brennan would not meet his eye. He massaged his throat in the terrible quiet.

The inspector could not afford the luxury of disgust, or the bile that rose in his gullet. He whistled softly to keep it at bay . . . *Charlie is my darling, the young chevalier.*

'This gentry. What did he look like?'

'He kept to the shadows,' said Brennan eager to help now, wrongly thinking the worst was over. 'Silver hair, tall enough but not as me, in a doorway, black gloves, he wore black gloves.'

'Anything else?'

'He smelled of soap.'

'Scented?'

'Carbolic.' Brennan nodded wisely. 'Thought I to myself, that's an odd thing.'

'How so?'

'Gentry don't use such. My mammy washed me in that soap.'

'Not clean enough.'

The inspector walked away to put some distance between them. Mulholland slid in again. 'Anything else about him?'

Brennan shook his head, Mulholland persisted. 'What about his voice, you said he spoke to you, what was the sound?'

'A whisper only. Slow words. But born to command.'

'An Edinburgh voice?'

'I'd hazard . . . not of the Celtic strain.'

'From the South? English?'

'Born to command.'

'What else?'

'Not a bit. I've racked my brains for you, I can remember no more.' Brennan sighed heavily. 'He put the coin payment in my hand, I walked back into the tavern. A mysterious event.'

'*Mysterious?*' McLevy laughed but it was a harsh bitter sound, a terrible twisted anger inside him. 'Ye sold the poor auld whore, left her defenceless, and while you were drinking yourself stupid on the proceeds, her body was being hacked to pieces!'

'That was terrible mischance for the unfortunate soul,' came the sententious response. 'And I blame myself something awful, but who can know the workings of God or the wiles of Satan?'

The flame in McLevy's eyes went out and a cold light replaced it. As he walked back to the table, Mulholland moved in reflex as if to intervene, then thought better.

'You're scum, Frank,' said McLevy. A dispassionate judgement more eviscerating than physical violence. 'At least when Burke and Hare sold bodies, they had the grace tae kill them first or rob the grave. When you sold Sadie Gorman she was alive, her heart was still beating, there was still mischief in her eyes. You are death's pimp. The very man to whom you sold her would be the man that took her life.'

'You don't know that!' cried Brennan.

'I know it,' was the cold response. 'And I'll

65

make sure everyone on the street does as well, every last sinner. Everyone of the Fraternity. When you look in their eyes, you will see what you've done. Not one person will be your friend. A ghost. A dead man walking.'

He went back to the door, opened it with the key and bawled out, 'Ballantyne!'

After a moment, the young constable appeared. He came into the room with some caution, eyes widening at the sight of his inspector in his red semmit and braces, then the after-reek of the farts wafted over. He gazed warily at the seated Brennan.

'Has this man soiled himself, sir?'

'Not yet son,' said McLevy. 'Not yet. Stick him in the cells.'

Brennan rose unbidden and walked on shaky legs to the doorway. A strange dignity had taken possession of him.

The young constable, not wishing to get too close, gestured him through the door but the big Irishman turned at the last.

'This won't make ye think any the better of me,' Brennan said in a drained voice, 'but I owe some such to her. The last three, four nights, Sadie thought someone was watching at her. In the streets. I didn't pay no heed.'

He looked at McLevy like a whipped cur hoping for a biscuit.

'Ye're right,' said McLevy. 'It makes you even worse.'

Brennan turned and left. Ballantyne followed. The door closed. Mulholland let out a long breath to relieve the tension in his gut and

McLevy began slowly to don once more his shirt and tunic.

'We can't hold him,' said the constable.

'I know that. Let him fester for a while. Something else may come to his mind.'

'I doubt it.'

'So do I. But let him fester anyway.'

'That old saying, sir.' The words popped out before Mulholland could get them back. ' "To err is human, to forgive divine' — it doesn't cut much with you does it?'

The inspector finished the last hook and eye then adjusted the hard upright collar of his tunic. Useful that collar in case somebody ever wanted to garrotte you from behind.

'Forgiveness?' he said. 'Tell that to the corpse.'

11

Go, and catch a falling star,
Get with child a mandrake root.

JOHN DONNE,
'Song' ('Go, and catch a falling star')
from *Songs and Sonnets*

The black cat hesitated in the moonlight; it was a neat decision. Behind the lighted window of the attic room was the possibility of succour, but she was a cautious female.

She padded across the oily slates of the roof. The dampness of a late March evening had filmed them to a disagreeable slickness, not at all to her liking.

A fastidious creature, she. Let other females, a lesser breed, fall into disrepair, fur matted, ears chewed, necks an easy target for the tomcat's teeth. She was above such careless rapture. She was a special case.

The cat reached her destination and yowled. After a moment the window opened just wide enough for her to pass through with dignity intact, and in she hopped. The frame came down smartly and it was as if she had never been.

Now, you see it, now you don't. Moonlight is deceptive.

On the other side of the glass, not long after, McLevy wolfed his poor man's supper, salt herring and potatoes, while the cat lapped daintily at a saucer of milk a discreet distance away.

They both finished almost at the same time. The inspector belched gently. Herring did repeat upon the breath but when a lowly constable he'd lived on that provender. Now and again he must return to the past.

He crossed to the fire where a coffee pot had been left to keep warm on the hob, poured some out into his cup, heaped in many spoonfuls of sugar — having a reprehensibly sweet tooth — then returned to his table at the window and sat to look out over his city.

McLevy stirred the black tarry mixture and reviewed events.

They had checked back at the tavern to find that Brennan's story held water. The man had indeed spent like a sailor and caroused until way past the time of Sadie's death. Under guise of questioning to find out if anyone had seen the supplier of Brennan's windfall, McLevy had let out what the big man had sold to gain such a fine recompense.

To judge by the reaction from some of the old biddies in the tavern, Brennan, once released, would be fortunate to survive with his chuckies intact. Bad luck.

Which left this mystery man.

Roach, on being given the report, had counselled against too much supposition on that score — nothing was known, only a payment. The lieutenant would still prefer a drunken navvy on his way home with a sharp blade to his shovel.

Mulholland nodded both ways. The boy would go far.

But McLevy did not approve of shadowy figures in doorways. That was his domain.

Had the man been stalking Sadie? Given Brennan his thirty pieces of silver to make sure the pimp was safely out of the way?

Was there something in her past life which might be the cause of her death or was it possible that she was just a target of a vengeful killing lust against all whores?

McLevy felt in his bones that the latter might be the true path. In his mind's eye he could see, as he had done in reality many a time, the proud stance of her on the corner.

That daft feather dancing in her stringy hair. Her unashamed proclamation, here I am, bugger the lot of you, ye've been in and out of me all my life, here I set myself, come and get it. The very swagger was a reproach to probity, sin laughing at virtue. Come and get it.

What darkness in the heart had been unleashed by that sight, a torrent so strong that it swept all before?

He closed his eyes and he was walking towards her, the weapon in his hand.

Mouth smiling, her eyes full of mischief, his heart seared with hatred, kill the harlot, kill the disease where it spreads. Hot blood.

Or was it a cold act? Detached. Watch her fall. Lie in the gutter like a dead animal. Just an animal.

The cat suddenly shot bolt upright, fur rising like a hairy nimbus from the back of her neck. A creaking board on the stairs outside. Gardyloo!

Mrs MacPherson, his landlady, up to get his dirty plate, though God knows she was always complaining about the stairs and hated the fact he had his meal brought up from the dining room.

He hoped most earnestly she wasn't accompanied by her West Highland terrier, Fergus, a decent enough wee tyke but representative of what McLevy considered a vastly overrated breed rejoicing in the name of man's best friend.

Fergus loathed the feline species and so, for his sake, did Mrs MacPherson, though she did not possess the dog's olfactory abilities.

McLevy quickly shooed the cat into his small bedroom, shoved the saucer of milk inside to keep company, and shut them both in just as a knock sounded at the landing door.

As he made his way to answer, something nagged at the back of his mind. Mrs MacPherson was a rap-a-tap-tap, that was just a rap-a-tap, what was going on here, surely the woman wasn't adjusting her habits?

He threw open the door, gaze automatically adjusted to the eye-level of the dumpy Dundonian frame of his landlady, only to find that he was, in fact, staring at a female bosom. Safely ensconced in material right enough, pale purple, deep collar, glimpsed behind the dark outdoor coat, but a not inconsiderable statement of undoubted femininity.

A polite cough brought him swiftly up to the face. The light from his room shone past his shoulder and illuminated her in the shadows of the hallway; the countenance was part hidden by her bonnet but the skin was clear, apparently unlined by travail, peaches and cream, and yet it had a tight stretch. Blue eyes, but there was a darkness to the colour. A troubled sky.

The mouth was firm, lips a touch on the thin side. A very beautiful face though. The kind you'd see in the old paintings, damsel in distress with young men dying all around her; fatalities of a misplaced desire to rescue what was perfectly capable of looking after itself.

McLevy's sympathy was always with the dragon lurking at the back.

As they stared at each other, the landlady's voice floated up from under.

'I hope ye don't mind, Mr McLevy,' she called. 'But the young lady says she knows of ye and I am covered all over in flour.'

'That's all right, Mrs MacPherson,' he shouted back. 'Tend tae your oven, that's the important matter.'

Sure enough, the enticing smell of newly baked bread could be discerned wafting up the stairway.

The dog barked below, perhaps it sensed the cat. The woman took a deep breath.

'Are you James McLevy?'

'You have heard me so identified.'

'I must apologise for disturbing your supper.'

He quickly wiped at his mouth with the back of a hand. Damn herring that left an oily spume.

'My name is Joanna Lightfoot. I . . . have great need of your assistance.'

He glanced doubtfully back into the recess of his room.

It wasn't exactly a midden but, not unlike his own mind, nothing seemed to know its place.

Seeing his hesitation, she took another deep breath, then her eyes closed and she slumped forward.

He grasped her by the elbow. They were stuck mid-portal. The indignant cat started scratching at his bedroom door.

Between women. A fine predicament.

12

Tell me, where all past years are,
Or who cleft the Devil's foot.

JOHN DONNE,
'Song', op. cit.

The cat cast a final, baleful, slant-eyed glance at the female sitting in the cracked leather armchair by the fire, slid out of the open window then ghosted off into the moonlight.

McLevy closed the frame and remained gazing out over the rooftops. He could feel the heat of the woman's gaze on his back but resisted the urge to turn round immediately.

'I'm sorry,' she murmured. 'I am not in the habit of giving in to weakness.'

'Neither am I,' he muttered.

Now he did turn and gave her a long hard scrutiny, making no attempt to hide the fact.

'What is the name of your cat?'

She was not ready to begin. Not yet. He could wait.

'Bathsheba, I call her. But she's not mine. She just visits. Like yourself.'

She looked away into the flames of the coal fire. He was not deflected and redoubled his examination.

'Ye're not as young as you first appear.'

The blunt statement seemed to amuse her.

'Appearances can be deceptive.'

'I've often found that so. In my profession.'

She had taken off the bonnet. Her hair was done up in a chignon of sorts, with stray golden tendrils escaping from the general confinement. Under the outdoor coat that now lay open, her gown was of a crushed silk material, the bodice a darker purple than the rest.

It was quality. Expensive. The style promised freedom to the body, not yet delivered but . . . a certain yield to the swelling pressure. Very fetching. A bonny picture. The itemised Eve.

'I am approaching thirty years of age.'

'I can believe that.'

She sat at once upright and there might have been the slightest narrowing of the eyes.

McLevy whistled cheerfully under his breath as he retrieved his coffee, making no effort to offer her a cup.

He could not to himself say why he was acting in such a boorish manner, though, to be truthful, he didn't ever have to stretch too far to attain such an attitude.

Perfection often annoyed him and he loved to give it a wee dig in the ribs but that wasn't the whole cause.

Anyhow, a swooning woman was grounds for deep distrust, as was the rare and perplexing sight of a female by his fireside. He could sense complication. A feminine psyche going back right tae the very caves themselves. A psyche whose ruthless inner certainty it was his bounden duty to disrupt.

He sniffed. She was wearing perfume. A rose

fragrance. Reminded him of Jean Brash. Females and their odours.

'Or is it just because I possess beauty?' she said.

His turn to narrow eyes.

'What was that? I must confess I was lost in thought.'

'The reason for your lack of manners.'

'Oh that? No, that's nothing to do with beauty. That's just . . . part and parcel.'

'I am glad to hear it. Most men take me at face value. It is so . . . inevitable, I suppose, given their limitations.'

One in the gut for him and nothing he did not deserve but why did he feel an obscure danger threatening?

Maybe she was right. Just beauty. In pale purple. That would be threatening enough. Ah well, cheat fair.

'What is your preference in coffee?' he ventured.

'Black.'

'Sugar?'

'A small plantation.'

McLevy smiled suddenly, a beguiling glint in his eye. It was rather alarming. Like the wolf in Red Riding-Hood.

He brought her the coffee as directed, put it almost meekly into her hand, then retreated to regard her from a secure distance at the other side of the fire. She took a gulp. It was like bitumen.

'Joanna Lightfoot. Mistress or Miss?' he asked.

'Miss.'

The merest flicker of an eye but she caught it. 'I know. At the prime of my life and still not married. Such a waste. I am tortured night and day, waiting for my Prince Charming.'

McLevy sensed some twisted truth in her words and a hidden barb. Perhaps directed against herself. Women were the very devil to read. Like the Sargasso Sea.

'I would nae place ye from round here.'

'You may place me from Liquorpond Street, in London. That is where I was born,' she said quietly.

'I've heard tell of that location.' It was a notorious slum quarter, mind you nothing to the Via Dolorosas of his own fair city. 'You've come up in the world.'

For a moment it appeared as if she thought to say something then she lowered her eyes.

'Ye remarked you had need of my assistance?'

Her fingers plucked at the bodice, which gently constrained the soft, no doubt sweet, flesh that poets eulogised and McLevy kept his mind resolutely free from contemplating.

'I read in the evening newspaper,' she stopped fiddling for which he was most grateful, 'about a murder in Leith. Yourself, the investigating officer.'

'I am indeed,' he replied. And waited.

'The death blow was most . . . singular?'

'That's one description. Sadie Gorman was split like an old apple tree, but she did not bring forth sweet scent.'

He chuckled to himself in a macabre fashion but his eyes never left her.

She rose from the chair, walked restlessly away from him into the centre of the room and looked around. The wallpaper seemed to be composed of brown flowers. She'd never seen *brown* flowers in all of her life. The place had an air of neglect, like an empty box. The ceiling had cracks running all over like a spider's web, two threadbare carpets lay like dead animals on the bare floorboards, the place was clean enough but sterile. As if McLevy lived his life somewhere else. Not even a picture on the wall, and, more importantly, not a mirror to be seen.

'This lacks a woman's touch,' she said.

'As Samson did Delilah's?' McLevy muttered as he shook the coffee pot hopefully and received a dry response. With a disappointed grunt, he banged it back on the hob.

The inspector was getting fed up with all this. A small fishbone had lodged in one of his back molars and he was dying to hook his thumbnail in there. Manners maketh man, however.

'Did you come up here to talk about decoration or murder? There's only the one that interests me, so declare yourself.'

The colour heightened in her cheeks for a moment, then she suddenly stamped her foot on the floor.

He noticed her boots were in the latest mode. Boots strangely interested him, of Italian leather he would surmise, tight to the ankle, the laces looped so neatly.

Her feet almost as large as his own. In fact . . . he walked towards her so that they were face to face. She was near the same elevation as himself, now what would all this equality produce?

She looked him straight in the eye, then delivered a body blow.

'Thirty years ago in Leith. There was a similar death, was there not?'

13

Teach me to hear mermaids singing,
And to keep off envy's stinging,

JOHN DONNE,
'Song', op. cit.

Leith, December 1850
Sergeant George Cameron lay in a hospital bed of the Edinburgh Royal Infirmary, what a place to end your days.

He had no relatives to gather round and dab their eyes, for which he thanked his Protestant Redeemer. They were all up in the Highlands gutting trout and chasing sheep.

What a scunner. Some drunken fool in a tavern brawl sticks a pen-knife in his leg, the blade snaps off, the young doctor, Jarvis by name, just qualified, full of mince, opens up his flesh but cannae find it.

'Dropped out,' he says. 'It must have dropped out.'

But it hadnae dropped out, the stupid bastard had missed the damn thing entirely. It had lodged just below the back of the knee and by the time inflammation had alerted Cameron, the thing found and removed from its hidey-hole, his blood was evil-poisoned.

Amputation had been suggested — that would be nice, on the saunter with a wooden leg. But even for that, the fever must abate, and it had not abated; it raged through him like a forest fire.

A hand came down with a big white hankie and wiped the sweat off his face. Dabbed the tangled eyebrows. Constable James McLevy. All his damned fault.

He should have been Cameron's rearguard, what happened though he'd got carried away and had not observed the eleventh commandment. In matters of communal violence, always stay back to back with a fellow bull's-eye.

Somebody'd nipped the helmet from the young man's head, he'd gone on the chase and while he was thus engaged a drunken sailor had stuck his 'baccy knife into Cameron's nether limb.

See the big white face staring down, the agony and guilt in his eyes, serve the bugger right. At least he would be alive to feel such agony. A spasm of pain went through Cameron and he reared up in the bed, then collapsed back.

God help him, he was like a gaffed fish.

'Well now, what have ye got to say for yourself?' he demanded fiercely. Well he meant it fierce but it came out more like snuffed mutton.

'I wish it had been me who suffered the blow.'

'So do I, son. So, do I,' muttered Cameron. 'But for some reason the Almighty thought otherwise.'

Another spasm took him and the young man stood helplessly by, like a mourner who didn't know where to lay the plate of funeral meat.

'Shall I fetch the nurse?'

81

'For God's sake no! She's a Paisley woman, what comfort is there in that?'

The constable gently mopped the soaking brow again.

'I am truly sorry,' he said.

'Sorry? Sorry's not good enough!' Cameron glowered up, his pupils dark with pain. 'Now you listen to me, the next time I close these eyes o' mine, will be the last. I'm not opening them another go.' His gaze went inwards and his voice lost power.

'Too much suffering, Jamie. I'll be giving up the ghost. Now here's what you must do. You must tell our noble commander Lieutenant Moxey that I am to be buried with full honours and attendance.'

'I'm not sure the lieutenant will pay much heed to me,' the constable replied. 'But I'll stand in front of his face until he does so.'

Damn the boy, and damn this dying, George would have enjoyed teaching him the craft.

'Just mention a bawdy-hoose, name of the Happy Land. Then ask after his wife. He'll do it.'

By God he would, the dirty auld leglifter — ever since his good woman had taken to her bed with a wasting disease he'd been at it like a fornicator reborn.

'Now, on the day, the burial day, you must pray for rain. Buckets of it.'

Cameron laughed painfully at the look on the boy's face.

'Rain?'

'Aye. The high heid-yins, the powers-that-be,

will all be standing there. I would wish a long service, a deep-ribbed minister who loves his own words, and the east wind blowing a sleety lash in their faces so they all may catch their death of cold.'

This time the laughter racked him so deep with pain that he had to stop even his last pleasure. Down to the real business. He beckoned the constable in close and pointed to a small mother-of-pearl box which lay on his bedside table.

The young man brought it to him with due solemnity as if it contained the ashes of his ancestors.

'That box was a nuptial gift to my own good mother, pity it wasnae a gun tae shoot my father on the wedding night,' the sergeant announced heavily.

'Then ye wouldnae be here,' said the constable.

Damn the boy again. Damn his gallows humour. Damn the tears stinging at his eyes. He didnae wish to disgrace himself, let the boy see strength. Strength was everything.

Cameron fumbled for his eyeglasses, stuck them on his nose, opened the lid with impatient trembling fingers and took out . . . a fragment of thin black cloth.

'Ye remember this?'

'I do. From the murdered girl. In her hand.'

'That was the bond, Jamie. Between us. We looked at death thegither then. Now, we do so once more.'

He put the fragment back and pressed the box

83

into the constable's hand.

'It always irked me, the vicious bastard, I never brought him in to kiss the hangman's rope. Poor wee lassie, it was her first time a-whoring, did ye know that?'

'I was there when her brother told you.'

'So ye were, so ye were.' The sergeant's eyes began to droop and with an effort he prised them open again. Behind the thick glasses, magnified, they blinked like an owl.

'It was in all the papers, you 'member that?'

'I do indeed,' replied the constable.

A silence fell. Cameron stared into space and the young man produced a headline from memory.

'A Lamb to the Slaughter,' he quoted solemnly.

Cameron's head jerked back as a shaft of pain burnt through his body. He looked up at the constable.

'The case is yours. One day you will solve it. I charge you so. Don't fail me, now.'

'I promise I will do everything in my power.'

'Until the day ye die!' demanded Cameron.

'Until the day I die,' came the pledge.

Cameron leant back exhaustedly on the pillow, his mind was beginning to go, the poison dancing in his veins, what was that air he always enjoyed? Tam Lucas of the Feast, damn me but he could not recall the tune.

'Can ye sing?' he demanded hoarsely.

'I know very few melodies,' was the response.

The sergeant waved his hand in decree, he could not trust the words to emerge.

Damn it, he was on the verge of weeping buckets, this was not the way to go.

'Sing!' he commanded

The constable, with quavering voice, gave issue.

Shock pulled Cameron from death's door.

'That's a Jacobite air!'

'A friend of my mother, she sang it. Jean Scott. When I was a wee boy. It's the only tune I can carry.'

'Was this friend of Jacobite persuasion?'

'I never asked her.'

The sergeant smiled crookedly.

'Tell ye the truth, son, I sometimes wished I could have fought by Charlie's side. I'd rather die from a bayonet than a bastard penknife.'

He motioned for more melody, then a random thought struck and he laughed with a feverish glee.

'But, it wasnae the knife that did for me, it was the blackness crusted, the tobacco on it that poisoned. A dangerous damned thing. Tobacco.'

He closed his eyes without farewell and James McLevy sang the Highlander out, tears dripping down his face.

'Charlie is my darling . . . the young chevalier . . .'

The thick glasses glinted. But the light was gone.

14

And find
What wind
Serves to advance an honest mind.

JOHN DONNE,
'Song', op. cit.

There was one man who could put fear into Joanna Lightfoot by the blankness of his gaze; now she had found another. She took a pace back as McLevy slowly returned from where her words had transported him.

'Mae Donnachie,' he said, voice slurred from a muddy past. 'Her first night out whoring. She was fifteen years old. She had a family to support.'

He turned away and shook his head as though to rid it of certain images then swung back and reached out his hand towards her, fingers crooked, as if to hold her by the throat. Then he dropped the hand and was perfectly still.

'How do you know about this?'

She had her nerve back now. A calm reply.

'Tell me what you found, and I shall respond in kind.'

He moved to the fire and, using the tongs, carefully put individual lumps of coal one on top of the other, building a fortress amid the flames.

'She'd come down across the bridges from the Royal Mile, the competition would be too savage up there. She didnae know the streets of Leith, she was just a young lassie. Desperate. Her brother's lungs were shot tae hell, she wanted to get him medicine; the father drank what the mother earned with washing and the like. The mother had six further children. Lived in the one room, eleven feet or so each way. One o' the wynds off the High Street. A common enough tangle.'

'What a dreadful life.'

He sensed a distance to that remark, just a wee touch of looking down from on high; so he jumped on it like a dog on a bone. Teeth first, arse to follow.

'Ye must have seen the same in Liquorpond Street, if what you tell me is true, that you were born there?'

'I was . . . removed at an early age.'

'Lucky you. Mae Donnachie stayed where she was.'

He crossed to a small cupboard, and banged the side of his fist against the wood. The door sprang open and she jumped a little at the unexpected noise. As he scrabbled inside for something, he carried on the tale.

'It wasnae our parish but the City police were a wee touch on the brutal side, so we broke the sad tidings to the Donnachies ourselves.'

'We?'

'Sergeant Cameron and me. I was a babe in arms then.'

'Hard to imagine.'

He ignored the remark, and brought out something wrapped in tissue paper. He held it cupped carefully in his hands, as he made towards the table at the window.

'The brother was stricken with guilt. He died soon after. A short-lived family.'

'Terrible times.'

'They have not changed.'

'Surely there are civic policies on hand to alter all that? Improvements?'

'They must have passed me by,' McLevy said dryly.

'But surely, Social reform — '

'Politicians have no interest in the poor. The poor have no power. They cannot vote. The only choice they have is which bucket to be sick in.'

He had laid a small mother-of-pearl box on the table; it was a pinky-white colour which took on some of the radiance of the moonlight coming in through the window pane.

McLevy blew upon the casing and wiped away a minuscule speck of dirt with the tissue. He concentrated his gaze as if the box contained some deep secret and seemed to have completely lost interest in their conversation.

'Mae Donnachie, how did she die?' Joanna prompted.

'Split to the bone.'

'Did you find the murderer?'

'Not a trace.'

He straightened up and smiled. 'But you would know that, surely?'

She avoided his eyes for the moment. She was beginning to catch on to his methods. Always keep the subject off balance, come in from an angle, break up the rhythms, truly the fellow was more devious than appearances warranted.

'You must have found something?' she ventured.

'A man was seen running through St Andrews Street, towards the Kirkgate. Well dressed, a fine head of hair.'

'Hair?'

'He was seen from above, through a dirty window by an auld wifie on her last legs.'

He laughed but there was a bitter edge.

'So far gone, she didnae even mind talking to the police. We knocked on every door, stuck our heads to places a starving dog wouldnae creep in to die. We'd have talked to the very rats themselves, had they but been witness.'

'It sounds a personal quest.'

'You might put it that way.'

He was now looking at her with a measure of hostility. That suited Joanna just fine.

'So the result of your labours, was . . . nothing?'

'A drunkart claimed he saw a man o' that ilk, but the fellow was in delirium with bad whisky, kill-me-deadly, he would have sold his birthright for another drink.'

'Which you gave him?'

A wolfish grin.

'The price we had to pay, Miss Lightfoot. The price we had to pay. He claimed the man near jumped over him where he lay on the ground. The man was clad in black, a red stain all down his front. He didnae glimpse the face. The man ran off towards the Maris Chapel on Constitution Street.'

'But you did not believe him? This . . . drunk-ard?'

'Oh, I entered into the Catholic church right enough, Sergeant Cameron wouldnae go near the place. Just built. New. Ye could smell the Pope everywhere. There was a young priest, Father Callan. I made enquiries of him but he could not help me. Ye know these Romans, the confession box or bugger all else. And the place was white as snow, the only red was the altar wine.'

He laughed but he had a memory of Father Callan's face, a soft moonlike priestly visage though the eyes were honest enough. And there might have been something hidden in them. Obscured by the calling. A shadow on the wall. He'd pressed the priest as hard as he could but came up against a profound, sanctified silence.

Of course he was only a constable then, but even now, at the height of his considerable powers, he doubted if the little priest would have told him more. A Catholic silence is like no other.

'So you ended up with bugger all?'

'Precisely.'

If she had hoped to knock him back by repeating the swearword, it had no discernible effect.

'It wasnae much to begin with, but the trail died that night. The man had vanished.'

She thought that he would say more, but nothing came. The room was utterly still. Rooted to the spot.

Sadie Gorman's body on the slab. McLevy

wondered then, had the past come back to haunt him. Time would tell.

'The location of this . . . dreadful murder. Mae Donnachie. Was it . . . nearhand to the . . . recent event?'

'Oh, aye. Back of the Markets. A few streets between them. Thirty years and a stone's throw.'

'And the present . . . victim. Was she also young?'

'Sadie Gorman?' he laughed suddenly. 'I don't think she would describe herself as such. She was at the other end o' the sliding scale.'

He laid his hand on the mother-of-pearl box, and ran his fingers gently over the surface. 'That would appear to be me, Miss Lightfoot. Now how about yourself?'

'What lies in the box?' she asked.

Make him wait. Make him wait.

'Relics.'

He opened it and brought forth a broken white feather that he held carefully between thumb and forefinger.

'This came from Sadie Gorman. She wore it in her hair. A silent witness.'

He held it up.

'As you can see, it has also suffered injury. The proud head chopped off.'

Joanna showed little interest. He returned the feather to the box.

'And this?' He produced the fragment of black material. 'This was clutched in Mae Donnachie's hand. A remnant. A killer's legacy.'

Her face went white at the sight of the scrap of fabric. She jerked forward convulsively and

91

almost snatched it out of his hand, fingers trembling, holding it up to her eyes by the light of the fire.

For a moment he feared that she would throw it into the flames and tensed to hit her arm a blow which would divert any such intention, but after a moment she seemed to come to a decision. She handed the scrap back and spoke quietly.

'Could that have . . . come from a stock? Such as would cover a finger, or part of a hand?'

'I had thought about that. Not a glove; the material is too fine for that. Perhaps a stocking, or a cravat, a scarf of sorts even, but . . . it might be part of such a covering.'

He scrupulously replaced both relics inside the box and closed the lid.

'Why do you ask, Miss Lightfoot. What is on your mind?'

'What if I told you a story, inspector?'

'I like stories,' said McLevy. 'But I don't always believe them.'

'I don't ask for belief,' she replied. 'All I desire is that you listen and form your own opinion.'

She crossed back to the leather chair in front of the fire and sat herself down. McLevy warily followed suit to ensconce himself in the sister armchair opposite which had, however, a broken spring jabbing into his backside. They faced each other like subjects at a séance.

She thus began. In the manner of a story.

'This is about a man who sat in a railway compartment with his daughter's coffin, all the way from Euston to his own father's house in the northern slopes of the Mearns, between Dundee and Aberdeen. A long, long journey.

'The girl was five years old. Her name was Jessy. The medical explanation for her death was meningitis. She had lingered most cruelly for two weeks, until,' a deep, bitter note entered the voice, 'she was compassionately taken by her Saviour into the fold of his peace.'

'That's nice,' said McLevy.

'His own words. Please refrain from interruption.'

He glanced longingly at the empty coffee pot. This could take for ever, he'd never yet known a woman frugal in expression, their details tended to multiply like the Hydra's teeth.

She continued. 'He closed the blinds down in the compartment, so that he could be alone with her and his thoughts. His Christian thoughts.

'But suppose his mind shifted and the demons came to feast? What if his sins had caused her death? What if it was God's punishment for his surrender to temptation? The temptation of the flesh. How could he cleanse that from his soul? Suppose his mind was near deranged, unbalanced, trembling on the edge of the abyss?'

She took a deep breath. 'And when he reached his father's house, things went from bad to worse.'

15

If thou be'st born to strange sights,
Things invisible to see,
Ride ten thousand days and nights,
Till age snow white hairs on thee.

JOHN DONNE,
'Song', op. cit.

Fasque, Mearns, 13 April 1850
The woman squirmed and twitched against the leather straps restraining her on the bed, the dark hair plastered against her brow. Her legs fought against the bonds, aching to spread and let Jesus in, eyes wild, as the addiction bit deep. O sweet opium, bring me your beautiful dreams, let me walk in fields of gold, let me taste the honeycomb, let me kiss the purple hem, let the incense burner trail its perfect smoke around my naked body, let the Holy Wafer melt in my mouth with fine indulgence, let Christ's blood flow in the firmament, let me bathe in it like Cleopatra in the ass's milk, let my Faith shine free!

Dr Purdie moved away from the writhing figure towards the man who stood watching, helplessly, as his sister continued the inner dialogue with her present God.

Both manner and dress proclaimed the doctor to be a tightly buttoned Presbyterian, but he was not an unkind man.

'I'm afraid she took the death of your daughter Jessy very badly, Mr Gladstone,' he said. 'She evaded the scrutiny of her nurse and, as far as we are able to ascertain, imbued herself with near to three hundred drops of laudanum. It is a massive dose. We have had to hold her down by force while the leeches were applied and now we can only wait and pray.'

'How is my father?'

'Sir John is . . . resting. Upstairs. In his bed. He wishes to conserve his strength. For tomorrow.'

Outside, the rain beat against the windows, adding to the gloomy spectral air of the room which was shrouded, the dark drapes pulled tight.

A bedside light was the only illumination and it cast their shadows on to the pale violet walls where portraits of family ancestors looked down in no great approval, as the woman jerked convulsively.

The nurse, starched like a nun, and a brawny specimen to boot, laid a cold compress on the brow. It provoked an outcry and a shiver.

Purdie noted a response from the man, hand clenched to a fist, nails dug into palm. The whole family would be on medication soon.

The man's voice was slow, sonorous, it betrayed little of the dreadful tension within.

'Tomorrow Jessy will be buried in the family vault. I would not wish my sister Helen to attend.'

'I do not think her capable, sir.'

'I would not wish it in any case.'

95

'A wise decision,' murmured Purdie who had a sudden outlandish vision of the patient in her nightgown, leaping on to the coffin and scandalising the granite slabs. This madness was catching.

'Has she asked for me?'

The doctor coughed.

'Not immediately. She did, in her . . . perturbation demand the presence of a priest but I thought it better to wait until yourself or Sir John might advise me on the matter.'

It was as if he'd shoved an iron bar into the rectal region. Purdie knew that Helen Gladstone had converted to Catholicism some eight years ago, and though the family was High Anglican, a priest would be as welcome in this house as a rat with the plague.

'I would like to be alone with my sister.'

A command Purdie hastened to obey. He would be glad to get out of the place, the very walls seemed to be closing in and there was a feeling of being constantly observed and spied upon, eyes everywhere, the servants of the house more like sentinels. Besides the man oozed a kind of baleful power, and it was said that when he rose to speak in the House of Commons, opponents feared his oratory as they would fear a projectile from the sky.

The good doctor, who had no wish to be projected upon, signalled the nurse to leave also.

Apart from one curious glance as she passed the man by, Eileen Marshall, for that was her name, did as she was bade.

The room was now empty, save for the rigid tense figure of the man and the restless dreamer.

16

Thou, when thou return'st, wilt tell me
All strange wonders that befell thee,
And swear
Nowhere
Lives a woman true and fair.

JOHN DONNE,
'Song', op. cit.

A frenzied series of barks in the distance
downstairs broke the spell. Fergus must have
burnt his nose on the hot oven.

Joanna Lightfoot had fallen silent.

McLevy was like a wee boy with his face
pressed up against the sweetie-shop window.

'What followed after?' he demanded.

'That is for someone else to say.'

'Such as who? The sister?'

'She died not long ago. January past. Events
may have once more been set in motion by that
particular death.'

Joanna sighed and threw back her head to
reveal a white throat, where McLevy could make
out the faintest beating of a pulse just above the
purple collar.

The fishbone was driving him mad. To hell
with it.

While her eyes still glazed up at the mottled
ceiling, he dug a thumbnail into his back teeth,
hooked out the offending fragment and flipped it

surreptitiously into the hearth.

Now, as George Cameron would have put it, let's get tae the real business.

'I assume you are referring to William Ewart Gladstone here.'

A sardonic edge cut under the grandiose words. 'Yon Muckle Great Liberal. About to take Midlothian by storm and carry all before like a speeding train? Are ye talking about him by any chance? The People's William?'

'God help me, I am indeed.' She replied with some feeling.

'And are you trying to draw some connection between this pillar o' rectitude and these two murders?' McLevy abruptly shot out of the armchair and almost danced in agitation around the room as he continued. 'Because so far nothing you have said would in the smallest part convince me of anything other than the fact that you possess a fearsome imagination, Miss Lightfoot.

'Dinnae mistake me. I enjoyed the recitation but it amounts to damn all. Not worth a spit in the fire!'

She looked at him levelly, unmoved by his apparent indignation.

'In 1843,' she said, 'William Gladstone shot the forefinger off his left hand in a hunting accident. He has worn a black stock ever since, to cover the loss.'

McLevy thought for a moment. 'Serves him right for such intent tae slaughter.'

A sudden smile. Those lupine eyes caught colour from the flames and for a moment took on a yellow sheen.

'But a scrap of cloth proves nothing.'

Joanna Lightfoot spoke in formal tones as if laying out the terms of a will.

'The night his daughter was buried, the 14th of April, William Gladstone, informing everyone that he had sore need of solitude, went through to Edinburgh New Town to stay at the family winter house in Atholl Crescent.'

'I know Atholl Crescent,' cried McLevy suddenly. 'Not a kick in the arse from Leith!'

'Not to a man who considers twenty miles on foot to be a mere stroll,' she replied.

He smiled. She realised her response had been too eager. Damnation.

'Go ahead,' he said. 'It's your story.'

Nothing for it. No turning back.

'William Gladstone did not remain at the house. The servants were told that he was too restless, he needed to walk, to clear his head. He left just after supper and returned at two o'clock in the morning. On that night Mae Donnachie was murdered.'

'Oh there's no argument about the date,' said McLevy almost placidly. 'Just the rest of your insinuations.'

He whistled softly under his breath, despite his better judgement he could feel a wee wriggle in the breadbasket.

'Accepting for a moment, which I do not, not remotely, nevertheless, let us entertain a postulation that some of the events you describe may possibly have occurred, you mention a fragility of mind brought on by the weight of guilt, itself a result of a surrender to temptation.

99

'Sin. I believe you may have even used the word . . . sin. What sort of temptation, Miss Lightfoot? What kind of sin are we talking about here?'

My goodness, he thought, was that a blush on her fair cheeks? Or were maybe her drawers getting too much warm air from the fire?

And why, he further thought, his mind entertaining these mad notions a wee touch further, would the killing of a pavement nymph expiate such sin? Then he remembered his own words to Mulholland, *'These pillars of genteelity, they need their whores but they despise and hate themselves for it. And some of them hate the whores even worse.'* Was he wiser than even he knew? Was that possible?

He almost laughed aloud. His mind had that effect on him sometimes.

He looked into her blue eyes. There was an anguish of sorts lurking deep within, but whether it had connection to this present moment was impossible to gauge.

'What kind of sin, Miss Lightfoot?'

She took a breath, a shudder of sorts.

'I hope to bring you proof of that shortly. One thing I can tell you more. After addressing the crowd at Waverley Market last night, Gladstone retired to the house the Earl of Rosebery has taken for him. In George Street.'

'That's in the New Town as well. What a coincidence!'

Joanna ploughed on, in measured tone, regardless.

'He insisted that he was too enlivened by the

adoration of the people to rest indoors. He embarked upon an evening walk. For the good of his health, he said.'

'When did he return?' asked McLevy in an idle fashion.

'After midnight.'

'How d'ye know all this?'

'I have a present connection. On hand.'

He waited for more but she bowed her head as if too weary to continue. 'And what about thirty years ago? Ye certainly werenae on hand then. Hardly even in conception!'

A coarse laugh which she dismissed.

'Please do not act the vulgarian, inspector. You demean both yourself and me by pretending to a brutish quality you do not possess.'

'Oh, I would not be too sure of that and ye havenae answered the question.'

'I cannot. Not at this moment.'

Joanna lifted a small lady's reticule she had laid beside her on the chair, opened it and took out a folded piece of paper.

'But, I would implore you to visit the person whose name and address are contained therein.'

She held out her hand but he did not respond in kind and she remained rather foolishly with outstretched arm.

'Therein?' he said mockingly. 'What's therein tae me?'

'The truth. I must find it out.'

'Then pursue for yourself.'

'I am too personally involved.'

'Are ye now? Do tell.'

Her arm was beginning to ache and her temper rising.

'It is everything I have in my life. I must know the truth, you are the only person I can trust!'

'Why me?'

'I am told you will not be deflected from justice, high or low. And, in this case, a case of murder, you are the investigating officer.'

He pressed further. 'A cold trail, a warm murder, and Willie Gladstone. What is your interest in all these?'

'As I have told you. It is personal.'

'In what way? What secret do you hug tae the bosom, Miss Lightfoot?'

For a moment her eyes glistened and her outstretched fingers trembled.

'Come along,' said he. 'Ye can trust a policeman.'

'I already have. Please. Do not make me beg.'

He still made no move. Her hand closed convulsively round the paper.

'Take or leave. Go to hell, inspector.'

She threw the paper towards the flames of the fire, snatched up her belongings and was through the door in a trice while McLevy stood completely flummoxed by the sudden change in events.

He made as if to follow her then realised that the paper was curling up in the heat and hastily fished it out at the cost of a singed index finger. As he blew upon the injured digit, the outside door of the house slammed shut and he went swiftly to the window and threw it open.

Down below in the street he made out the tall

figure of Joanna, who banged her hat upon her golden hair and strode purposefully towards the corner then round and out of sight. She had a somewhat mannish gait, strange he hadn't remarked that fact. He stuck his head out into the night and strained to listen.

Yes. Faintly. Jingle of a carriage. The mysterious Miss Lightfoot, like Cinderella, had a coach at her disposal.

Interesting. A hansom cab probably and she'd been with McLevy a fair passage, that would cost, these buggers wait for no one a length of time without their pockets being lined. Money to burn, eh? And her clothes were expensive.

Was she being kept? And, if so, who was keeping her? Who was up to what with whom?

Somewhere in the night, a cat shrieked as if in terrible pain. McLevy hoped it wasn't Bathsheba. After mating, the male would be withdrawing its member and the barb at the end would be causing sore agony, a dirty trick nature played on the female of the feline species.

He produced the paper slightly blackened round the edges, shuffled it open, and peered at it in the moonlight.

It contained a name and address. At least that much was true. But only that much.

17

The Diary of James McLevy

They say the child is father to the man. I shall not dispute that assumption.

My own childhood was spent staring into the face of a madwoman. My mother.

Madness is such a strange visitation. The mad do not realise that they are so. They merely see a different world where everyone else is a demon in disguise.

It took some time to realise the insanity before me. It was quiet and insidious. I wonder how much seeped into my soul, a fear that never leaves me.

Most of the time, she was normal. A dressmaker. Good at her job. The room was clean. Then her eyes would shift to a far country and she would pour poison in my ears.

She would take to her bed and lie there in the most terrible stillness, her hair raven black on the pillow.

Black as the Earl of Hell's waistcoat. So said our neighbour, Jean Scott, a wee round woman, scolding and kind, who took pity on such a boy as I was, birthed to insanity.

She lay on the pillow. Maria McLevy. Her mother was Italian, her father was bog Irish and my own father, she insisted, was an angel of God who came to her one night.

The son of a madwoman and an angel. Who am I to argue?

18

As who should say, 'I am Sir Oracle
And when I ope my lips let no dog bark!'
WILLIAM SHAKESPEARE,
The Merchant of Venice

The accustomed early morning hush in the parkland of the Earl of Rosebery's Dalmeny estate was broken by the biting sound of an axe on wood.

A sycamore tree shuddered under the weight of the assault as the blade cut deep, wielded with great force by a man whose white hair waved accompaniment to each precise and fearsome blow.

The face was a mask of concentration while he hewed at the timber as if his very life depended upon the process.

Shirtsleeves rolled up above the elbow, the left hand gloved, but his weskit more than held its own, fob chain aglitter, as he lifted up the axe and crashed it home.

William Ewart Gladstone, three score years and ten with the vigorous strength of a man half that time-span, wrenched the blade free from the deep wound inflicted, sighted down the edge, then once more swung with such desperate, savage energy that it seemed as if he were trying to eradicate some insult perceived in the innocent grain of the tree.

It being spring, the sap oozed from the wounds of the tree like arboreal stigmata but he cared not a fig for such fancy. Up went the blade and down it chopped.

The splinters of wood flew over his shoulder and fell brokenly to the ground.

There had been times when enthusiastic followers collected these splinters like holy relics, but for this moment he was observed only by a gentleman, one of his private secretaries, and a woman who had the great man's frock-coat draped over her arm, lightly pressed against her body.

'The forest suffers Mr Gladstone's desire to work up a righteous sweat,' murmured the secretary.

The woman made no response except to press the grey frock-coat a little more firmly to her angular frame. The secretary glanced down at her with no great relish.

Jane Salter suited her name. She was a stooped skinny virgo intacta, he observed. Lank brown hair scraped in a middle parting, pointing the way to a sharp nose which sniffed a little dismally in the dank dew of early morning. Perched on the nose was a pair of pebble glasses without which she was practically blind.

The secretary, Horace Prescott, took a deep draught of air, exhaled, and watched with interest as the released breath smoked from his mouth like ectoplasm.

He was tall, languid, silver locks swept over the brow, adopting the aristocratic air of his master the Earl of Rosebery. Prescott had been affiliated to Gladstone's staff to help with the campaign and under his ironic affected tones could be discerned a certain bitterness.

He had the appearance of a leader of men, but not the power. That lay elsewhere.

Jane Salter studied him from beneath lowered lids. How deep did that bitterness go? Despite Rosebery's apparent total commitment to the Liberal champion, she could detect a tension from the earl and his followers.

Nothing in politics was what it seemed and friendship only lasted till the next broken promise. Treachery was rife. Like the plague.

The Great Man, she knew, held himself above such venality, but it only made him the more vulnerable to betrayal. High moral ground. A slippery slope.

The figure, silhouetted by morning sun, raised the blade like a pagan priest at a sacrificial offering.

Gladstone's energy was astounding. He had arrived by carriage this early hour from Edinburgh almost in a frenzy, woke the whole household, then grabbed an axe and got to work as if the Furies were after him.

One more blow would suffice, calculated the People's William, as the sycamore lurched. The knack was in knowing when to strike and escape the consequence. One more blow. A look of almost fiendish glee fell over his countenance and he peeled back his lips to show his teeth as if prepared to bite through the very bark of the tree.

Some four years before, Disraeli had calculated he was secure, that Gladstone was too old and would never again lead the House of Commons. Disraeli therefore considered it safe to accept the offer of a peerage from his adoring queen. He would still remain prime minister of course. But lead from above.

Lord Beaconsfield, he was thus dubbed. But much good it had done him. At the opening of Parliament, this very February, his emaciated figure had struggled to carry the Sword of State in the official procession. Could the Jew not carry a sword? Then Gladstone would swing the axe.

From the French windows of Dalmeny House, the stately figure of Catherine Gladstone emerged, a woman of some humour, great loyalty, and an ability to ignore what she did not wish to contemplate.

'William?' she called. 'The kidneys will congeal on your plate and I cannot be held responsible.'

He straightened up. For a moment he looked like a predator cheated of its quarry.

'I shall arrive,' he announced, stood back, then delivered the final *coup d'etat*. The axe chopped in and, after some hesitation, as if yet holding on to its green life, what had once been a proud growth of nature crashed to earth, shuddered like a stricken animal, then was still.

All four people watched, then Gladstone raised his right fist in the air like a triumphant pugilist.

'The arm of the Lord is bared for work!' His resonant tones echoed in the silence.

Catherine Gladstone shook her head in

exasperated amusement and disappeared back inside.

William rolled down his sleeves and, with measured tread, approached Jane Salter who held out the frock-coat for him to don as if he were a medieval knight who had just slain the dragon. He nodded a dignified thanks.

'Have you partaken of breakfast, Miss Salter?' he asked.

Prescott concealed a slight shudder of distaste. For some reason the old man had a soft spot for this desiccated creature who had attached herself to the campaign in the last few months. A volunteer. An amateur.

'I rose early and broke my fast with some bread, Mr Gladstone,' she replied, her voice low-pitched, a pleasant and merciful contradiction to the rest of her as far as Prescott was concerned.

William's face, which was deeply fissured in lines like the cracked side of a cliff, frowned in some concern, the mouth downturned to indicate gravity of situation.

'Bread is not enough. We shall need all our strength in the days ahead.'

His right hand, he felt, might blister up tomorrow, but it was worth the pain. With suffering came release.

He glanced back at the felled and fallen tree.

'The Tories are incorrigible, impotent for reformation, a parasitic growth. But they will *cling*. You cannot cut them down without sinews of iron.'

He shot out his sleeves in a strangely

flamboyant gesture, perhaps even in the manner of a Mississippi gambler, but the faint smell of his morning soap, the disinfectant odour of phenol, discouraged further comparison.

Prescott had thought Gladstone's flight of fancy a mite over-burdened but William's fierce gaze precluded any niceties of discrimination. The statesman turned and stomped off towards Dalmeny House.

'Fuel in the boiler, Miss Salter,' he called back. 'Politics is a field of Christian action. Action cannot sustain itself without fuel in the boiler. Although . . . '

He came to a halt as if struck by a sudden insight.

'What Mr Disraeli nourishes himself upon these days is open to conjecture, wouldn't you think?'

Gladstone suddenly emitted a harsh laugh and then continued on his way pursued by a rather flustered Prescott.

'I have mapped out your timetable for the day, sir.'

'And I shall observe it, sir, but I must warn you that at the hour of five I address the good people of West Calder and I shall need a quiet interlude for preparation. I have a long speech fomenting and I feel . . . '

He turned back again and looked at the woman who was watching them both.

'I feel . . . not unlike a loaf in the oven.'

His mouth quirked in what might even have been the ghost of a smile. She lowered her gaze and the same ghost crept across her lips.

He resumed his march and Prescott though longer in the legs, struggled to keep up with the energetic steps of the older man as they breasted the hill.

Jane Salter observed them leave, then walked slowly over to peer down at the tree. The sap was still flowing and the axe had been driven into the bark so that it stood up at an oddly phallic angle, which she affected to ignore.

The second time this week William Gladstone had cut a sycamore down. It gave him life, he said.

Fuel in the boiler.

19

As Tammie glowr'd, amazed, and curious,
The mirth and fun grew fast and furious.
                    ROBERT BURNS,
                    'Tam o' Shanter'

Constable Mulholland was not a happy man. His Aunt Katie had once put it in a nutshell.

There's the lion's mouth, go on make a name for yourself.

Of course you had to hear the underlying *scathing* tone to fully appreciate, but the meaning was clear, the advice infallible, and his own inspector hell-bent on ignoring such nuggets of wisdom.

They were on the wrong side of Princes Street for a start, out of their parish. They had headed over the North and South bridges towards Guthrie Street. For God's sake, Walter Scott had been born in that street! It was no place for entertaining weird notions about — notions he couldn't even bring himself to think on, so full of the danger of demotion were they. *Fearsome* notions.

But just because some female had landed up in the inspector's shanty and some big Highland sergeant had kicked the bucket thirty years before, a death Mulholland had never heard brought to mention till near this moment, here they were in a respectable sitting room where

113

they had no right to be, on the point of discussing events they had no conceivable right to be on the point of discussing.

It was a parlous state of affairs.

The big woman had made them a decent cup of tea right enough. Lapsang Souchong. A Chinese brew. Smoky as a tinker's fire. It appealed to the connoisseur in Mulholland but McLevy was near choking on the stuff, a measure of some compensation to the constable.

She had received them cordially so. Now she waited.

Her hair had once been chestnut brown, thick and lustrous. Now it lay in white scallops on her head. The eyes were steady upon them. A dispassionate gaze.

Seen every side like a nail in the slaughter-hoose, thought McLevy. Her name on the paper he had read in the moonlight. Eileen Marshall.

'You were nurse tae Helen Gladstone, were ye not?' he began formally.

Mulholland sighed. Here we go.

'I was indeed, God rest her soul.'

Eileen had a deep almost mannish voice and, unlike many women of McLevy's acquaintance, a stillness of carriage not induced by whalebone.

'When did you last see her?' he asked.

'Dead or alive?' she answered.

A hint of graveyard humour in the hazel eyes.

McLevy half-smiled in response, this might make up for the hellish tea which had left a taste in his mouth like chimney soot. The Chinese have much to answer for.

'Alive, if you please, ma'am.'

114

He noticed that her hands, placed peacefully in her lap, were big-jointed and strong. No wedding ring. Like himself. Still in the stream.

'I nursed her till she was cured and then she later withdrew to a convent in the Isle of Wight and thence to Germany, where, after many years, she died,' Eileen replied somewhat carefully.

'Cured? Of what ailment?'

His eyebrows rose in what was almost a parody of the inquiring investigator. From Joanna Lightfoot he had a very good idea what particular ailment, but play daft and maybe you'll get in for nothing.

'An addiction to laudanum, indeed any drug which promoted oblivion,' was the unruffled response.

'Laudanum? That's the very devil, is it not?'

His remark hit a nerve and, for a moment, there was a flash of anger in her eyes.

'The doctors dole it out to women who are troubled, restless, unable to hold their . . . place in society. It helps them . . . accept the unacceptable.'

'And incidentally often renders them addicted?'

She nodded.

'And that in turn supplies more work for the doctors, curing the sick they themselves have created. I'm in the wrong profession!'

McLevy let out a bray of laughter. Mulholland winced at the lack of sensitivity but Eileen didn't even blink.

'Helen Gladstone was not cured by medical means but by the knucklebone of a female saint.'

Now it was McLevy's turn not to blink. He sat

115

as if turned to a wax representation of himself while the hairs on Mulholland's Protestant neck were beginning to prickle.

'Monsignor Wiseman, who was the agent of Helen's conversion to Catholicism, arrived at the house after Mr Gladstone had finally returned to London. The Monsignor brought with him a holy relic.'

'The said knucklebone?'

Another nod. Eileen continued.

'Her jaw was locked, the whole body in paralysis. He performed a truncated service, touched the relic to her jaw and effected what can only be described as a miraculous transformation.'

Mulholland spluttered as if something had got stuck in his throat but McLevy's face was unreadable.

'God works in mysterious ways,' he opined. 'But I wouldnae think William Gladstone was any too pleased at the source of this . . . miracle.'

Eileen smiled thinly. 'I think Mr Gladstone was grateful to have his sister recovered. Back in the fold of the family.'

There was a deal of black irony in these last words that McLevy registered with some relish. Things were hotting up. Just the way he liked them.

'Do you believe in such things?' he enquired.

'I am a Protestant,' was the composed response. 'But I saw what I saw.'

'A miracle of sorts?'

'Of sorts.'

Their eyes met. McLevy scratched his nose,

absent-mindedly, like an old man on a park bench.

'What did Helen do, back in the fold?' he asked mildly.

'She looked after their father, Sir John, until the old man died in December of the following year. I was her companion more than her nurse. By that time.'

The last three words hung in the air. Eileen seemed to have withdrawn into herself. McLevy sensed many conflicting emotions behind that calm exterior.

She was a stern, handsome woman but her face had softened, the lower lip extended . . . just a touch.

He put his finger to his own lips, part in thought, part signalling a fidgety Mulholland to a continued, still, silence. They waited. The silence grew.

The door to the sitting room creaked open as if a ghost had been summoned and an elderly, rather fat labrador dog waddled in, plumped itself at Eileen's feet and, catching McLevy's jaundiced gaze, growled softly. Eileen reached down and scratched the beast.

'Albert's getting old,' she said. 'Like myself.'

But you don't smell as bad, McLevy thought unkindly, as a whiff of doggy emanation smoked his nostrils.

'What was she like?' he asked. 'Helen? The little sister. Helen . . . Gladstone,' he pronounced the name quietly, like an incantation. 'What was she like?'

'She . . . found peace in Germany. In a

convent. We . . . corresponded. Until she died.'

Mulholland noted that the woman had never yet answered the inspector's questions directly. It was as if she was responding to other enquiries that she alone heard. Then he abruptly chided himself for that flicker of interest. None of this was of any consequence. Out of their parish.

The dog whined. Eileen had stopped scratching. It wanted more. So did the inspector.

Her replies were cautious, considered, judicious. McLevy therefore, like a pig after truffles, suspected treasure to be found in the digging.

'Between Helen and her brother, what transpired? At the time of Jessy Gladstone's death. What . . . transpired?'

'I don't know what you mean, Mr McLevy.'

'I think you just might, Miss Marshall.'

He smiled. His face open, like a child's.

Mulholland had seen the technique before but it never ceased to impress; this was not the monster who had stared down at Frank Brennan.

'What was told to me was told in madness. In delirium. Once she was cured, Helen never spoke of it again. We never spoke of it again.'

'That's the terrible thing about getting the cure. You're never the same person,' said McLevy.

He smiled again. She did not respond.

'But she did speak of *something*, did she not?'

Eileen Marshall shook her head as if denying the words she had recently uttered. McLevy pressed further. Gently does it though. Firm but merciful, that's the ticket.

'I am engaged upon an investigation, Miss Marshall. My authority has been granted from the most high office.'

Mulholland gulped at the bare-faced lie. The inspector, as usual, was hanging from the window with the backside out of his trousers.

'Anything you confide will remain completely . . . at my discretion.'

Which meant if McLevy thought the conviction warranted such, he would haul the poor woman, dog and all, up before the judge like a tub of guts.

'I am asking for your help. Without it, I cannot proceed.' McLevy bowed his head, a forlorn figure.

That much was true and who is to say that Eileen Marshall had not been waiting to tell her story for all these years?

Even those without Romanish tendencies long for the face behind the grille to which they may unburden their soul in blessed relief. The only drawback with James McLevy in such function was that a hand might come through the holy orifice and arrest you where you genuflect.

No trace of that ruthless impulse on the inspector's face now, however, a kindly receptacle only.

The dog had fallen asleep, bubbles of saliva gathering at its mouth.

Eileen Marshall made her decision, took a deep breath and began. The underlying harsh tones of her voice softened slightly, with memory.

'The day after wee Jessy Gladstone had been

119

buried at Fasque, Helen and I were alone in her bedroom. Her father was asleep upstairs, as was her brother, William. He had returned from Edinburgh that evening and spent some hours with Helen before retiring.

'It was past three in the morning but she could not rest despite a strong sleeping draught. I thought her dark suffering was because of withdrawal from the drug, weaning from laudanum is an agonising business.

'But the cause of her pain was more than that. I feared her mind would crack. The demons had her. They were dancing on the grave. Dancing with delight.'

20

This ae nighte, this ae nighte,
Every nighte and alle,
Fire and fleet and candel-lighte,
And Christe receive thy saule.

TRADITIONAL BALLAD,
Lyke-Wake Dirge

Fasque, Mearns, 15 April 1850
The two women lay in bed together, Helen Gladstone mewling like a small animal, her face pressed into the starched white bosom of the other. This was not according to medical textbook but to hell with it, Eileen was at her wit's end.

Dr Purdie had gone home to his, no doubt, adoring wife and family, the other two Gladstones were upstairs deep in conventional slumber, and she had been left atween pit and pendulum.

Above was the portrait of a male of the line. He had the Gladstone features, some great-uncle no doubt, looking down his bulbous nose, eyes deep in sockets, mouth pursed at the goings-on.

Below, Helen burrowed frantically as if trying to conceal herself under the nurse's body. She seemed terrified, her breath coming in short gasps, then all at once she raised her head. The pupils of her eyes were perfectly round, the irises a black purple.

'He has washed his hands,' she said. 'In blood he has washed them. He told me so.'

'You should try to rest, Miss Gladstone,' murmured Eileen, suddenly and acutely conscious of the impropriety of their situation. Thank God the household was asleep. If someone had entered and found her splayed out on the sheets with arms around a patient, all hell would have broken loose. All hell.

But it was her own thoughts and feelings that were causing the commotion. Helen was drenched in sweat yet the nurse found it a sweet smell, a fertile fragrance, and Eileen ached curiously, disturbed by a tenderness which seemed to flood her very being.

William Gladstone, on his evening return from Edinburgh, had demanded that Dr Purdie administer a strong sedative to his sister and then closeted himself with Helen in the bedroom.

He had announced to all and sundry that he wished to impart to his sister the details of the funeral she had not been strong enough to attend the day before, conveniently forgetting that he himself had expressly forbidden her to do so. The tension in him was almost palpable, his manner peremptory. But, given that he had yesterday buried his own daughter in the nearby family vault, it was an excusable state of mind.

Nevertheless Eileen had felt uneasy, for no reason she could put her finger on. There was a wildness in his eyes and she noted that he had changed his mourning attire for a light waistcoat and brougham trousers beneath the still sober frock-coat. Catching her gaze, he folded his arms protectively over the differing garments and dismissed them all, his face white against the dark sideboards which framed it down to the clenched line of his jaw.

The doctor had left, post-sedative. William Gladstone had at last emerged after a period of near two hours' seclusion with Helen and retired upstairs without another word to join his father who was already abed and asleep.

Sir John had been a strong and driven man all of his life but now, in his eighty-fifth year, the worm of frailty was busy in the flesh.

Age withers us all, strength or no. The worm must eat.

William was forty-one. He had nothing to fear yet. But the worm is patient. An opening will present itself.

Eileen had come back to the room to sit in the chair by the bed and snatch what sleep she could, when suddenly Helen had shot bolt upright, eyes staring, as if a fever inside would not let her rest, as if she dreaded what the darkness might bring. She began to speak in tongues, a mad whirling storm of guttural words that made no sense.

That had been many hours ago and now Eileen herself was tired almost beyond endurance. Her attempts to manage the circumstance had fallen short, and the only action which had quieted the woman was when the nurse had, rather rigidly it must be admitted, yielded to Helen's entreaties, and stretched out beside her on the bed.

123

Silence in the room. The thick curtains gobbled up the small scratching noises of the wind outside.

Helen had fallen back, her head just under Eileen's chin, the damp curls tickling at her neck. They lay in quietness together. Somewhere in the house, a grandfather clock struck four. The witching hour.

When Helen began to speak, the voice was so small and disembodied that it seemed to come from somewhere else, as if a child had crept under the bed and was playing a trick upon the two of them.

'Jessy and I, our souls are as one. She has gone to heaven. It is God's judgement that her father may go to hell.'

Outside, a small animal shrieked as a predator struck home. Even through the drapes, it was a sound to freeze the blood.

'She was punished for his sins. He told me so. He told me many things. He thought I was asleep. He always thinks I am asleep. Always. And then . . . he feels free.'

Helen giggled. A sly treacherous smile on her face.

'About wickedness. And lust. And pictures in his mind. And how the world was full of blood, dripping from the walls of Babylon.'

She suddenly turned on to her back and raised both palms into the air like a saint about to give a blessing. Eileen was transfixed.

'He thought I was asleep. And wept. And told me of his sins. And women of the street who came to him in darkness and touched his flesh.

And how he scourged away the sin. With blood. Silly man.'

For a moment, gazing at the hands above her, Helen laughed again, then she cried out in fear and once more whimpered her way back into the nurse's side.

The nape of Eileen's neck was ice cold. Helen reached up and laid an unerring hot little hand upon it.

'I have prayed to Mother Mary,' she said brokenly.

Her forehead was against the other's throat and she began to cry, scalding tears, warm in the cold night, which trickled down inside the collar of Eileen's uniform and on to her bare skin. She could feel the rivulets spreading over the collar-bone, the clavicle, that was the medical term, best to keep medicine in mind.

Despite her small frame, Helen had surprisingly heavy breasts, a pocket Venus. They pressed against Eileen's arm, one on each side, in the Spanish style. Even though she was sheathed in a nightgown of thick flannel, Helen's nipples were visible, erectile tissue is so hard to contain, and her haunches, the material stuck to them like a second skin, rounded and curved in a way which would have delighted the Ancient Greeks. Or even Romans.

Romans, Greeks and clavicles, thoughts that were not proper to this situation, were filing in an increasingly disorderly fashion through Eileen's mind. Hallucination. Delirium. What was she catching from her charge?

'I have prayed to Mother Mary,' said Helen,

'that he may be forgiven. Though I would wish him first to suffer great pain. Like Christ on the cross. Who died for all of us. And gave His blood.'

Her hand still rested on the nape of Eileen's neck. She could feel each fingertip.

Eileen shivered, the contagion of madness, or desire, shook her to the bone.

A floorboard above creaked and she listened tensely for the sound of footsteps descending the staircase. Or footsteps anywhere. She had a feeling of being watched constantly — the various servants of the house seemed sly, observing, recording all that passed.

But mercifully nothing. Helen snuggled into her and laid one leg across so that extrication was . . . forestalled.

The patient comes first. A dictum Eileen had always observed. On an impulse she removed her nurse's cap and the rich brown tresses cascaded down around her shoulders.

She closed her eyes, the better not to see.

21

Cover her face; mine eyes dazzle:
She died young.

JOHN WEBSTER,
The Duchess of Malfi

Eileen Marshall had told some of this, but not all, to her visitors, Enough to intrigue the inspector, and alarm Mulholland.

She had stuck to a bare recital of facts, the nuances of feeling remained her own business. McLevy could sense such, but that was not his interest.

'You're saying that when William Gladstone returned from Edinburgh he had changed his clothes?'

'He had.'

'That's not unusual,' Mulholland butted in. 'Travel stained.'

'Stained indeed,' said the inspector. 'But what might be a wee bit unusual is the other stuff that Helen told you, about scourging out sin with blood.'

'But that was said in madness!' cried Mulholland.

'I have known many things said in madness,' replied McLevy. 'Things to scar the soul. But the truth is like that sometimes.'

'And sometimes not. True or false, who knows? It was all so long ago,' said Eileen. 'I myself may play you false, inspector. Memory shifts.'

'Aye, it does. Like a dog with fleas.' McLevy grinned but his eyes were hard as pebbles. 'Have ye spoken tae another about this?'

'Not since that time.'

McLevy's head was spinning. Why had Joanna Lightfoot pointed him here? Why had she not come herself? Was she afraid of what she might find, was she using him as an instrument to find the truth, or just a blunt instrument?

And how would she have suspicion of what happened thirty years ago?

The dog groaned in its sleep.

Mulholland had sunk back into his chair. He knew exactly how it felt.

'Ye said that the house felt full of spies, eyes everywhere?' McLevy would grind this down to powder.

'Yes. The servants. As if we were watched. Observed.'

But where would these observations go? And how would they survive the passage of time? McLevy shook his head.

On the next meeting with Joanna Lightfoot — and there would be one, of that he had no doubt — he would have a few questions that might set her Italian boots a-tapping.

He roused himself. A remark Eileen made had lodged like that fishbone. Time to dig it out.

'And dead?' he asked suddenly.

'What?'

'I asked when you last saw Helen Gladstone. *Dead or alive?* ye said. Ye've covered the live part.'

Her face tightened, no graveyard humour this time, the memories had taken care of that.

'She died this January. Her body, like wee Jessy's, was brought back to Fasque for burial. I was at the display.'

'Display?'

'It was a display of sorts.'

'And you were there. Friend of the family, eh?'

McLevy was being obtusely familiar thought Mulholland but he'd have a reason. He always had a reason.

'On Helen's deathbed, one of her last requests was that I should attend. Mrs Gladstone, who is a kind woman, informed me of such. And Helen also wrote a letter to me. When she knew her powers were . . . failing.'

'What did she die of?'

'Old age. And the ravages of the past.'

'I don't suppose I could see that letter?'

'It was personal,' was the uncompromising response.

'And so . . . ?' The inspector's mind was darting around like a wasp near jam. 'There ye were, dressed in black, the coffin lowered, the family vault. January is a bugger of a month, ye must have all been chilled to the bone, eh?'

No response. He was losing her. Try a leap of faith.

'Who performed the ceremony, Monsignor Wiseman?'

'He died some time ago; it was the Archbishop of Westminster. And it was not a Catholic service.'

McLevy's jaw dropped comically as if he could

not believe his ears. He said nothing, however, childlike bewilderment on his face. She took the bait.

'According to William Gladstone, Helen had recanted her Catholicism just before she died. She was buried in the Anglican tradition.'

'Did you believe that?'

'To me it does not matter. To Helen it meant a great deal. Her faith was everything.'

A sniff from Mulholland. Either he was expressing an opinion or he had just got a whiff of Albert.

'So that would be the display part?' McLevy's eyes gleamed with mischief. 'The Anglican tradition, eh?'

Eileen nodded grimly.

'Five years before she died, Helen wrote to me that her brother had visited her in Germany and they'd had a conversation of thirteen hours, chiefly on the subject of, as he put it, the dangers of post-Vatican Council Roman Catholicism.'

'And had it changed her mind?'

'Not that she expressed in the letter. She merely described him as fanatical on the subject.'

'Thirteen hours is a long stretch, right enough. What a strain on her tonsils.'

'She would be listening mostly,' was the dry retort.

'And did you express these . . . misgivings to William Gladstone?' asked McLevy.

'It was family business,' came the terse reply.

'But ye must have said something to him? I don't see you letting it go. For old time's sake.'

The inspector leant forward, a winning smile

on his face. Eileen Marshall was provoked enough to reach up and hammer in the nail.

'I told him that Helen and Jessy, when he died, would be waiting for him. That their souls were as one. They would know all things. They would be waiting.'

McLevy whistled softly.

'No escape, eh?' he said wryly.

'No escape.' Her eyes met with his. 'But you must know that, inspector. Professionally speaking.'

'Retribution,' said McLevy. 'My faith in a nutshell.'

He laughed softly.

Mulholland was cross-eyed now. These two had gone down some path into a forest within the like of which he had no desire to play the little lost Hansel.

It was that damned mystical side to McLevy which took him, as Aunt Katie would have put it, *away with the fairies*.

The inspector and Eileen Marshall gazed across the room at each other.

'What was Mr Gladstone's response to your offer of condolence?'

'He looked as if he would like to strike me to the ground,' she said. 'A dreadful anger in his eyes. But then I had never found his favour.'

'Because of your influence with Helen?'

'Because of many things.' Her mouth tightened in recollection. 'He turned his back on me and walked away.'

McLevy noticed that her ankles, under the hem of the dress, were somewhat thick and

131

misshapen. Circulation maybe not so good. Too much sitting by the bedside.

'I saw him two nights ago,' she said suddenly. 'At Waverley Market, addressing the crowd. He is quite an orator. His voice rings out like a bell.'

Such ambiguity was there in her tone, but what was behind it? A delicacy of purpose, but what?

'Did he see you?' the inspector asked.

'I believe he did. I was right at the front. I got there early, walking is difficult for me so I took a cab. It was surprisingly expensive. For such a short journey.'

A smile on her lips. McLevy had it now. Vengeance. What had drawn her. A neat measure of vengeance.

'How d'ye *know* that he remarked your presence?'

'He faltered in his speech. His eyes met mine. He lost his way.'

McLevy could see it in his mind's eye. Gladstone roaring like a righteous lion, the inspector had read in the paper twenty thousand people and those who fainted handed back over the heads of the crowd as if dead, and then in that ocean of adoring faces he finds the one he did not want to see.

Eileen Marshall, flanked by two ghosts.

'Maybe,' he ventured disingenuously, 'ye reminded him of something he'd just rather forget, eh?'

'Or he may have just stumbled. People do stumble. Words can be treacherous,' she said. 'But — it may have been my imagination of course — but I swear I saw such anger in his eyes. Dreadful. The same as the day of Helen's funeral. The same as when he came back from Edinburgh, the night after Jessy had been buried. Anger. Burning. As if he would wish to strike me to the ground.'

The prospect did not seem to alarm her but give some cause for satisfaction. Not much. But as good as she would get until the day of judgement.

There was a long silence.

Two funerals, thirty years apart. Two murders, with the same separation of time.

McLevy had many other questions in his mind but he felt, somehow, that he had gained as much from the exchange as he might reasonably expect to deserve.

The dog whimpered, paws scrabbling against the carpet and Eileen looked down at it indulgently.

'In his dreams, he believes he is hunting. Still a young dog.'

'That's nice,' said the inspector motioning Mulholland to rise, who, as he did so, spoke his first words in a long, long time.

'It was a very splendid cup of tea,' he said.

Like a good hostess she saw them to the door. They said their goodbyes but then, perhaps because McLevy's unexpected cessation of further questioning had left a hunger gnawing at her, she reached round her neck for a locket which he had noticed much earlier; its thin gold chain and ornamental heart-shaped purple case rather at odds with the plain and simple dark-green dress she wore.

'Helen gave this when she left me,' she said, and opened the case to reveal a photograph inside.

A young woman stared out at them. Even in the formal pose, it was a troubled and, it must be said, quite sultry face.

McLevy nodded. Mulholland craned over.

'Let's hope she's at peace,' he said doubtfully.

Eileen gave him a look which set his head jerking back, then closed the case with a snap.

The dog almost woke up, then returned to its scrabbling.

'He's still hunting,' she murmured, looking back.

'It's always the way,' said McLevy.

For a moment he looked at her with such compassion that Eileen knew it must be her purest fancy, then he turned to go. Her hand went to the nape of her neck. And rested there.

22

All her hair
In one long yellow string I wound
Three times her little throat around,
And strangled her. No pain felt she;
I am quite sure she felt no pain.

ROBERT BROWNING,
'Porphyria's Lover'

Certain discreet apartments in Edinburgh Castle had been reserved for visiting members of Her Majesty's government who craved seclusion.

At a pinch the quarters might even admit certain *shadowy* figures, not exactly members as in the sense of connection to the trunk of authority, not exactly branched projections in any politically priapic sense. No. They were more insubstantial forms, and yet, at the same time, so very necessary for the *constancy* of things. The continuity of power.

The Serpent was one of those shadows. Those he served valued him above all others. He preserved that continuity.

He stood in the middle of the room and pondered the nature of his task.

For what had said Benjamin Disraeli?

'To uphold the aristocratic settlement of the country.'

The prime minister's main agenda and one consistency.

'To maintain the empire and protect the constitution.' In Disraeli's own officially recorded words, the purpose of the Tory party.

Many other things Disraeli said and the Jew was a man to reckon.

In his noble guise of Lord Beaconsfield, he had kissed goodbye the Commons and walked out into the streets in a long white overcoat, even though it was August in London.

The Serpent smiled. Not his style, but to each his own.

The very name had given rise to a portmanteau noun, 'Beaconsfieldism', clumsily created and pejoratively used by one William Gladstone to denote an unchecked, unbridled, profligate, imperialist, naked lust for power.

But power it was, and evermore shall be.

Change must be resisted. Truth kept in a pretty little box with red ribbon, wrapped around. Securely bound.

Gladstone waved it like a flag but the Serpent knew the truth for what it was. A trinket. In a box.

A bottle of burgundy lay on the table, reasonable vintage, with hunks of bread and a plate of cheese.

Rather too *Scottish* a selection for his taste, hard-rinded Knoxian Cheddar, goaty Highland fare, a decent Brie violated by a wash of whisky and another Cheddar which seemed to be wrapped inside what might only be described as a tartan bandage.

This was his lunch. All other creature comforts, all carnal compensations to be

136

forsworn until the matter was done and dusted. The stakes were too high, the risks too great to admit prolonged *personal* contact. This was what must be observed. Religiously.

And yet he missed his little fleshly beast. The surrender in the eye, the biting of the lips, and when he laid bare the creamy skin and cupped the softness, such shameful trembling then ensued as they fell into the pit of hell together. Wantonly, deliberately, damnably, ate of the forbidden fruit. Predator and prey. Each in turn.

He wrenched his mind away from pictures that might fire the blood with their sweet obscenity, poured a little wine into the glass, swirled it round and sniffed the bouquet. *Pas mal.* Perhaps a little *earthy.* But it would have to do, let it breathe.

And he would have to wait. Who knows what sharp edge would be sharpened from the whetstone of patience? What variations of a hungry, oblique desire might rise to the surface? Anticipation is everything.

Paper contact. Nothing more. He had picked up the report from their agreed drop-off point and left a little offering in return. A very important little offering with precise instructions as to its usage and the time to throw it in the mix. Not part of the original plan, a touch of improvisation on his part, but it would augment, convince and, with a bit of luck, bring death and destruction.

He emptied the glass, little finger crooked in the air to amuse himself no one else being on hand, and put it down with a flourish. That'll have to do, old chap, more where that came from, that'll have to do.

He reached into his inside pocket, pulled out his operative's report, read it again and sniffed the paper. The faintest trace of perfume rather overwhelmed by the odour of cigars from the case he often kept in the same pocket.

A single page. Short and to the point.

All was proceeding according to calculation. The subject was not easy, the objective difficult, but so far, so good. He smiled. It was a phrase he himself often used to cover a multitude of sins. There had also been a strange coincidence, which the operative had seized upon and indicated that luck might be with them.

Either that or they might have the truth on their side, perish the thought.

He laughed at that notion, then crossed to the fire where half a forest seemed to be burning in the hearth, dropped the paper on to the flames and turned to warm his backside, surveying the room at the same time.

Severe masculine lines ran everywhere like the North British railway. Dark mahogany ruled the roost. A heaviness of purpose to furniture and fittings — but what else could one expect from such a regimental billet?

On the wall, a glassy-eyed stag's head stuck out like the prow of a ship, its antlers raised to no great purpose since they had signally failed to stop a well-aimed bullet.

A symbol of Christ, the stag. According to Pliny, it drew serpents by its breath from their holes, and then trampled them to death. A reprehensible practice.

There was a full-length mirror set into the panelling just by the door, and he crossed to look at himself in the bilious, rusty glass. The plenitude of length was to check on the rigours of the kilt, he supposed, and the ugly rust to discourage any narcissistic leanings.

He scrutinised his own face. All things to all men. A Protean plasticity of feature. Despite his years, his many troubled years, a trim figure, well enough dressed, nothing too ostentatious, Jermyn Street never shouts its wares.

A boyish cast. *Puer eternus*. The eyes light blue, not holding much warmth, but then death is such a cold affair and they had seen so much of death.

The hair above a silver-yellow, the mouth below, a cruelly sensual slot. Not without humour. A smiling assassin.

An abrupt turn left his image to its own devices and he moved to the window. It was criss-crossed with thin lead piping of sorts and the glass, pale ochre, lent the scene outside a tinted quality, like an engraving.

He was looking out over the esplanade, the approach to the fortress where Lady Jane Douglas, the most beautiful woman of her age, had been burned to death in the sight of her son and her second husband; accused of attempting the king's life, James IV, by dint of poison and sorcery. Her real crime was, of course, being a Douglas.

And many witches on that very esplanade had been, as they so quaintly put it in these parts, 'worryit at the stake', that is strangled and burned after scant trial for — as they were accused and found guilty of — renouncing their baptism and dancing with the devil. Five at a time, no less. Save on firewood. Thrifty folk, the Scots.

Dancing with the devil would seem to be a most unhealthy pursuit unless . . . authorised.

The other window of the apartment looked out and down towards the Lawnmarket where the Serpent knew that in James's court lay a tall house called Gladstone's Land. It had been acquired in 1631 by one Thomas Gledstone of that hallowed family. Know thine enemy.

From high on the castle to look down on the people below was to observe them as so many ants, crawling about their predestined pathways.

He could lift his foot and crush them all, but wholesale slaughter was not his style.

You must identify, isolate, and *then* destroy. Without emotion, as a curious child might pull the legs one by one from an insect and leave it not dead precisely, but powerless, incapable, twitching on its back.

A crack of sound as the gun on the half-moon battery on the eastern front of the citadel signalled one o'clock, Greenwich Mean Time, to all the good citizens of Edinburgh.

He had been about the streets late the night before and accomplished much.

Like Wee Willie Winkie, crying through the lock. Are the children all in bed?

A vision from the previous night came into his head. Good fun. Out by the skin of his teeth, but

140

it had been good fun. Splendid to be back in the field.

Time for a spot of lunch. Time for a spot of lunch, old boy.

23

My soul, do not seek immortal life, but exhaust
the realm of the possible.

PINDAR,
Pythian Odes

The body was dead, no doubt about it. Dead as
a doornail. The room smelt of stale sweat and
whisky, the cadaver sprawled out on the mattress
as if just fallen heavily to sleep.

McLevy observed the corpus. Mulholland was
outside taking notes from the live members of
the household and the inspector was grateful for
the solitude. The constable and he and were
scarcely on speaking terms owing to a slight
disagreement of procedural intent.

It had manifested itself in this respect.

As soon as they had been deposited outside
Eileen Marshall's door the young man, seeing
the way the investigation was heading along with
the squinty-eyed demeanour of his inspector,
made what he considered to be an important
point. More than just important. *Crucial.*

'What do we tell Lieutenant Roach?'

'Nothing,' came the response serene.

'Nothing?'

Mulholland's eyes were near popping from his
head and McLevy regretted ever bringing him
along in the first place. A weakness on his part.
The need for witness.

Even though he had underplayed the exotic frissons of his exchange with Joanna Lightfoot and presented it more as a stark narration, the look on his subordinate's face had not been one of confidence. And it was even worse now.

'*Nothing?*' repeated the constable, his voice rising to a high note so that a passing carthorse neighed in reply, thinking to have heard a fellow labourer.

By this time they were heading up Chambers Street, ready to turn into a cold whipping wind coming up the bridges from the direction of Waverley Station. But the wind was nothing compared to the coldness Mulholland felt in his bowels. A fell dank creeping chill.

'I know that look on your face, sir. Somewhere you are entertaining the impossible possibility of a link between one of the most important political figures of this age and murders which occur at thirty-year intervals.'

McLevy smiled at a passing young woman who was clutching at her fashionable *chapeau* as the wind picked up.

'Hold on to your hat,' he advised.

Mulholland was not to be diverted.

'And why did you not tell me of this George Cameron business before?'

'I like tae keep things up my sleeve,' was the nonchalant reply.

'That's for magicians!' Mulholland said sharply. 'I'm supposed to work along, not guess magic tricks, leave all that prestidigitation to Pope Leo. This is nothing less than a weird and crazy fantasy, not one shred of proof!'

'Of course it is,' agreed McLevy blandly. 'Stories, supposition, ghosts and mirrors. We can't tell that tae the lieutenant, he'd have a heart attack.'

'He'll have one of them anyway when he finds out what we're up to and he'll tell you what I'll tell you. Stop. Right. Here!'

McLevy did so. A piece of paper had blown against his face and he had automatically caught at it. It was an election pamphlet, a picture of William Gladstone, arm raised, finger pointing. The words below the image said simply, *The People's William. He is the man.*

The inspector crumpled the paper up and threw it into the air so that it sailed over the side of the South Bridge, which they stood upon now, down to the Cowgate below.

He watched as it gave the appearance of life, dipping and swooping, but it was at the mercy of a stronger element, a force of nature which would not be denied.

'It may all be moonshine,' he said quietly. 'But I made a promise to George Cameron which I must try to fulfil.'

He brooded further as they walked on, Mulholland shaking his head like a cow plagued with flies.

'If these two murders are connected in any way, and there is any chance, no matter how strange and fanciful it might all seem, of finding the perpetrator, then I shall go right tae the end.'

'Ye'll be on your own, then,' said the constable bitterly, still smarting about being kept in the dark.

'That doesnae worry me, I was born so.'

McLevy was equally bitter, feeling he'd been let down.

'I asked you along because I value your opinion but if this is all ye can offer, then the least you can do is keep your mouth shut and not clipe on me tae the lieutenant.'

'I am not a clipe,' said Mulholland stiffly. 'I do not betray, but I have my duty.'

'So did Pontius Pilate,' was the caustic response.

Both noses were out of joint and, to tell the truth, there were deep feelings of disappointment on either side. As George Cameron had been towards him, so McLevy may have wished to be to the constable, father to son.

But that was to overestimate the young man's need for a parental shadow, and also somewhere evidenced a refusal on the inspector's behalf to acknowledge that he lacked the same generosity of spirit as the big Highlander.

In frozen huffy silence, they had traced their path back to Leith station, a nondescript building even more nondescript inside. Sergeant Murdoch at the desk, half-asleep as usual, dust motes floating in the air around him.

Ballantyne with his tongue sticking out of the side of his mouth was attempting to write up a report. He did give them a quick glance, paused as if to say something, then got his head back down swiftly as the highly polished door which led to Lieutenant Roach's inner sanctum, the only door in the place with a shine worth the mention, swung open and out

145

stepped the man himself.

Roach often put McLevy in mind of a crocodile for some reason. The lieutenant possessed a long jaw which he habitually worked from side to side when perturbed, and bulging slightly bloodshot eyes which hinted at sins suppressed.

The man's neat white collar and black tie peeped out of the open neck of the official braided frock-coat.

Stiff and tidy. McLevy had never seen him out of uniform, and wondered idly what he wore. Perhaps a scarlet cloak and boots of Castilian leather?

Roach pursed his lips. 'You've been out all morning, McLevy.'

'On the case, sir. On the case.'

A jovial reply and swiftly in, lest Mulholland blurt out his procedural misgivings.

A wintry smile from the lieutenant, the man had something on his mind, something in the back pocket.

'My suspicions were correct,' he said bleakly.

McLevy blinked. Surely Roach hadn't got wind of what he was purposing, who could have told him? And yet the lieutenant had an uncanny knack of sensing when McLevy was up to mischief. A knack developed by dint of the fact that Roach usually was the one who got it in the neck.

Mulholland stepped forward. 'Suspicions about what, sir?'

The big lanky unctuous bastard was going to betray him, McLevy was sure of it.

Roach took a deep breath.

'At the lodge last night, Chief Constable Grant laid his hand upon my shoulder and said . . . *Women chopped in half are no great advertisement for our fair city, lieutenant. Murder is a blot. Clean it up. Sooner before later.*'

The lieutenant jerked his jaw in painful memory.

'And I have to say the way he was looking at me confirmed my worst fears. As if I had the pox.'

'A grand suspicion, sir. I remember you saying the very words. A plague carrier, did you not say?'

A sidelong glance at McLevy indicated where Mulholland thought the source of the pestilence might lie but, to the inspector's relief, he added nothing to the above words.

In fact, McLevy was a little ashamed of his earlier accusation. Mulholland might well sook up, but he wasnae a clipe. Not yet. The inspector was safe. No one would tell on him. He was safe.

His ears were buzzing and the ground seemed to move beneath his feet, surely Edinburgh wasn't suffering a tremor of the earth?

He closed his eyes and in his mind he was a wee boy looking up at his mother; her mouth opened and shut; he couldnae hear the words but the spittle was fair flying in his direction.

She raised both her hands, fingernails like talons, but then her face changed to that of a desperate sanity. She crossed to the door, locked it, put the key on the table, then turned towards him.

The woman reached out tenderly to touch the boy's face and then snatched something up from the table, flung herself away into the alcove bed set into the small room, and pulled across the curtain.

The wee boy stood alone. He was hungry. He went to a chair, clambered up on it and sat carefully by the table.

Maybe if he was good, nothing bad would happen? He waited. Time passed. The curtain was closed.

McLevy came out of this disquieting reverie to realise that Roach had addressed a question to him. Both lieutenant and constable were awaiting a response.

'I am sorry, sir,' he muttered. 'I have not quite grasped the implication of your last remark.'

Roach's eyelids blinked down, then up again, the skin a thin membrane; by God the man *did* look like a crocodile.

'A simple query. You are the investigating officer, McLevy. What is the progress of the said investigation?'

'I have suspects in mind, sir. When I am more certain, I shall acquaint you.' Mulholland sniffed audibly. 'And now if you will excuse me?'

He badly needed to sit down, dizzy spells were a bad sign, too much coffee the night before, a fractured sleep, his fast not broken, the portents of a gathering obsession.

'You will not be excused,' said Roach with a

148

certain grim relish. 'D'you know of a woman . . . Bridget Lapsley?'

'Keeps an auld hoose in Meikle John's close,' replied McLevy promptly, glad to get back on even ground. 'Rents the rooms tae all and sundry. When in drink, is prone tae caterwaul all night. Hence her familiar — Biddie Yammerlugs.'

'Your knowledge of Leith's depraved and lost souls never ceases to amaze me,' said Roach bleakly. 'She sent in word not half an hour ago. I was almost on the desperate point of rousing Sergeant Murdoch, when into the station you fortuitously march.'

'What word did she send?' McLevy muttered.

'One of her lodgers has died in bed.'

'I'm surprised she didnae throw the body out the window, rent and be damned.'

'Well, she did not. You are to inspect the corpse.'

'Are the circumstances doubtful, sir?' Mulholland attempted to supply an interest singularly lacking in his inspector.

'McLevy will tell us that.'

Roach turned to go back into his room. The inspector was still a little shaky; what he wouldn't give for an aromatic cup of Arabian best in Jean Brash's garden, the early roses matching her red hair, listening to the fluting calls of the whores as they hung out the morning-washed bed linen.

'Could one of the constables not pay a visit?' he said with a hopeful glance at Mulholland.

'It is your concern,' said Roach. 'It is connected. As you are so fond of telling me,

149

everything in Leith is connected.'

On that cryptic remark, the door closed, leaving the inspector hanging out to dry like the whorehouse sheets.

'You're not the only one keeps things up the sleeve, eh?' said Mulholland.

24

When boys go first to bed,
They step into their voluntary graves.
GEORGE HERBERT,
'Mortification'

And looking down at the dead body of Frank Brennan, this one hour later, he had to acknowledge the accuracy of the constable's observation.

It was common knowledge, even the lieutenant would have heard, that McLevy had fingered the big Irishman as being morally if not physically responsible for Sadie Gorman's death. Roach must have enjoyed the thought of the inspector suffering, he would most earnestly hope, terrible qualms of guilt over the result of his machinations.

McLevy did indeed feel a certain queasiness in the pit of his stomach but rather than pangs of conscience he would more put the attribution down to the stench in this grimy box of a room.

There was the memory, however, of the appeal in the big man's eyes, when he had tried to make amends by revealing that someone, so Sadie told him, had been watching at her and Brennan had paid no mind.

As McLevy, in turn, had paid no mind to that pathetic effort of atonement.

Frank Brennan had died unshriven. The

151

inspector would have to live with it.

He brought his mind round to the present. One question only. Was the death natural?

He gazed down at the pasty white face of the corpse, still dressed in shirt and trousers and lying where the man had, no doubt drunkenly, fallen on to the mattress. At least he'd managed to kick off his shoes; the Irishman's big toe stuck comically out of the frayed and holed sock.

Was the death natural, accidental as it were? Was it suicide? Was it murder? From his examination, he thought he knew the answer. Brennan's eyes stared open. He reached forward with his fingers and gently closed them.

The door opened and Mulholland entered, his head near touching the ceiling of the narrow room.

'I've seen more space in a prison cell,' he announced.

The constable then fell silent. He was still in the huff. McLevy took note and sighed.

'I realise I have caused offence with my accusation of yourself being a clipe. I now take it back. You may be many things, constable, and undoubtedly are, but a clipe is not one of them.'

This, from the inspector, was the equivalent of the legendary Ashes of Contrition, and Mulholland, realising such, bowed his head in dignified acceptance then delivered.

'I spoke to everyone in the house, never met such a disreputable assembly in my whole life, ye could not believe one single word spoken. And Biddy wants the room back.'

'She told me that earlier.'

To Mulholland's previous annoyance he had been dispatched to question the rag-bag collection of labourers, sailors and one-eyed trollops that made up the lodging-house inhabitants.

McLevy had meanwhile closeted himself to interview Biddy before chasing her out to annoy the constable. She had followed Mulholland from room to room, complaining loudly of the inspector's lack of esteem for a decent respectable woman, the like of which she fondly imagined herself to be.

'Still on about that, eh? Is she going tae fumigate the place?'

'I wouldn't know, sir.'

'Well, she'll have to wait,' grunted McLevy. 'This may be the scene of a murder.'

'Murder? There's not a mark on the man, he died natural, unless you think poison?'

'No. I do not think poison. See the lock on the door over there?'

Mulholland shook his head. 'But the door was ajar late this morning, the reason Biddy stuck her head in to discover the dead body. And let out a fearful scream she told me.'

'Aye, so she did. That must have been something tae hear.'

Mulholland still didn't move to the door, so McLevy indicated to the only other piece of furniture in the place, a spindly three-legged chair drawn up near to the dirty mattress, which lay on the floor, acting this moment as bed and bier. On the seat of the chair lay a large key.

'What does that tell you?'

153

'Brennan came in drunk, fell to bed and forgot to secure the lock,' said the constable.

'Yet Biddy said he was fierce particular about that, she was surprised tae find the door pushing open.'

'That's true enough,' said Mulholland rather snidely. 'He'd be in fear of his life what with you telling the criminal fraternity of how he betrayed one of their own.'

McLevy ignored the barb. 'He kept the key by his bed, close to hand. Drunk or not, I don't see him forgetting.'

He pointed silently at the door and Mulholland crossed without further comment to crouch down and examine the lock.

'Well?' demanded the inspector.

The mechanism was black-encrusted, a wonder the thing worked at all, but there were two fine scratches, just newly made by the looks of it, of a type the constable had seen before in his travels. He looked over at the other.

'Lockpicks, d'ye think?' said McLevy.

'Could be,' replied the constable slowly. 'Hard to tell, but . . . could be.'

He thought further. 'However, if crack open and enter why not secure when leaving, unless . . . ?'

Something one of the lodgers had told him, Archie Galbraith, a retired cooper who still held on to some vestige of dignity while drinking himself to death on what he used to watch being put inside the barrel.

'I got up in the middle of the night, tae answer the call of nature, ye ken? Dark. But my aim was

good, right in the middle of the bucket. I heard a door creak, shouted out my name, 'Archie Galbraith here!' in case it was somebody with drink looking for good company. Went and looked, near knocked the damn bucket arse-over. The hall was empty, naebody on hand, but I could have sworn the door tae the outside close had just shut. A draught of cauld air. Gives ye a terrible thirst, man. Cauld air.'

'It was in my mind to tell you, sir,' he said as McLevy gave him a basilisk stare after this was related. 'But the old fellow's so far gone, you couldn't put credence on his words.'

'Yet his call would interrupt, ye'd have to get out the door quick. Intae the close. That would explain why there was not the time to use the skeleton keys to lock it up again, after the deed was done.'

'What deed?' asked the constable in some exasperation. McLevy had his *I know a secret* face on, a most irritating sight to behold. 'There's not a mark on the fellow!'

'Oh yes there is,' said McLevy.

He signalled the constable over and they both knelt down by the body as if in prayer.

McLevy tilted the man's head back with some difficulty, to reveal the neck. On each side, just under the jawbone, was a small bruise.

'I near missed it myself,' he muttered, 'though I expect the eagle eye of Dr Jarvis would have brought it to our notice.'

Mulholland peered closer, in truth he wasn't sure why the inspector was putting such weight upon what looked, to his eyes, innocuous enough.

155

'It's hardly a death wound, sir. Could be the result of a fall or anything really. Louse bites even, and the man scratching.'

McLevy looked at him as if perplexed by such monumental ignorance, then remembering that the two had but presently repaired the rent in their professional rapport, heaved a magnanimous sigh and, in the manner of Moses on the Mount, revealed what he considered to be the imprint of God's incontrovertible evidence.

'Thumb marks,' he said. 'Pressing each side on the carotid artery. Unconsciousness is instant. An eastern practice, attributed to the Thuggee system. Assassins. Indian, by nature. Followers of Kali, the Goddess of Destruction.'

'How would you know all that, inspector?'

The constable seemed unaware of the implied insult in his question, so McLevy, not for the first time, decided to give him benefit of doubt.

'The aforesaid practice was almost inflicted upon me by an opium runner who had a den by the dockside and specialised in getting his customers doped to the eyeballs, practising his black art to knock them out, then killing them, robbing the bodies and dumping the cadavers weighted down with rocks through a trap-door at the back into the sea where they nourished the denizens of the deep. Coal-fish and crabs mostly. Bottom feeders.'

McLevy had a sudden vivid memory of the man leaning over him, face contorted in a hideous delight, sliding his thumbs up each side of the neck.

'I had been sent in under guise of an opium

156

user, by dint of my complexion. I think Lieutenant Moxey, my superior officer at the time, was trying to get rid of me.'

'Did you have to puff the pipe?' Mulholland asked eagerly, fascinated by this racy anecdote.

'I did not inhale,' was the stern response.

Although, mind you, there was a certain heightened aspect to his recollection. McLevy could have sworn the man had a tattooed serpent on his face, but at the trial it had mysteriously vanished.

'And did he kill you, sir?'

'Obviously not.'

'No. I mean. Sir. How did you effect escape?'

Again the memory, the thumbs tightened, the yellow teeth bared in a murderous smile, then the man shot up over McLevy's head like a cork out of a bottle and landed with a crash on two far-gone addicts who lay peacefully behind them in the smoke-filled, opium-scented den of iniquity.

Case concluded. Of course Moxey took the credit.

'I used a technique,' said the inspector gravely, 'called Kissing the Clouds.'

'Is that Chinese?'

'No. It comes from Leith. It is adapted from the leg movement of a hanged felon. I'll show it you sometime.'

Back tae business. He looked down at the body.

'Once Brennan was safely insensible, the killer finished off the job.'

McLevy anticipated Mulholland's next question by picking up the dirty, ripped pillow from the mattress and displaying a reddish stain which lay in the centre of the cloth.

'This mark is recent, even still a wee touch damp. If you examine Brennan's mouth . . . well go ahead, examine the damned thing!'

This sudden flash of temper indicated to Mulholland that all was back to normal. He peeled the lips of the corpse apart, peered inside and winced at the rotting stench.

'Worse than a dead badger,' he muttered.

The inspector smiled happily. 'The by-product of gingivitis; observe the gums and you will see another result of the inflammation.'

The whole mouth was in a terrible state but the gums were especially caked with smears of dried blood where the irritation had wreaked havoc.

Mulholland nodded. It made a sense of sorts. He let the mouth fall shut with a hollow clack.

'The man was potentially smothered,' he said.

'Exactly! And the blood in his mouth left marks where the pad was pressed.' McLevy's eyes gleamed.

'And I'll tell you one more on top of that. It was not a member of the fraternity, they'd just cut his throat and to hell with it. This is professional. High class.'

'There's not much in the way of actual proof, sir. A wee bit scratch, a couple of bruises and a stain.'

'Uhuh. So, you say,' replied the inspector.

The unspoken question in McLevy's mind was, of course, why kill the man anyway? Was it some sort of . . . clean sweep?

The door abruptly flew open and the squat form of Biddy Lapsley stood framed, arms folded. She opened a mouth like the gates of hell.

'I want my room back,' she bellowed. 'This man's been dead long enough.'

Then. Astonishingly. Tears started to flow down the veined and mottled face.

'I had hopes for him,' she muttered brokenly. 'He was such a fine big specimen. Meat on the bone. He put his lips upon my hand in the hall. A real gentleman. I could have raised him high.'

The policemen looked back at the corpse. It showed no sign of resurrection.

25

When the stars threw down their spears
And watered heaven with their tears:
Did he smile his work to see?
Did he who made the Lamb make thee?

WILLIAM BLAKE,
Songs of Experience

Sir Henry Ponsonby had been in the Queen's service these nineteen years. He'd arrived as an equerry to the Prince Consort but his exuberance, intelligence and good nature had quickly endeared him to Victoria so much that she almost at once took him over.

For the last ten years he'd been her private secretary; he'd heard the bell of St Paul's toll the death of her Prince Albert and listened through a door as the Queen cried like a soul bereft. He had seen her through the John Brown scandal, various illnesses, various wars and various threats of abdication if she did not get her own way.

When Victoria became interested in spiritualism after the death of her beloved husband, Ponsonby had even taken part in the darkness, but at a mock Household seance had disgraced himself by laughing so hard that the tears came through the obituary section of *The Times*, it being part of a newspaper blindfold he had been obliged to wear at the occasion.

Risen through the ranks. First a colonel, then

hailed as general and now knighted. But, in his mind somewhere, he was still a decent soldier. Loyal to the bone.

Eliza, as he irreverently called the Queen to others, had valued him as a friend, confidant, and rock upon which impetuous seas might break in vain, most of them being the seas of her own temper when thwarted. But value him, she had most dearly. Until now.

Now he was outside a ring of iron. For he possessed a grievous fault, a terrible sin which had been raised to confront him like a spectre. He was a Liberal.

Of course, he'd always been of that persuasion, proud to be so, pepper the court with the cannon fire of some common sense and a smidgeon of humour. But what had once been regarded with affection, indulgence and, God help him, sometimes even acted upon, was now viewed in the words of one of the Queen's own telegrams to no less than the Dean of Westminster as 'opposition proclivities' to be corrected.

His own wife Mary was also under suspicion but she, God bless her, threatened to go around with a mysterious look on her face as if in hourly communication with the forces of darkness.

Ponsonby could not afford that luxury. He was a servant of Her Majesty, once a most intimate servant, now excluded and distrusted. The Queen had been poisoned against him and he knew the man responsible. As Ponsonby fell, so the other rose in her affections, higher and higher.

161

Insinuations smeared his good name. That he had carried messages to the enemy, not true, not true, in the midst of Tory plots and opposition counter-plots he took no sides, he steered the middle course.

Much good it did him. He was no longer trusted. It was like a witch hunt. The court of Elizabeth Regina had set the treacherous template for the present one.

Well, mustn't bleat and moan, one would battle on somehow but it was a damned hard grind.

He looked out of the windows of Osborne House. As happened quite often in the Isle of Wight, there was a fine mist of rain swirling and falling. It was the kind of drizzle that could soak you to the skin. Sly. Insinuating.

Two figures were in the garden. One, tall, emaciated, like a funeral director, by God, held a large black umbrella to protect both himself and the other who sat on a small garden chair and worked busily at a border of flowers.

Yes, he had her under protection all right, humbugged to such an extreme that she detested and feared anyone with connection to the Liberal cause. The very word Liberal, in its essence generous and noble-minded, had been turned into a leprous epithet.

Gladstone in particular was to be reviled and shunned as if he carried that deadly plague. The mere mention of his name caused the Queen to shudder as if someone had walked across her grave.

Ponsonby's pale, rather protruberant eyes

creased in pain at his predicament as he gazed down at the instrument of his fall from favour. The funeral director. Blast and damn the man.

What was that play? His wife had dragged him to it, *Hamlet*, that was it, lasted an eternity, but there was a moment when the player king fellow had poured poison into someone's ear. Fatal. Yes. Shakespeare was nobody's fool.

As the rain smudged its way down the window pane not quite blotting out the view below, the secretary's lips moved in what was either imprecation or prayer.

In the garden, Benjamin Disraeli swivelled his head to see the pale face jerk back at the upstairs window.

Yes, the fellow was still spying, but Ponsonby could not discern the words exchanged, not unless he had left his ears under the rhododendron bushes.

Normally this observation would have a tinge of humour, but the prime minister did not feel humorous today. He felt like a hunted animal.

His umbrella twitched. Benjamin Disraeli hated the damp. He yearned for a perfect climate and never attained such.

He could almost feel the lining of his bronchial tubes thickening by the second. Another coating of moist slime, courtesy of the English weather.

A drop of water trickled down the hook of his nose and dripped off the end. Prospects indeed were dismal in all senses, marooned on this benighted island.

Yet, if he was being candid with himself,

although he only usually used honesty as a facade to confuse his enemies, he had somewhere welcomed her summons to Osborne.

Ostensibly it was to consult him on various matters of state before she left for Germany to attend the confirmation of her motherless granddaughters, diphtheria having removed her beloved Princess Alice some two years before, but really she wished to be reassured by his company.

The nation was voting. In England they were now at the polls and Scotland would follow some days later. A strange and staggered system but God guide their hand and, if not, Disraeli, his representative upon earth, was her man in a crisis. He would bring the ship home.

Disraeli's lips quirked a mixture of chagrin and bitter amusement. Yes, what a colossus he was to be sure. Had Count Bismarck not hailed him at the Congress of Berlin as *der alte Jude, das ist der Mann*?

Of course the Iron Chancellor was somewhat in his cups at the time and ballooned with flatulence, but it was a compliment to be savoured, was it not?

He remembered the scene well. Bismarck awash with champagne and black beer, stuffing himself with seven different kinds of sausage, and Disraeli himself wreathed in cigar smoke as a measure of protection against the flood of indelicate stories being poured by the chancellor into his isolated ears.

'*Put not your trust in Princes*,' Bismarck had also told him.

164

Ah, where would we be without the irony of God?

Another drip fell from his nose to earth. Back to the present. The election. Yes. The election. Well, well.

As for himself, he could do no more. The game was over. It was up to the country. Already, in England, they had begun to vote. The game was over.

In a strange way, at this very moment, he needed Victoria as much as she him.

They trusted each other as much as either of them could ever trust anyone. Lord Beaconsfield and the Queen.

He had arrived to find her flitting around in a state of almost hectic gaiety. She had immediately dragged him out to the garden and, wrapped in waterproofing, thick gloves to hand, was engaged in digging up some of his favourite flower, the wild primrose, which grew in abundance here.

For him to take home. To enjoy. In triumph.

Victoria struggled with some difficulty to rise from the low chair; between her growing plumpness and the myriad layers of clothing which encased the Royal person, to lever oneself up these days was a daunting endeavour.

Disraeli had the same problem. In their earlier days he thought nothing of throwing himself upon his knees and proclaiming his eternal loyalty to his Queen but now it would take a hoist to get him back on his feet.

He offered a spindly but chivalrous arm for her to lean on and, umbrella hovering overhead, escorted her to a garden table where she carefully packed the primroses and their earth into a shallow basket.

She looked up at him and smiled. Her small stolid form was in odd contrast to his attenuated frame.

'I am so glad you prefer the primrose,' she said.

'It is all the better for being a touch wild, and so retains its beauty for a longer time,' he replied.

As he smiled the skin stretched tight across his cheekbones like papyrus.

She worried over his health. 'You smoke too many cigars, Mr Disraeli,' she admonished.

'All men have their vices.' A cynical droop to the eyelids provoked her to laughter.

She spun, surprisingly nimble-footed, away from the sheltering umbrella into the lush perfection of Osborne's immaculate lawn.

'Your Majesty is unprotected, and runs the risk of saturation,' he called as she whirled farther off.

'Nonsense! It is only God's rain,' she replied sharply.

'God rains on earth and the Queen in England,' he punned a little riskily.

Her frown vanished and she laughed once more, trailing her heavy skirt through the wet grass like a child at play.

'When I return from Baden-Baden, you will be once more prime minister, and we shall have a celebration. A masked ball perhaps, I shall arrive as Titania and you as Oberon.'

Disraeli regarded her fondly, but he understood the root cause of these extremities of spirit.
Fear of the unknown. Ah well, adopt an earnest
tone. Though what is earnest is not always true.

'Indeed, ma'am, to the confusion of our
enemies, we hope to have much cause for
celebration.'

Reassured somewhat, she smiled, then looked
upwards and clasped her hands together in
supplication.

'Observe, prime minister. The rain has
stopped. It is an omen! Our diligence must be
blessed!'

Disraeli peered out cautiously from under the
still dripping shade. He was dressed in black and
his resemblance to a crow was unmistakable.

He furled the umbrella, struck a pose as if it
were a walking stick to hand, and responded to
her fervour.

'We shall prevail, ma'am. And I am reminded
of something Your Majesty was gracious enough
to confide in me in her letters. We must adopt a
high tone at all times. William Gladstone will
never be a man of the world.'

There was an element of self-parody in this
bombast but the Queen seized upon the literal
meaning.

'There are tales he is a secret Papist and a
. . . libertine!' she exclaimed.

Disraeli smiled inwardly. Indeed Gladstone's
'rescue' work amongst prostitutes had long been
the most fertile source of innuendo, and if
Beaconsfield had not actually given birth to
these rumours, he, when they reached her ears,

167

had certainly never contradicted them.

Over the years, he had made it his business to lace her thoughts with poison, wherever possible, as regards his bitter rival and, though he said it himself, he had made a splendid fist of it.

Fear gives rise to anger. Both can be manipulated. The art of politics.

Victoria brooded upon Gladstone's faults.

'He would *reduce* the empire. We must be prepared for attacks and wars, somewhere or other, *continually*. He would deny this. Moreover, he treats me like a public *function*! He is *worse* than the Russians!'

Her own words triggered off an alarm close to hysteria and she gazed at him with near-naked entreaty in her eyes, the previous comfort she had found in his assurances gone as if it had never been. Like the rain.

'You must be my chief minister for ever. I demand it!'

He could not look her in the eyes. He felt he did not have the strength.

'I am sure the people will choose wisely.'

'But if they do not?' she almost shrieked, then walked off abruptly to compose herself in a corner of the garden.

Indeed, thought Disraeli, if they do not, what could he offer her? His mind shifted to a conversation, held in a private club near St James's Park. A private room, wreathed in cigar smoke, where he had sat with a man he had met barely half a dozen times. A man who moved in the higher, more secret, circles of power. Not yet at the top, but ambitious to be so. A man recommended.

It was not long after he had declared the election, and Disraeli was wondering if he had made a mistake.

They had spoken for near an hour and, at the end of it, the man had leant forward and said, '*And how may I best serve the Queen?*'

'*In whatever way you see fit,*' was Disraeli's response.

No. He could not offer that. Best take refuge in whatever wit he might dredge up.

He walked across the grass, leant over, and confided.

'With any luck, Your Majesty, after a resounding defeat, Gladstone will emigrate to Siberia and remain there like an extinct volcano. Forgotten and fossilised.'

Not very good and part-pilfered from a much wittier phrase he had once coined, but it was the best he could manage at short notice and it had the desired effect.

She nodded happily at such a prospect and seemed to have fully recovered her spirits.

Disraeli was anxious to repair inside. He was rather exhausted, his very bones were aching in this damp, God-forsaken universe and a glass of port wouldn't go amiss.

But Victoria had one more surprise in store.

'Can you command a waltz, Mr Disraeli?' she asked.

For once the silver tongue was tied.

'I — I — have done so at one time without causing offence or accident,' he finally murmured.

'Prince Albert danced the waltz quite beautifully,' she murmured.

She stood. Not looking at him. Gazing into a pleasant middle distance. Disraeli at last comprehended the nature of the silent invocation. His own wife had adored to dance but she was more inclined towards the polka, the rhythms of which he found . . . most unappetising.

He laid aside the umbrella and approached his Queen.

'Would Her Majesty consider honouring her most humble servant?' he almost whispered.

Without more ado, she held out her plump little arms, still encased in waterproofing, her hands safely covered from fleshly contact by the stout garden gloves. He took one of them in his, and put his other arm round her back in a discreet curvature.

They waited in silence. Somewhere high above, a seagull screeched mockingly. Finally Victoria began to hum a tune under her breath.

Disraeli, slowly, like a grandfather clock creaking into motion, began to move gingerly to the melody.

She followed suit. They danced. Ghosts in a garden.

Upstairs, Ponsonby could not believe what he saw. He bit hard into his knuckle to disprove hallucination, and then looked out once more.

The figures still waltzed before his sight. Victoria and the funeral director.

He would have found a measure of comfort, however, had he been able to catch the look in

Disraeli's eyes as he gazed over the head of his sovereign.

They were bleak. Like a cornered beast's. Fixed upon an uncertain future.

A shaft of pale sunlight broke through the clouds and illuminated the dancers. The rest was gathering gloom.

26

He saith among the trumpets, Ha, ha;
and he smelleth the battle afar off, the
thunder of the captains, and the shouting.

JOB, 39:25

Gladstone had begun speaking at five o'clock precisely, was near an hour into his speech and appeared to be just warming up.

He had first covered in intricate detail the financial profligacy of the Disraeli government turning an inherited surplus of six million pounds (a surplus created by a Liberal government in which Gladstone had been simultaneously prime minister and chancellor, one head being better than two, and a canny recognition that every chancellor's sweetest desire was to dance on the dead body of his own PM so the only person you may have even the faintest hope of trusting is yourself) into an eight-million-pound deficit during six spurious years of unchecked imperial-ist annexation, *false phantoms of glory*.

He then had a passing swipe at Victoria being declared these four years past the Empress of India, *theatrical bombast and folly*, although he was careful to lay the blame for that at Beaconsfield's door.

Now he was engaged on raising his audience to an almost mystical communion against the evils of plutocracy.

But if truth be told, the People's William was far from an egalitarian. The opportunity to make large fortunes did not arouse his moral repugnance, indeed it had his full approval. What he was sore against, however, was the flaunting of it. And his indignation over such display had a practical streak. Don't shove your wealth in the faces of the poor, it may stir them up to resent their lot. They may rise against you, pitchfork to hand. And stick it in.

His ideal would be for one to live well within one's modestly acknowledged vast fortune and plough the money back into the land, or nurture the urban wage-slaves by building another factory to enhance their existence.

However, if unable to aspire towards such philanthropy, then at least balance your books, refrain from coveting thy Afghan or Zulu neighbour's land, don't pick a fight with foreigners, and, when at home, don't show off.

Most especially round your wife's neck.

And yet, almost despite himself, the *bain de foule*, the adoration of the masses within which he immersed himself with growing addiction, aroused an evangelical fervour which lifted him to address the people directly, over the heads of the aristocracy, landed interest, the established Church and even, most specifically, the Queen.

If Gladstone was aware that Victoria had always regarded direct address to the people as her prerogative and therefore the Royal nose had been put well and truly out of joint, he gave no sign of it.

His oratorical style was at times ponderous, monolithic, but the slow sentences built up, fuelled by a boundless physical energy, till they created the impression of a mighty sea rolling in, wave after wave after wave.

McLevy watched from amongst the crowd. All this oratory was giving him a blinding headache although he was prepared to admit a certain prejudice.

The inspector detested politicians. Scavengers who would sacrifice their own children if they thought it would advance them one small step nearer to kissing the rancid arse of power.

Gladstone, luckily, was unaware of this jaundiced view from at least one of his audience as he launched into a final but still lengthy salvo, on the subject it would seem of 'the *nation* against selfish interests'.

'We have great forces arrayed against us,' he began, before dismissing out of hand the afore-said aristocrats, gentry and Church, ' . . . wherever there is close corporation, wherever there is a spirit of organised monopoly, wherever there is a sectional and narrow interest apart from that of the country, and desiring to be set up above the interest of the public, there, gentlemen, we, the Liberal Party . . . '

Aha, thought McLevy, moved from the nation tae the party, have we?

' . . . have no friendship and no tolerance to expect.'

Gladstone paused for a moment. Earlier parts of his speech had been somewhat elevated and erudite, littered with Latin, marbled by Greek,

174

but now he was moving in for the kill, the axe raised high.

'But, above all these, and behind all these, there is something greater than these — there is the nation itself!'

Now, we're back tae the nation, McLevy reflected, the auld bugger's faster on his feet than he looks.

A prolonged burst of applause had allowed this seditious thought some room to express itself.

McLevy glanced sideways at Mulholland who was apparently enthralled by this spouting torrent of words, this vast ocean of promises. The inspector, as previously noted, did not trust the ocean because he could not swim.

Gladstone took a deep swallow from a glass of water and returned, refreshed, to the fray.

'This great trial is now proceeding before the nation. The nation is a power hard to rouse, but when roused, harder still and more hopeless to resist . . .'

There was a buzzing in McLevy's ears. It could not be a lack of sustenance, for early afternoon in the Old Ship he had treated Mulholland to the constable's favourite repast, boiled sheep's head, though the inspector himself preferred it burnt black with the hot iron.

Strangely enough, the dead body of Frank Brennan had given them both a fierce appetite, and after arranging for the body to be taken back to the mortuary to await examination, they had bolted for the tavern.

Mulholland's eyes had lit up at the contents of his plate, much the same as Herod's viewing the head of John the Baptist, while McLevy looked on benignly.

This had been a necessary sop before dragging his unwilling subordinate, by coach, some sixteen miles to West Calder, within whose townhall William Gladstone was making his last election address on the Saturday before the Monday poll. Sunday being the holy Sabbath, where all chicanery ceased under the stern eye of God.

West Calder was not even in Gladstone's Midlothian constituency but he had tramped the length and breadth of Scotland and, for some reason, this homely venue brought out the best in the People's William.

The place was packed up to the rafters, near up to fifteen hundred souls, all shapes and sizes, mostly honest working men and women in sober clothes. The town's economy was based on oil-shale production, not the most romantic of occupations, indeed a grinding prospect, but their faces were alight with a hope and belief which may well have helped cause the painful vibration in McLevy's head.

Most of the poor buggers were not even franchised to vote, yet here they were being elevated into thinking they had a serious judgemental duty to exercise. A delusion of democracy. Gibble gabble.

He could see Gladstone's mouth opening and shutting but a curious feeling of numbness and separation came over him. It was as if his eye had become a lens which swept the scene in front of him like a telescope.

This feeling of separation, as if seeing what was ahead like a screen upon which images were projected, had come to him in his life before but each time he contrived to pull shut the curtain of memory because it linked in some way with his mother; a certain gruesome picture at the back of his mind which brought with it a sense of vulnerability and childlike fear.

But what was to fear at this moment? Nothing. So let the lens roam.

Behind Gladstone on the platform various figures were seated and behind them others stood even farther at the back, almost out of the circle of the light.

Beyond them were no doubt more diverse shapes in the darkness, and behind them even other shadows. Going farther and farther back till they lost accountability. Such is the nature of the political animal. One face after another till the mask drops and all that is left is a vacant space where something may have once been. Or stood. Like a ghost.

Seated to the side was a self-composed elegant figure McLevy recognised as the 5th Earl of Rosebery, Archibald Philip Primrose to be precise. It seemed as if Rosebery had a bad smell under his nose, surely not the proximity of the People's William? The earl never looked directly towards Gladstone but at a spot some two feet in front of the great man, which was where, according to rumour, one day he would wish to find himself positioned, ruling the roost as cock of the party.

But for the moment Rosebery had to rest content with acting the great Scottish grandee who was hosting and masterminding the campaign. His eyes were half-closed giving a somewhat reptilian cast of feature and it was said he never slept. Too busy plotting perhaps. Spring is a great time for the plotting.

A gaggle of private secretaries swayed to and fro in the background like the fronds of some underwater plant and one in particular caught McLevy's eye. Tall, silver haired, he was in marked contrast to the stunted jobsworths who scuttled around him. He brought to the inspector's mind Frank Brennan's account of the doorway gentry who paid a price for Sadie Gorman that the poor old whore paid later.

Though even Gladstone himself might fit that particular bill. But had not the doorway gentry said . . . a friend? He was making the purchase on behalf of a friend. And was Brennan killed because he might remember the half-seen face or the smell of carbolic soap? What to believe? That was always the problem.

The silver-haired man moved out of the light and his place was taken by a woman who clutched some papers to her bosom as if they were a precious child.

A stooped, pinched body, God knows the misfits this game attracted, but there was something familiar about her. Of course, the glasses, the thick glass put him in mind of George Cameron.

A dig in the ribs brought him back. Mulholland frowned over as another burst of applause rent the air.

'You were grunting,' he said accusingly.

'I was not,' replied McLevy, annoyed to be brought out of his reverie. He looked back to the platform to find that the woman, also, had vanished.

'You were too, sir. Like a pig at the trough.'

The inspector ignored this bucolic simile. His attention was fixed on the stage where Gladstone had raised his right hand and held it in front of him as if he grasped the globe of the world in his cupped fingers. As he drew breath to speak, McLevy noticed that the left hand, resting quietly by his side, was indeed covered with a black stock.

The crowd kept a profound and impressive stillness as the sonorous voice rolled like thunder, the slight trace of a Lancastrian accent from childhood upbringing under the commanding Shakespearean tone. The man's physical magnetism almost palpable, an eagle's swoop of grandeur to lofty cadence. William in the high reaches.

'Our nation is called to undertake a great and responsible duty. A duty which is to tell, as we are informed from high authority, on the peace of Europe and of the destinies of England . . .'

What about Scotland? wondered the inspector.

' . . . we have found its interests mismanaged, its honour tarnished, and its strength burdened and weakened by needless, mischievous, unauthorised and unfortifiable engagements of war.

The nation has resolved that this state of things shall cease, and that right and justice shall be done! It shall — be — done!'

Gladstone threw back his head like an actor who had delivered a successful speech — which, McLevy cynically supposed, was exactly the ticket. Playing a role. Like a mountebank selling quack medicine.

For a moment there was silence then a full-throated roar of approval indicated a successful conclusion to the last act. Mulholland, caught up in the general enthusiasm, shouted something to the effect of, 'Well done, that man! Fine words. Fine words. Bring home the bacon!'

McLevy sometimes forgot how young was his constable but, at this moment, it was only too obvious and oddly touching to see his face alight, the blue eyes sparkling and the large hands, which had grasped many a criminal collar, clapping together for all they were worth.

The inspector turned away and looked at the applauding audience behind them, perhaps Joanna Lightfoot would be amongst the worshippers, waving her drawers in the air or even brandishing the further proof she had promised McLevy.

But he failed to see her tall, fashionable beauty amongst the hempen homespuns. Then his eyes narrowed.

Father Callan. Coat up to his neck. Also, like the inspector, not putting his hands together. The little priest was unaware of McLevy's scrutiny and his gaze was intent upon the platform where Gladstone was gravely acknowledging the adulation of the masses.

What was going on here? A secret admirer? A Papish plot? Perhaps he was going to unveil himself and declare to the world that William, admittedly an unpromising name for such, had knelt and kissed the hem of the Pontiff? Or was it something quite other?

As if McLevy had shouted out his name through the noise, the priest started, turned and looked straight at the inspector, listening to God on a full-time basis must bring its own acuity. His moonlike face registered a brief smile as McLevy's eyes bored into him, but, in the manner of his calling, the countenance gave nothing away.

In McLevy's experience few of the Romanish icons did. Except Jesus. You could trust that agony.

His priestly collar still hidden, Father Callan melted back into the crowd like a holy wafer on the collective tongue as they roared approval.

Mulholland was standing by, with the dazed, slightly foolish look of someone who'd been running with the herd.

'I didnae know ye to be such a radical,' said McLevy.

'I got carried away, sir. Glorious sentiments.'

The constable still retained a rapt look in the eyes and McLevy had an obscure craving to puncture the dream.

A malicious desire which did not speak well of him, but perhaps he was jealous of the young man's expression of unstinted admiration for

181

another. Few of us are free from jealousy; it follows us home like a black dog.

'Sentiments is exactly what ye got. A hogwash of figmentation,' the inspector remarked somewhat harshly.

Mulholland's face darkened but just before he opened his mouth to deliver one of Aunt Katie's homilies of remonstrance, to wit, *a man without belief is a dung fly in the midden of his own mind*, the inspector noticed that the entire platform entourage, minus the Earl of Rosebery who had shot off in another direction, was moving through a crowd of well-wishers towards the side door.

'Come on. Now's your chance!'

McLevy hustled the bewildered constable on a course of interception and practically shoved him into Gladstone's face as the great man was about to exit.

'My colleague here has been riven tae the core, Mr Gladstone!' he bawled like a fishwife. 'He cannot resist the impetus tae tell you so in person, and commend your message to the nation. Go ahead, Mulholland!'

A couple of the secretaries stepped forward protectively to shield their leader from this bellowing lunatic and his gormless beanpole companion, but Gladstone was apparently unperturbed. McLevy was struck by how much like a death mask his face now seemed. On the platform, his eyes had radiated energy and blazed with moral indignation, but now they were sunken back in his head.

He seemed spent, a sheen of perspiration

over his face, and looked all of his seventy years. Mind you it was the end of a long campaign and one and a half hours in West Calder might well be equivalent to ten in any other venue.

Then, were a switch pulled, the man sparked into life as if a current had been shot through his body.

He gazed keenly up at the tongue-tied, befuddled Mulholland.

'I am gratified that you approve my humble offering, sir,' he boomed. 'Let us hope that your sentiments are shared by many, and we carry the day.'

'It was fine, fine,' mumbled Mulholland, wondering how in God's name he found himself in such a pass. 'You brought it home. My Aunt Katie always says, you can do no more than bring it home. That's what God does.'

Gladstone was not to be outdone in the nuts and bolts of deific referral.

'And the same Almighty, in his wisdom, has wonderfully borne me through,' he pronounced.

He clasped his hand to Mulholland's shoulder in order to indicate an end to the exchange, it was half past the hour of six and he had many more hands to shake.

As Gladstone turned to go, however, McLevy had other ideas.

'We are policemen,' he said, out of the blue.

This caused a momentary hesitation in the acolytes who had turned as one man and woman to leave with their leader.

Who amongst us has such unspotted conscience that the word 'policeman' will not cause

183

just the merest tremor in the soul? The shadow of a passing sin?

McLevy put on his idiot face and slid forward to confront Gladstone. He was near enough to sniff but all that came to him was a slight sour odour of sweat from the great man.

'We are from Leith. We keep the streets safe. Do ye know Leith, Mr Gladstone?'

'My father was raised there,' was the somewhat formal response. 'Before he left for pastures new, he had the honour to be a merchant of that parish.'

'I never knew that. Did you know that, Mulholland?'

McLevy turned away, addressing the remark to his subordinate who wished the ground to swallow him up such was the buffoon his inspector was presenting.

'And what did he trade in, sir?'

Gladstone's face had set in rather stony lines, the cause unknown, the effect plain for all to see. He replied with the one word.

'Corn.'

McLevy took a deep breath and stepped off the edge of the precipice.

'And d'ye ever come back, sir? Tae the auld place? Walk the ancient streets as it were?'

Gladstone made no response. A flash of anger in his eyes. The silver-haired secretary stepped into the breach.

'Mr Gladstone has many demands on his time,' he said ambiguously. 'Now, if you will excuse us?'

'Oh, aye, aye, definitely.' McLevy now

184

appeared to be crushed and rather obsequious. 'It's just that we came all the way. From Leith. Tae see you, Mr Gladstone.'

'And now you have, sir. Now, you have.'

There was a moment when the two men's eyes locked, bulls in a field, then Gladstone made his exit.

Most of the entourage followed, leaving only the tall secretary and a few stragglers. The official looked down with barely concealed disdain at this dolt of a policeman now standing alone, Mulholland having retreated as far back as he could without actually fleeing the scene.

'What is your name?' the secretary asked abruptly.

'McLevy. Inspector McLevy. At your service, sir!' The inspector straightened up in what was perilously close to a parody of military readiness. 'And whom do I have the honour of addressing, sir?'

'My name is Horace Prescott,' was the clipped response.

'Horace? What a splendid appellation. Very close tae Horatius. The Captain o' the Gate!'

There was a cough from behind Prescott, it may even have been a smothered laugh, coming from a wee, fat, rather dissolute-looking cove who certainly was no great advert for the party of morality. The secretary's cheeks pinked up but he decided to treat McLevy like the idiot the man undoubtedly seemed to be. Though when he attempted to introduce a silky menace to his tones it was inappropriately tinged with a growing petulance.

185

'I assume you have a superior officer?' McLevy nodded his head vigorously. 'What is his name?'

'That would be Lieutenant Roach, but it's not worth your while talking to him. sir.'

'Why not?'

'I'm afraid he votes Conservative,' said McLevy. 'Always has, always will. Ye'd be wasting your time.'

From Prescott's view, the implication that he would be trying to curry election favour with some nonentity of a police officer left the man almost gasping for breath.

There was another sound behind him, this time verging on a definite snigger. His lips tightened and without another word he prepared to make a dignified and dismissive exit. But McLevy wasn't finished yet.

'I could swear I've remarked ye some time in Leith, sir. Have you ever visited, down by the docks maybe?' Mulholland winced as the inspector ploughed gaily onwards. 'There's some pretty sights. When the ships come in.'

Prescott had never met such a profoundly irritating person in his life.

'I know little of the place,' he snapped. 'And I am happy to keep it so.'

He strode off, the wee fat fellow after him with a broad grin on his face. The rest of the stragglers followed in an untidy scramble on the outside edge of which McLevy briefly glimpsed the woman with the thick glasses, body still hunched over her papers. Then she and the rest were gone. As if they had never been.

While the inspector whistled softly to himself,

an outraged Mulholland returned to his side.

'You made a terrible bloody fool out of me!' he accused bitterly.

'With God's help and your own efforts, the situation may yet be remedied,' came the opaque reply.

McLevy looked past his indignant constable into the body of the hall. It had not yet emptied, people stood around in clumps still chewing over the words of William Gladstone, but he did not see a likeness he recognised.

'Don't think I didn't fathom what you were up to,' Mulholland said through gritted teeth. 'You wanted to look in his eyes. Well. What did you see?'

'Power,' replied McLevy. 'But for good or ill, that I do not yet know.'

The constable threw his arms to the heavens that McLevy could entertain the slightest doubt over a man so widely regarded as the sentinel of truth and probity, but the inspector's mind had shifted back to the small, windowless dining room of the tavern where they'd filled their bellies.

The dried skulls of the sheep had been arranged all round the walls, lighted candles placed between the horns.

It was meant to be decorative but had struck him as just so many intimations of death.

27

Come forth thy fearful man:
Affliction is enamoured of thy parts,
And thou art wedded to calamity.
                    WILLIAM SHAKESPEARE,
                         Romeo and Juliet

The Serpent held out a hand before him and noticed the fingers to tremble a little. That was good. Nerves. A man without nerves was a fool who deceived himself.

He moved over to the window and looked out over the lights of the city glittering fitfully in the darkness. He had already been out earlier in that darkness, to set the scene as it were. But now he had returned to wait for the appointed hour.

Some solid banks of fog were beginning to build up. That was good, good for business. What was it the old fellow, regimental batman, ancient mariner, whose gnarled hands were supposed to attend to his every need, had said this morning as he scraped out the ashes?

'We'll hae a sea haar the nicht. I feel it in my bones. Cauld as the grave, sir.'

He mimicked the near-incomprehensible accent perfectly, speaking aloud in the silent room, then moved restlessly away from the window to regard himself once more in the stained, cracked, full-length mirror.

Now, there was no going back. Now, it had to be done.

Had the word from the South been cheerier, the early election forecast more promising, he may have considered a halt to the mission. But no, let's be honest old chap, even with the advent of good tidings, the matter must run its course. He had the taste for blood now.

And it was such splendid sport, to be out in the field once more, not sending others out to risk for him.

It was all a matter of timing. When to play the cards.

On an impulse, he tried to mould his features to those of Benjamin Disraeli, the drooping eyes he could manage but not that splendid nose, that would need some construction. The mouth was possible, hinted at a certain lubriciousness, a delving into dark corners. The reflected mouth smiled at the thought.

For had Disraeli not written, possibly on his knees at the time, to the comely Lord Henry Lennox, 'I am henceforth your own property, to do what you like with . . . '?

He dropped the pretence and sneered at himself. But was he not the same? A creature to be used? An instrument, not of pleasure though, but of ruin? His potency dependent on those above? In this case, not even the dignity of direct command, a suggestion here, an implication there, an elegant oblique silence after a subject raised.

A creature. That was all.

The Serpent was suddenly filled with the

189

venom of self-hatred. He spat, quite deliberately, into his own face and watched as the saliva slid down his mirror image.

Then he cheered up immensely. Good to get that off one's chest. Think of the rewards from on high. Favours bestowed. The power granted. Beyond his peers. No one would deny him. He would be *indispensable*. Above all others.

Nerves, that was it. Before going into action. Not long now, this was the tricky one, trick o' the light, all depended on the timing, repeating himself, not a good idea.

He moved away from the mirror and took stock. He knew the time and place, the mark was set, part of the money paid, the route reconnoitred; all he had to do . . . the Serpent took a deep breath. Relax. Not the first time, old chap. Think of yourself . . . as the Hand of God. Royal appointment. Relax. That's the stuff to give the troops.

He summoned up a picture that always turned his bones to water. The first time she had come to him, the little fleshly beast.

The Serpent had been asleep and awoke, heart pounding, to find her at the foot of his bed, golden hair loose to her shoulders. She wore a nightdress he himself had approved and bought. Appeared chasteness itself in the shop, a thick cotton swathe behind which youthful modesty might rest, but now it seemed the very emblem of temptation.

And then it fell, by some strange motion, as if a snake had sloughed its skin, to the carpet.

A naked female is the most terrifying mystery.

She was part in shadow, he could make out the shape of her long young body glowing in the dark. But all that was immediately visible, a shaft of moonlight through a high window playing the pander, was one bare foot.

One slender white foot, on a red carpet.

And then it moved. Towards him. And all else followed. Foot, ankle, calf and thigh. Then perdition.

He'd tried to resist, to protest, but such speech is difficult when the mouth is so otherwise occupied.

From far below the castle walls, there came the sound of laughter. Harsh, jeering laughter from an unknown source.

The Serpent found his lips dry. Surely a cigar was called for? His case was on the table. He crossed, took one out, Dutch, can't beat the Dutch, lit it up, and found he was calm again.

The operative had her part to play. And so had he. Flesh could wait.

Somewhere a church bell struck nine hours. Not long, now. Not long, now. Action.

28

Behold, I shew you a mystery; We shall not
all sleep, but we shall all be changed.

I CORINTHIANS, 15:51

The Old Ship was one of the finest taverns of the
Leith port, not like some of the other dives in
and out of which McLevy had fought his way,
hauling to a reckoning many a thief, while the
man's lava Venus hung on to the back of the
police uniform trying to scratch his arresting
eyes out.

Indeed there were drinking dens in the
harbour area which fell silent and lost half their
customers at the sight of himself and Mulholland
walking through the door.

The constable was feared for his hornbeam
stick plus the skill with which he wielded the
implement and McLevy for his fury of response
should violence threaten.

The story still did the rounds of the night he,
as a young constable, and Henry Preger, a
notorious lifetaker and close-quarter mangler
whose massive fists had smashed many a
policeman to his knees, battered hell out of one
another in the Foul Anchor tavern while Preger's
wee pillow-wanton, Jean Brash, looked on in
pure amazement.

Preger had made a sneering comment about
the death of Sergeant George Cameron, and his

hope that the worms were crawling up a certain orifice to enjoy a fine Highland feast. Teuchter pudding.

Then, as Milton put it so poetically, all hell broke loose.

Some say the fight lasted near one hour and a half, some say longer. But, at the end of it, Preger lay bruised and writhing on the sawdust planks while Jamie McLevy walked out of the door into the night without a backward glance.

That night, he made his name. He had taken everything Preger could throw at him, and, at the end, danced a wild jig round the body of his foe, howling out a Jacobite song, and putting the fear of God into all who watched.

McLevy was not so sure he could do it now. He was carrying a bit of weight these days, but that could work in his favour. Ye might assume the bulk would slow the motion, but he still possessed fast hands. And feet.

McLevy had a dram of peat reek whisky set out before him. He lifted it and drank. A dark thought came. It is often so with whisky.

Fast hands, but they hadnae been fast enough to save George Cameron. His vanity had seen to that. Perhaps one day he would forgive himself, perhaps one day, when the promise was fulfilled.

The inspector sighed and looked around the tavern.

The Old Ship. He felt at home here, well as much home as anywhere. The place had a generous size to it, great staircases, thick walls and the cosy rooms panelled with moulded wainscot. He loved the big stone fireplaces that

193

had witnessed many a deep carouse, and appreciated most keenly the wooden cubicles where a lone man might be private unto himself.

On return from West Calder, Mulholland had sprung a surprise on him. Often it was their custom to share a glass at the end of a week and chew the fat till closing time, but it would seem that your man had begun to develop social pretensions to go with his general sookin' up, and he was away to a musical recital in a respectable house. The Roach house no less. This very night.

Seemingly the constable had a fine tenor voice and Mrs Roach, the good lieutenant's wife, had noted his prowess in their church, which Mulholland had chosen to attend, no doubt to ingratiate himself even further.

Despite the constable's lowly office, she had roped him in with a view to future duets amidst some of the young ladies of her artistic circle. Tenors being in short supply.

McLevy had been firmly discouraged from any possible attendance in case he brought down the tone, an element of revenge for Mulholland after his being made to look like an imbecile at the Gladstone meeting. The inspector told himself he did not mind because he hated that tight-arsed cultural genteelity which had no connection to any kind of life he had ever come across.

Though, truth to tell, he was a bit sore nevertheless at the exclusion. McLevy disapproved people keeping secrets except, of course, for himself.

He had wrung from the constable at least that

Mulholland would make no mention of their tiptoeing to West Calder should he be offered a shortbread biscuit by the man of the house, but say merely that the investigation was continuing its course.

It comforted the inspector somewhat that Lieutenant Roach would have to sit through the entire programme of high-flown musical tributes to the sensitivity of human nature, because one thing that he and Roach shared was a profound distaste for such functions.

The lieutenant's wife was one of these women who were always doing good or something approaching it, and spent her life wrenching the poor bugger from one committee meeting to another when the man would rather have been at home reading his golfing periodicals or out on the course.

Doing good. The unco guid. What they preach, they do not practise. McLevy's lip curled. The dirty squalid world they sought to alleviate was created almost entirely by a financial system and usage that they themselves supported with great enthusiasm.

If you scratched these good folk hard enough, you would find nothing but a fear of contamination. They would seek to forget the painful, suppress the disagreeable and banish the ugly. The city council was even now, under the Chambers Improvement Act, engaged on pulling down the slum buildings and erecting in their place so very little and, such as it was, laid aside for those they considered honest hard-working artisans and the like, so that the poor were more and more crushed together like rats in a cage.

And the respectable citizens of the New Town who had left so much of the Old Town to rot, walked on the maze of small bridges and pathways above, making sure that no one was keeking up their skirts.

They looked down on the seething mass below, pitied their lack of religion and morality, which was surely the cause of this misfortune, and met in committees to shake their heads and consider guidance.

McLevy took another dram of whisky and shivered slightly as the raw spirit hit his throat as hard as Preger had done, all these years ago.

Twice, in the fight, he had almost given up the ghost, the once especially when he had found himself face down on the dirty floor of the tavern spitting out blood, with the crowd howling and the man's boots planted in front of him, one drawn back to finish the job. Then the memory of George Cameron on that hospital bed and strangely enough a wink from Preger's wee whore, glimpsed through the V in the man's legs, drove him on. He slipped the kick and punched up into the bastard's groin. A hammer blow.

A man on the ground is not necessarily a man defeated. McLevy looked down to find that his hand was clenched into a fist. A woman's shadow fell across it.

'How the hell did you know I was here?' he demanded.

Joanna Lightfoot managed a faint smile but the haunted look he had noticed on their first meeting seemed more pronounced.

'Your landlady said I might find you in this place. It being your custom of a Saturday night,' she replied.

'That is private information she had no right tae divulge!'

He looked at her indignantly and made no move to invite her to sit, but she did that anyway, feeling the heat of some curious glances from the tavern regulars. She'd had to gather up her nerve in order to enter in the first instance. Women of her class were simply not seen in such an establishment.

She slid into the cubicle seat opposite him, taking off her bonnet, and put her small bag upon the table. He glared at her as if she was the last person in the world he wanted to see but Joanna had some knowledge of him by now.

Enough to discern that his first impulse would be to put her at disadvantage.

'Is that whisky?' she questioned of the glass.

'It most certainly is.'

She reached forward and drained the contents in one gulp. McLevy's eyes popped. She sat back.

'There is no time for such nonsense,' she said firmly.

'What nonsense?'

'You know very well.' Joanna closed her eyes as the aftertaste of the whisky hit home.

'I am being followed. I am certain of it,' she said.

'Who by?'

'The protectors of those in power.'

'Such as William Gladstone?'

'That, I do not know.'

She shrank back as a burst of noise from one of the upstairs rooms indicated some revelry afoot. McLevy watched her keenly; this had better be worth his purloined drink.

But by God she was beautiful, a hectic colour to the cheeks, the dark blue eyes almost purple or was that reflection from the high collar of her dress? She wore the same outdoor coat as last time but, as she loosened it at the neck to take a long shuddering breath, he could see beneath a different colour where the white of her throat met a dark reddish blue, the crushed silk material rustling as her bosom heaved.

Bosoms, thought McLevy. Just a menace.

'Ye dress a treat,' he said. 'Who buys for ye?'

'What?'

He watched as she tried to repress a belch brought on by the harsh liquor. Eructate. Ladies do not belch they eructate.

'You heard. All done up like gingerbreid. Ye didnae get that at the Grassmarket. Not married, one of Jenkin's hens, a spinster, howtowdie, that was your proud assertion. Are you somebody's fancy keep then?'

This time she did, belch. Eructate. While she brought out a dainty lace handkerchief and dabbed at her lips, McLevy checked out the tavern. Mostly regulars; no strangers to his sight. There was one fellow worth the noting, wee Johnnie Martin, who had just sidled in from the other bar, but no one seemed to have followed her inside, no one was watching them.

Joanna finally found a response.

'It is none of your business, but . . . if you must know, if you feel it is of such importance, may I inform you that I have a private income!'

It was a lie somewhere. McLevy knew it. Never mind, he had her on the hop. That's the main thing.

'What d'ye want with me, Miss Lightfoot? Other than a free whisky?'

'Did you do as I asked?' she countered.

'I did. And found more of the same from the big nurse with the terrible tea. Stories, weird and wonderful, not a shred of proof. In-substantial.'

He leant over and peered into his empty glass in a disappointed fashion then shot out a question.

'How did ye know about this woman?'

'I was given her name.'

'Who by?'

'I cannot tell.'

'There's a lot you cannot tell.'

In the silence that followed, they appraised each other. It was a matter of trust. Or, more likely, an absence of same. Her fingers rested on her bag for a moment, and then she withdrew them. What was she going to conjure up this time?

'I saw your cat in the street. She hissed at me,' Joanna said as if it was of great importance.

'Bathsheba's in a bad mood these days.'

'Do you comprehend the cause?'

'Another cat. I have a presentiment that her neck has been gripped. There's a soft fold o' flesh. Once the teeth are in, she cannot move.

199

Often two males are privy to the act. One bites deep, the other performs. She may howl, but she is at their mercy. Then they change places.'

McLevy's eyes had a sardonic gleam and she sensed a depth to his being that he rarely revealed. What he had just delivered was not merely a zoological footnote and it seared her like a hot poker.

'But does she not invite that?' she asked. 'By her very nature. Who can resist their own nature?'

The door to the tavern banged shut and they both whipped round but it was only an old fellow, well enough dressed and a little the worse for wear, who was greeted in familiar terms by the barman.

'Aye, Andra — what is tae be your pleasure?'

As the old fellow made that known, McLevy turned back to Joanna.

'And so, Miss Lightfoot,' he said. 'What is to be your pleasure?'

There was a mocking glint in the slate-grey eyes and for a moment she felt an obscure stirring of desire in a place she would not care to mention. Damn her predilection for the older man. Deep breath.

'I need you to promise,' she said, 'that what I show you will be returned to me.'

He said nothing. Joanna took that for yes.

She pulled a couple of dog-eared vellum pages from within her bag and laid them carefully on the table.

'These are indications,' she almost whispered. 'No more than that.'

McLevy squinted at the pages; the light in the tavern was poor and he was beginning to wonder if he might not need reading glasses. He tilted the paper towards the light and perused the words as best he could.

The two pages, though loose, seemed to be in diary form, the entries dated by day and month but not by year. There was a strange marking by some of them and the words used were cryptic, cut-off, with some Latin and Greek thrown in by the looks of it, as if something was to be hidden from the reader.

Her finger tapped at one entry and, as he muttered the words under his breath, Joanna Lightfoot spoke over this.

'In 1850, the year that the first murder was committed, William Gladstone had been visiting prostitutes in London.

'Often he saw them in the streets, late at night, and went to their rooms, his wife away in the country, and he stayed there, in their rooms, for many hours.'

There was a breathless excited quality to her speech which McLevy found unsettling; he wished she would hold her tongue because it was the devil's own job to decipher this writing. He muttered what fragments he could make out.

'Saw *P.L. A singular case indeed. More harm . . . trod the path of danger.'* Another entry caught his eye. *'I have . . . courted evil . . . deluded in the notion of doing good.'*

Again Joanna spoke, this time in the curiously formal manner which he recognised from their first meeting.

'It is common knowledge that Gladstone would walk near the Argyle Rooms in Great Windmill Street where the upper classes indulged in every kind of dissipation. He would approach these women of the night under the guise of rescuing them from a life of sin, at least that is how it was presented to the outside world.'

She moistened her lips with the tip of her tongue and swallowed hard as if some vision in her mind had perturbed her, then got back on track.

'But these entries might show that when he was alone, feasting his eyes upon them . . . who was the sinner, and who was sinned against?'

'Aye. A fallen woman's a great temptation,' said McLevy cheerily. 'But even if he did. What then?'

In response she pointed at one of the curious markings at the foot of an entry. McLevy strained to make sense of the words which came before the sign.

'My trysts are carnal or the withdrawal of them would not . . . leave such a void.'

Then after that came *'Returned to . . . '* followed by the strange symbol.

'It looks a wee bit like a whip,' he hazarded.

'It is the Greek symbol lambda. The letter L. I believe it represents the lash. The whip, as you say. The scourge.'

McLevy's eyebrows shot up; this was approaching value for his lost whisky. 'Are you saying these women *whipped* him?'

'No!' she said impatiently. 'It was self-administered. He scourged his own body. Many times. To drive out the terrible guilt. The impurity within. To suffer is to be released. But only for a time, and then it returns, even stronger.'

Her eyes upon him were hot and zealous; McLevy felt as if he needed space to draw breath.

'I knew an embezzler had one of those leathers,' he said, with a scholarly air. 'Studded with nails. I think he got it from France. I believe they were all the fashion.'

Joanna would not be deflected.

'There were many women, Emma Clifton, Elizabeth Collins, you may find their names, and he writes of his sympathy being corrupted, how he must limit and scourge himself, but back he goes, again and again!'

She took a deep breath to control what seemed to him to be a rising hysteria. 'And then . . . came the punishment of God. In the middle of all this, his daughter died.'

Joanna had alluded to this in their previous tête-à-tête but it was another turn of the screw.

'Ye think this might be the root cause of our two murders,' he mused. 'You cannot control the guilt within, so you kill the cause of it, without. First his daughter, and then the sister's recent death set it all off again.'

'He may not even know he does it,' she said. 'He may be split from it. Like the branch from the tree.'

McLevy sniffed. He had no time for these

sorts of daft notions; anyway part of his attention had shifted to a scene about to happen at the bar.

No. Not yet. The recent arrival, Andra, had turned from the counter to survey in benign fashion the tobacco smoke which spread like a cloud through the bar.

The old man added to it by lighting up his pipe and puffing contentedly. The chance has gone, Johnnie. Wait for the next time, eh?

'How did you get these papers?' he asked suddenly.

She hesitated. 'A friend. They were loose inside one of his . . . official diaries.'

'You have someone in Gladstone's employ?'

She nodded unwillingly.

McLevy sat back. No point in asking the name of her provider; she would return to 'I cannot tell'. There would be a time, either in the interrogation room, or when he had some leverage on her, like a headlock perhaps.

He smiled at the thought but was there not some element of attraction in this vision? Her head against his chest, his arm across her throat? And did she not invite this, by her very nature?

He flicked the pages over to her with an idle finger. 'It's a good read, what I can glean, but it says nothing. Proves nothing. Nothing worth a damn.'

His voice was flat, his face stony, as if he had completely lost interest. She tried to hold down her mounting desperation. He had to believe her!

'There is another book. A private diary. Kept under lock and key. Always. If I can get my hands on it, I know it will contain his innermost thoughts and deeds. Then we will know the truth. You must help me, you must — '

His hand shot out like a snake and grasped her firmly on each side of the jaw. She shuddered as he bent her face close to his, like lovers.

'The truth?' he said softly. 'What is your commerce in all this, Miss Lightfoot? Tell me your own truth, and I will see where to lay the brand of justice.'

Without taking her eyes from his, she reached into the bag and took out another page of the paper. He let go her face and she bowed her head as he looked upon the page.

'Saw P.L. indoors and said it must be the last time. My thoughts of P. Lightfoot must be limited and purged.'

He looked up to find a single tear finding a path over the high cheekbone down to the corner of her mouth, where she licked at it like a child.

'Pauline Lightfoot,' her voice was low and agonised. 'My mother. She left this vale of tears when I was five years old.

'She had given up the streets when I was born, a sum of money had been settled on her. When she died, I was taken away by a guardian and looked after till I was old enough to make my own way in the world.'

Joanna let out a sigh which a softer heart than McLevy's would have found quite piteous.

'I told you the truth. A private income, I have, of sorts. Each month a sum was deposited in a bank account under my name. My guardian arranged this, but, like my mother, would not tell me the identity of my father.'

The inspector's eyes were watchful, this woman was full of stories. They all are.

'So, you have fixed on the People's William?' He whistled a melody under his breath as he awaited her answer.

'God help me. I have.'

'Why in particular? Your mother must have had many . . . visitors in her time?'

She looked away, and put her hand up to her throat.

'When my guardian died, this is most shameful to relate, I went through all of his papers. I found evidence that a large sum of money had been passed to him from a lawyer acting on behalf of an unnamed benefactor. The money was to be settled on my mother and myself. The rest was easy.'

'Was it now?' McLevy's eyes widened in what she had come to recognise as his idiot look. 'And how did ye persuade the lawyer to divulge the name of this here benefactor? They are mean-mindit, small-mouthed creatures. Their whole profession is dedicated to guarding others' secrets. How did you do that, I wonder?'

Joanna smiled crookedly.

'I seduced him, Mr McLevy. I came to his bed at night and dropped the seventh veil. These wiles are in my blood.'

McLevy again whistled softly under his breath and gazed back out into the bar. All quiet. So far.

'Since then, I have made it my business to find out every single thing about William Gladstone. I have used recommended . . . investigators and now I have my friend. A friend at court.'

'Would it not be easier just to go up and ask the man?'

A simple enough question but her eyes filled up and she bit into her lip with such force that he feared a bloody response.

'The name the lawyer gave me was by the spoken word. Not by written proof.'

'Your seduction had its limitations, then?'

'Yes,' she said quietly, then drew another deep breath.

'I am afraid he will deny me. And I am even more afraid that he may have committed murder. The least I owe myself is to know the truth of that before I knock upon his door.'

As McLevy brooded on this and turned his face once more away from her, she drew the pages towards her bag.

'He stays tonight in George Street. It is his habit to go walking of an evening. Who knows — ' her voice almost broke, 'what he may accomplish? I wish that you might follow him. Perhaps you may find out the truth this night. For me. And for justice.'

He made no reply, his eyes fixed towards the bar. She looked down to put the papers into her bag and when she raised her eyes once more McLevy was no longer opposite.

She looked out into the crowd and there was no sign of him. He had vanished into the smoke-filled room.

Johnnie Martin was good at his trade and on the point of exercising it. The mark was fuddled with drink which made the delving even easier.

He slid his fingers into the man's side pocket where he had previously noted the purse tae reside, prepared to lurch into him, blame the whisky, grin his apologies and be out with the lift before —

An iron hand gripped his where he held the wallet, and he looked up with a sinking heart to see McLevy's big face leering through the smoke at him like a warwolf.

'Well, Johnnie,' said the inspector softly, 'we'll not make a fuss. Slip the retainers on, just tae keep you honest, eh?'

The little man sagged back as McLevy deftly clipped the cuffs around his wrists, removed the wallet from his unresisting hands and tapped Andra on the shoulder.

'I think this belongs to you, sir,' he said.

The old man had noticed nothing.

'I must have dropped it on the floor,' he muttered.

'I think not,' replied the inspector.

Still holding firmly on to the pickpocket, he glanced back to see if Joanna had witnessed his small triumph.

The cubicle was empty. A draught of cold outside air hit him on the back of the neck, and the street door shook gently as if a ghost had left the tavern.

For a moment he was tempted to race after but she would be long gone with these long strides. Never mind. He would hand Johnnie over to one of the constables on the beat, and then go about his business.

'Can I see my way tae buy you a drink, sir?'

said the grateful Andra, puffing his pipe fit to bust.

'I believe I may have a whisky,' responded McLevy. 'I lost the last one in mysterious circumstances.'

29

Gather ye rosebuds while ye may,
Old Time is still a-flying.

ROBERT HERRICK,
'To the Virgins, to Make Much of Time'

Mulholland took a deep, soul-satisfied breath. This was the life. A grand destination.

He'd worried in the coach all the way back from West Calder, cursing the weakness for sheep's head which had let McLevy inveigle him out there in the first place, chewing a bitter lip that he'd be late — but no, just made it in time.

Slipped in at the back as the first note quavered in the air. This was the life.

The recital had unfolded with one sweet mystery after another. To begin. A succession of young ladies who held their violins like newborn lambs as they sawed their graceful way through compositions by various, by the sound of it, foreigners.

And then to follow some songs which delighted the ear, while the eye was being entertained as the daughters of the Muse swayed tastefully to the constrained passion of the melody. They never moved their legs though. Good breeding saw to that.

Madrigals and pastoral fancies, *chansons* and *saluts d'amour*, the notes ascended to the corniced ceiling like rose petals in a high wind.

One piece which particularly impressed the constable was *andante sostenuto*, slow and deliberate like a herd of cows coming home to be milked of an evening, steam rising from their flanks. The fellow must have had a decent farm somewhere in his background. What was the name now? He'd want to be wafting it in front of McLevy first thing in the morning, unless it was some false coiner from Naples.

Donizetti! Your very man. Italian by the sound but none the worse for all that.

Indeed had Mulholland known the fate of Gaetano Donizetti, the poor songsmith dying mad, eaten up by cerebrospinal syphilis, he may have reflected that fine music, like most things, comes at a cost.

But he did not know that. And his attention had been captured by one particular young lady who had played piano accompaniment for the various performers.

Emily Forbes was her name. Her father Robert sat at the front, stern but proud, a widower of three years.

The whole society seemed to be in mourning for someone or other, from the Queen downwards. A nation of glum faces, surrounded by black crape.

Mulholland had sat at the front beside Mrs Roach, the lieutenant holding to the outer reaches of the audience, and the constable could have sworn that Emily had cast some sidelong glances in his direction though she might have just been following the pages of the score.

There was the satisfied buzz of honey-laden bees as, recital over, the young ladies congratulated each other and were in turn complimented by the sons of upright citizens.

The constable found himself rather isolated, suddenly conscious of his low rank. These fellows were of a different breed, a confident assumption of their own self-worth wafting around them like horse-breath in November. Money does that.

One of them, a fellow Mulholland had disliked on sight, was making great play over Emily who seemed not to notice what a potato-head the man had on him and laughed, no doubt in pity, at some presumed witticism.

Roach, seeing his constable lurking like a night-thief at the back of the crowd, crossed over amid the tinkling of teacups and crunch of ginger biscuits.

The lieutenant's wife revelled in these evenings but his own patience was sore tried by it all. Just when you thought the damned thing was finished, up popped another song about trees bending in the breeze, decent enough on the course when such a wind had to be taken into account, but not worth such interminable musical spasms.

'Let us assume you have enjoyed the recital and not waste words, constable,' he said tersely. 'Where did you leave the inspector?'

'He was . . . heading homewards, sir,' was the careful reply.

'McLevy doesn't have a home, unless he carries it on his back like a tortoise,' muttered

Roach. 'What is the progress of our investigation?'

'We're gathering in all the strands, lieutenant.'

A baleful glint of humour surfaced on Roach's saurian features. 'You sound like a seaweed collector. What about Frank Brennan?'

'The inspector thinks it might be murder.'

'Murder? By what cause?'

'He may be better telling you himself, sir. In the morning. At the station. It's to do with opium dens and thumbmarks, and a goddess from India,' the constable offered with a straight face.

Roach held up his hand in reflex.

'Stop where you are. You're right. In the morning. After church. I'll get it from the cannon's mouth. I don't have the strength for an account of McLevy's meanderings. Not this particular night.'

If you knew what was going through his mind, the constable thought bleakly, ye'd die with your leg up.

'Gentlemen,' a voice broke into their exchange, 'I trust you have not descended to police business!'

Mulholland was relieved to see Mrs Roach bearing down on them with the smile of a born hostess. She was a small woman with a pretty face, like a doll, dainty and pleasant enough, but unable, as Aunt Katie would have put it, to sit on her backside for five minutes. She loved social gatherings, committees, conversation, culture, never stopped talking and had a laugh which trilled like a bird in the bushes.

God help him for the cruel callous swine he had become and it was all to do with spending so much time with McLevy, but Mulholland could not rid himself of the thought that she must be a truly terrible person to live with; always smiling, always busy, always fixing the woes of the world, not a shadow to be seen on her unremittingly cheerful face, no wonder Roach headed for the fairways. Ye needed a bit of grimness in a woman, not too much but just enough to prove that she was seriously worth the effort.

However, she was welcome enough now because not only did Mrs Roach extricate him from his lieutenant, she pointed the constable in the direction of Emily Forbes.

'That young lady,' she pulled Mulholland down so that his large pink ear was in whispering range, 'is possessed of a beautiful contralto voice. Together you may grace our recitals with the most exquisite renderings.'

'But I don't read music,' said Mulholland plaintively. 'I missed it growing up.'

Mrs Roach fixed him with a bright stare, like a bird with its beady eye on an emergent larva.

'There is nothing that cannot be solved by hard work and perseverance. The good Lord took seven days to create the world, musical notation is nothing to that.'

With this pithy homily, she ushered Mulholland away, without so much as a by-your-leave to her husband.

Roach watched his constable bow stiffly over Emily's hand, and even more stiffly greet the man with her, Oliver Garvie, who bore the unmistakable mark of his father's profession. A butcher's son. He had a certain beefy charm and a finger in many pies. An entrepreneur. Mulholland had his work cut out there.

Robert Forbes, Roach noted, was watching the foursome but nothing could be gleaned from his face, what else could you expect from an insurance adjuster?

The lieutenant watched his wife with a strange, puzzled affection. He had joined the force late, and married even later. Roach had been marked down to inherit the family undertaking business, but the customers were uncomforted by his brooding presence.

Roach's nature and looks precluded an easy belief in the hereafter. His brother Archie, round faced, moist-eyed and sympathetically solemn, at least provided some hope.

Thus the worm of life tries to wriggle off the hook before death bites.

The day after he laid out his own father, Roach left the business to Archie and joined the police force.

He had at first been welcomed with open arms, education and breeding to the fore, but somehow had never quite attained his cherished desire. He blamed his mother's soft nature. To be successful in the force, you needed a heart of stone. His had cracks somewhere.

They were childless. The act of procreation, despite Mrs Roach's chirps of encouragement and his banging away grimly like a man with his ball caught in a gorse bush, had produced nothing. No justice.

The lieutenant came out of these musings with a start.

It was worrying how he sometimes saw events through McLevy's eyes, the man was a pernicious influence.

All was well with the world. Keep it that way.

One of the young ladies of the soirée approached him, full of the joys of culture.

'All this must make you very happy, Mr Roach,' she informed him.

'Happiness,' said Roach. 'What is that?'

30

I met a traveller from an antique land
Who said: Two vast and trunkless legs of stone
Stand in the desert.

PERCY BYSSHE SHELLEY,
'Ozymandias'

The haar had settled on Edinburgh. Even the castle citadel, the king's bastion, 384 proud feet above sea level, was wreathed in a dense fog.

A large white gull waddled along the length of Mons Meg, the monster gun, four yards end to end, twenty inches diameter, but no longer fearsome since it had been fired and had burst in the year 1682 in an excess of joy at the greeting of the future King James II.

Such monarchical fervour had little interest for the gull, which deposited a large unpatriotic spatter of dung from its rear end on to the cannon before launching itself into the mist and disappearing like a carrier of ill intentions.

It left behind a curious sight. That which was meant to inspire fear in the enemy, covered in birdshit.

McLevy, meanwhile, was cursing under his breath in George Street as the raw, freezing sea fog swirled around, seeping into his very pores. This was a fool's errand.

He had stationed himself opposite the house which the Earl of Rosebery had so thoughtfully provided for William Gladstone, a house easily identified by the Liberal colours hanging from each window.

The front door was resolutely shut, and when the inspector had reconnoitred the place, he found a side exit which Mulholland would have been the one to cover if he wasn't so damned busy warbling like a canary. Cheep, cheep.

The inspector had tried to position himself so that he might cover both exits but it was increasingly difficult as the fog built up.

Add that to the dark of the night and it was just perfect conditions for surveillance — if, like the devil, ye had red eyes and could see through the smoke of hell.

What a foul pit-mirk. To match his mood. What was he doing here? Two hours he'd been breathing in the damp, rank vapour of the sea-fret. It caught at his throat and stung his eyes. What was driving him to make such a fool of himself? It certainly was not a tissue of stories from some woman in purple, no, and of course he had made the promise to George Cameron but . . . behind that?

There was something else. In his mind's eye, he saw a statue of overwhelming grandeur. And with a rope pull it down. And with a hammer break it apart.

A seagull let out a shrill skraich overhead, it would be seeing more than him that's for sure. The visibility was getting worse, as if a million incense burners had been let loose on the Protestant streets to drive the tight-lipped reforming faithful indoors. Must be working a treat because he'd not seen a soul this last hour.

Wait. He strained to listen in the dank muffled silence. Footsteps. Faint. From the side. Damnation!

He moved swiftly to the corner and looked down Hanover Street which cut through near to where he was standing sentry.

It was a well-lit thoroughfare usually but now seemed like an empty graveyard, the rays from a few street lights struggling against the fog and gloom.

But there he was. Stopped for a moment directly under one of the lamps as if posing for a picture. The man took off his tile hat and then replaced it firmly on his head.

White hair, grey frock-coat which matched colour and melded with the sea-mist, mutton-chop whiskers down the side of a face tilted away so that the features could not be completely seen.

'Turn round you auld bugger,' McLevy muttered. 'Let me put a mark on ye.'

The target lifted his hands, pulling up the collar round his neck to protect him from the cold or, more likely, unwelcome scrutiny. The hands were gloved. Black against the white hair.

Gladstone, it had to be. Surely? Though the inspector would not know for certain till he looked into his eyes.

Of course McLevy had no reason to gawp into the man's face, indeed no reason even to follow. This was just a respectable citizen out for a walk, in the dead of night, in the darkness, a constitutional, for the good of his health, it being such a healthy atmosphere.

The man turned and walked with swift sure steps into the blind of mist. In an instant he was gone.

McLevy took a deep breath, regretted it as his throat was caught raw, and plunged after his quarry.

Then followed a bizarre game of hide and seek as the fog twisted and spiralled around the two figures, linked by separate desires and a common destiny.

They prowled their way down East Claremont Street, past the Rosebank graveyard, down, always down, inexorably bound towards the narrow wynds of Leith.

McLevy could have sworn, in the few glimpses afforded by the moments when the fog shifted, that the man skipped along as if he was leading in a dance. Why would he skip, why would he hop? This was no dancing matter.

The streets were deserted, little cover save the mist and when it, of a sudden, dissipated, the inspector was marooned in strong light. The other was still in shadow and McLevy thought he saw the figure turn.

If so, he was discovered, and the policeman cursed silently as he moved to conceal himself. He could dog a man with the best of them but, in the changes of the haar, all things are equal.

However, there was no outcry, no accusation, no change of pace or direction, and the mist came down again. McLevy ploughed on, trying to keep a distance between them so that he would not blunder upon the fellow but near enough in touch not to be slipped like a fool.

The figure slipped over Great Junction Street, McLevy following as close as he dared.

Now they were in the back alleys and wynds of the lower part of his parish. The inspector was on home ground here but the mist suddenly thickened like a gravy sauce and any advantage was nullified.

McLevy came to a stop. He had been relying on the footsteps of the quarry, a firm strong sound on the cobbles, but now they had halted. Nothing. Silence.

His face was scammed with moisture from the mist, his clothes soaking. A feeling of complete isolation crept upon him, as if he was lost in a world where nothing was known, nothing was real, a thick grey world of cloud and silence.

It was like a nightmare. Then the silence was broken by a single scream.

He ran through the fog, feet slipping on the greasy cobblestones, his only guide a now silent cry of pain. The cloud thinned a little and he could see the Gothic spire of St Thomas's church sticking through the mist like a dagger at the top of Sheriff Brae.

A church bought and paid for by Sir John Gladstone of Fasque no less, what a bloody joke he thought as he came to a stop, gasping for breath, and listened with a growing desperation. Please make a sound. Betray yourself. Let me get my hands on you.

There was nothing. Something scuttled off at the side, a rat, a cat maybe.

Nothing. Then there was a gust of air. The east

wind. It had grown tired of the game, and raised the thick mist like a window blind.

The road before him was clear, like a ghost ship. Off to the side was a small wynd which he knew well. The nymphs used it to entice their clients in from the main street. It was as good a place as any to start.

She was sitting on the ground, her hand outstretched as if begging for alms. He could not tell if she had fallen thus or been arranged like some macabre depiction, like a print from Hogarth. *The Harlot's Progress.*

Her face looked up at him. A young face. Her name would come to mind. She was split through. Just like the others.

Something in the back of his head burst its banks and he howled in anger and grief. Like a wolf.

31

As for myself, I walk abroad o' nights
And kill sick people groaning under walls;
CHRISTOPHER MARLOWE,
The Jew of Malta

Leith, 1835

Jean Scott had been dozing in front of the fire when the noise cut through her sleep like a sharp knife. For a moment she was lost in an unfamiliar world, half between dream and awakening, then the sound came again, a high-pitched squeal such as she sometimes heard when she passed the auld slaughterhoose.

She was a stocky brisk woman, over forty years in age, who had already survived much in life, her husband Hughie dying an early martyr to strong drink. She buried him, spat on her hands, then made a new life for herself as a cook for Judge MacGregor's household, mustering a touch of surprising delicacy as regards desserts . . . Edinburgh Fog, Caledonian Cream and the like. The judge's wife had a sweet tooth, in contrast to her sour disposition.

Jean had saved good honest wages, reaching the point where she might look forward to a long peaceful roll down the hill towards the iron gates of Rosebank cemetery, but it would seem fate had other plans.

The noise grew louder as she came out and

crossed the hall to her neighbour's door. It was Jamie McLevy, she was sure of it, a quiet wee boy of seven years who kept his own counsel. The mother had probably been taken by one of her fits. Jean, periodically, heard her yowling away in what sounded like Latin. There was little danger of the woman being possessed of the devil though, not from the way she fingered that rosary.

A sharp tap on the locked door and the noise cut off abruptly.

'Jamie!' she called. 'It's me, Jean. Auntie Jean.'

She called herself so to him, though no relative. They knew each other fine well. The boy would visit and sit by the fire, with a wee home biscuit to keep him going, especially when the yowling was afoot.

She never asked and he never said.

The silence was profound on the other side. She tapped again.

'Jamie. I cannae get in if you cannae get out.'

This proposition seemed to do the trick. She heard him approach, then insert and turn the key.

The door opened slowly and she stepped inside.

The boy looked up at her. He had slate-grey eyes like a wild dog, and his face white as the judge's wig.

She smiled reassurance. 'Where's your mammy, son?'

He pointed wordlessly at the recess bed in the room where the curtain had been pulled aside.

Jean stepped carefully across the floor where various pieces of material were neatly laid out, with more spread on the table.

She'd never been in here before, just nodded in the hall. The place was clean as a whistle, a kitchen, workroom, living space, his wee bed over in the corner. She had to negotiate a wooden lay-figure which stood in the centre of the room, the bottom part swathed in a fine velvet skirt but the top as yet unclothed and showing its uncovered bosom.

Jean averted her eyes modestly, walked to the bed and looked in past the half-pulled curtain.

It was a sight to freeze the soul. Had the woman not gone and stabbed at her throat? With her own shears by the looks of it. The crucifix was stained all with blood.

She put out her hand to touch the cold skin on the wrist of the corpse. No pulse. The dead eyes could have told her so. She thought to close them but wasn't sure of the Catholic custom.

High above the bed-head was a representation of Pope Pius IX. Jean was a staunch Presbyterian but no fanatic.

Let each worship whom they may, she steered the middle course but she could not help thinking that Pius hadn't been much help on this occasion. The woman would have been better off knocking on Jean's door and sitting by the flames with a hot sweet tea.

Hughie had liked it strong. He liked everything strong. Gripped her so hard on their wedding night, he near cracked her ribs.

These thoughts had kept the shock at bay.

225

Now, she found she was trembling. How long had she been standing here?

And the boy? She turned away from the gory mess on the bed and pulled the curtains across. He must have seen it.

'I was hungry,' he piped up. His face was blank. Like a mask. The stone-grey eyes looked at her, but they were seeing something else. For God's sake, the child was only seven, how could his mother do such a thing in her own home? Could she not stab her throat in the chapel, let the priest mop it up?

Jean swallowed her anger. How can you ever know what people may do, or why they do so? God help the woman. She must have been desperate.

If you believed scripture, she was a damned soul. The devil had his claws in her and was dragging her into the pit of hell. Never to return. A damned soul.

She realised she'd been standing there muttering in front of the poor wee lamb, his eyes still fixed upon her.

This wouldnae do. Don't want him thinking there were two madwomen in the hoose. What was it, he said? Hungry. Aye. She could fix that.

'We'll go next door. Tae Auntie Jean's, eh? I have a penny loaf. I'll cut ye a slab with cheese. And pickle. Do you like pickle, James?'

Whether it was the thought of a knife cutting through the white bread or the kindness in her voice, the dam broke in his heart. He let out a cry of loss and bewilderment and hurtled across the room to bury his face into her broad belly.

'It was my blame,' he howled, his voice piercing into her flesh like a dagger.

'What was your blame, son?'

'At Easter. She would wait. Every time. He never knocked the door.'

Jean wasn't sure she'd heard the words correctly, his face buried so deep.

'Who never knocked, son?'

'The Angel. The Angel of the Lord.'

'Well,' said Jean, trying her best. 'Angels are busy folk.'

The boy lifted back his head and looked at her.

'It was my blame,' he said.

She had never seen such agony in a face and clutched him in close as if to shield him from all the horrors of this world. Her own eyes filled up with tears.

Then she sniffed hard. This would not do. Whatever madness had possessed the woman, whatever angel knocked or did not knock upon the door, whatever rived the heart of that wee boy so that he took the cares of the world upon his shoulders, she knew one thing.

Tears got ye nowhere.

She took a long slow breath to calm herself. What was to become of the boy?

The McLevy woman had no kin, she was sure of that, no relatives ever visited, not a friend in off the street; he would end up in a home.

As if he sensed her thought, the boy buried his face back into her body as if he could hide himself inside.

Aye, and there was room so. She'd never had

a child. Nae wee pap-bairn at her breast. Hughie was vigorous and regular enough but the seed didnae take.

It was the Lord's will she had told herself as the years passed, so maybe this was his doing as well.

Everything was his doing, was it not?

She could use the company right enough. She'd been thinking of a dog but it would chew lumps out of her best furniture.

This thought put a fierce smile on her face. Still holding the boy, she picked up a corner of her apron and scrubbed hard at her damp eyes. Here she was with a dead woman soaked in her own blood, a lost wee soul sticking his nose into her belly-button and all she could think about was furniture.

Still. Hughie always said she had a practical nature. That was her. Now, how to quiet this wee soldier? He was silent this moment, but inside there would be a storm raging.

Anger and grief. Two terrible thieves that can steal your life away, as she knew to her cost.

Thomas Imrie, the cobbler. He was a drinking pal of Hughie's and a terrible Jacobite, but he could carry a tune. Full many a time she listened with her arms folded as Hughie banged the spoons to accompany, not that he gave a damn about the Bonny Prince, but the cobbler did.

With a passion. And she was charmed by passion. In spite of herself.

What was his favourite now? She began a tune, a melody of sorts, her voice a bit trembling at first but gathering strength, And the boy, *listening, quieted down inside his bruised and broken heart.*

> 'Charlie is my darling, my darling,
> My darling. Charlie is my darling,
> The young chevalier.'

32

How pleasant it is, at the end of the day,
No follies to have to repent;
But reflect on the past, and be able to say,
That my time has been properly spent.
ANN AND JANE TAYLOR,
Rhymes for the Nursery

The Just Land was in full swing. Nothing beats a bawdy-hoose at midnight.

Jean Brash looked on with finely honed tolerance as her girls plied the clients with champagne. One of the Dalrymple twins poured the precious liquid in a stream from her dainty slipper into an election agent's eager mouth.

It was nice to see that mouth used for something else besides telling people a load of lies.

She sincerely hoped that Margaret (or was it Mary, you could never tell unless they were both naked, one of them with a mole just above her temple of delight) had washed her feet. Jean was a stickler for that sort of thing.

Standards are everything.

She smiled at the thought and looked around the huge reception room which occupied the entire ground floor of the house.

Worth every penny, the red velvet curtains, the exotic ottomans and plush divans. The leather armchairs were another nice touch, big enough for two, especially one atop the other. A piano tinkled in the corner where some revellers gathered round to exercise their tonsils. Big Annie Drummond whose liking for cream buns had rendered her, save for the odd Italian, too gargantuan for normal service, laid her plump but delicate fingers on the keys. She played by ear and rarely hit a false note. A musical colossus.

Culture was omnipresent. The carpets were Persian or very near the thing, fine paintings on the wall, goddesses and the like, mostly unclothed in amorous pursuits with cherubs and satyrs. Jean had enjoyed her fill of both, in years gone by. She retained the appetite but had shifted focus. Her last lover had been a surgeon, a lithotomist who relieved the agony of stones in the bladder by cutting without killing by surgical shock.

He was in the habit of tracing his finger across the flat plain of her naked stomach as if mapping out an operation. It had got on her nerves after a while.

Jean's eye was caught by another work which had pride of place in her art gallery. A masterpiece. *The Woman with the Octopus*. She had humphed that painting from brothel to brothel. It was her lucky charm.

She was proud of her establishment. It had class. She often thought with the curtains, armchairs and suchlike, if you squinted slightly, ye might mistake the place for a gentlemen's club.

Except for the girls. They made a difference.

A sweet disorder in the dress but nothing too overt, a bare shoulder for a man's lips to brush, a *décolletage* to encourage further investigation, a ripple of the loins behind a gossamer covering, but, for Jean's money, nothing could match a saucy glance and a quick tongue.

The quicker the better.

She had trained her girls well. They were a merry bunch and could trade a bawdy ribald wit with the best of them, provoking an appetite they were well capable of satisfying.

So, have at ye.

The place was heaving. Both Liberal and Tory electioneering operators, at each other's throats these past months, now united in a common cause, debauchery, enmity forgotten, the Sabbath tomorrow, on Monday the vote is cast, it's too late now. The battle is over.

Jean had a dozen kitties working the room and half as many upstairs on the bones. When that shift was over this lot would be well primed; and down in the cellar, flexing her muscles, lurked the French mistress, Francine.

She and her assistant, Lily, taught *le vice anglais* to their willing pupils. Jean had put down a lot of money for Francine, but the girl was a specialist. She could lay on more stripes than a tiger.

The group at the piano burst into song,

> '*Champagne Charlie is my name,*
> *Champagne Charlie is my name,*
> *Good for any game at night, my boys,*
> *Good for any game.*'

One of them, a wee sniggery fat sausage of a man who, as a Liberal agent, anticipated he had more reason to celebrate than the opposite party, began to prance around the room.

His name was George Ballard, a Birmingham cove, and despite his unprepossessing appearance, a key member of the caucus which had out-organised the Tories, spreading out from the Midlands like a rash all over the country.

His real leader was the ex-cobbler, screw-maker and hard radical, Joseph Chamberlain, who was looking to the future. He was the coming man and the National Liberal Federation, his power base, had done more to win this election than any other. Chamberlain's time would come.

George had suffered the condescension of the slimy toffee-nosed Horace Prescott and the rest of his cronies from the Rosebery camp, and had been forced to bite his tongue.

Now it was over, and he was off the leash.

He caught sight of himself in one of the gilded mirrors which hung in profusion round the walls, reflecting the starry gleam of the shining candelabra.

There he was, sweaty, red-faced, teeth like a ferret and twice as deadly.

He kicked his legs up, 'Good for any game, my boys, Good for any game!' he bawled.

The dance grew wilder to the extent that he was about to crash into something when he was suddenly grasped by the shirt front and sobered up rapidly as the music came to an abrupt halt.

The giant figure of Angus Dalrymple towered

over him, his huge hands holding George as if he was a rag doll.

'Ye'll do yourself a harm, sir,' he said solemnly.

George blinked, bobbed his head, then nipped back smartly to the piano.

The big ex-blacksmith turned, nodded politely to his two daughters and padded softly away.

Jean smiled to herself. Ye were never short of entertainment in a bawdy-hoose, no wonder she was so fond of the profession.

'Drink up, gentlemen,' she called softly. 'The night is young, the girls are keen as mustard, who knows what the future may bring?'

The company, which had been rendered a trifle subdued at this laying on of hands, perked up again and the gathering resumed its rush towards a hectic gratification.

A side door which led down to the cellar opened and Lily Baxter, Francine's wee rub-a-dub lovergirl, who enjoyed her ancillary infliction of pain with a vengeance, poked her curly head in and signalled urgently at Jean.

What was it now? Jean had spent a fortune on that cellar, the high point of which had been the purchase of the Berkley Horse. The apparatus had been shipped from London and arrived shrouded in thick white canvas like a piece of sculpture.

To go with such, the cellar walls were hung with an extravaganza of flogging implements — thongs, straps, an array of canes which ranged from thin and pliant to thick and thunderous — to say nothing of the prickly vegetation inside the Chinese vases. She made her money back

234

right enough, especially when the General Synod was in session, but the maintenance cost was excruciating.

Francine demanded the very best to dole out the very worst and was forever plaguing Jean with fresh demands.

The Frenchwoman regarded herself as a martyr to flagellation. She considered that had it not been for her God-given ability to stripe with such precision, she would have pursued an artistic bent.

Jean had seen some of her drawings. They were mostly of Lily's unclothed body, itself a delicious tribute to unbridled tribadism, and had a certain charm, but they were nothing compared to Francine's talent for scourging the toughest hides.

The Frenchwoman was also an expert on the dark skill of hook and pulley, calculating bodyweight as precisely as the hangman.

Lily signalled again and Jean, muttering under her breath, crossed the room.

She spoke slowly and deliberately. Lily was a deaf mute. Nothing wrong with the length of her tongue, it just did not produce words. But she understood them well enough if you took the time.

'What is it — you want — what is the matter with that bloody woman now?'

Lily grinned, then made a face to indicate a problem of some kind and beckoned Jean to follow her downstairs.

The cellar consisted of two large low-ceilinged rooms, one where the champagne was stored and the other for a wee touch of torture.

No question which venue Jean preferred though she felt her customary lowering of spirits as she trailed Lily below. It was dark and a bit damp, you could catch your death of cold in the place.

When she entered the chamber, Francine was leaning against the studded wall, arms folded, her self-made leather apparel skin-tight around her slim, sinewy frame.

She had based the design on a portrait of the Egyptian goddess Isis that she saw one time in a Paris museum. When the goddess's brother and lover Osiris had been cut into fourteen pieces and scattered far and wide by her other brother Set, who tended to be a bit on the violent side, Isis had painstakingly reassembled the whole of her lover, save for the phallus which had been eaten by a crab of the Nile.

For some reason this story appealed to Francine and so she recreated the dress of the goddess in black leather.

It left her arms and most of the bosom exposed while tightly sheathing the rest of her body, save for the one slash up the side that gave a necessary freedom of movement and through which a beautifully formed white leg emerged.

She had also toyed with the idea of a headdress, but found it somewhat impractical with the low ceiling.

Lily wore a simple white robe. Like a priestess.

Jean looked at them. They made a fine pair. So, what was wrong on this occasion?

Francine's dark tempestuous face was set in its

usual dramatic lines but there was also an element of puzzled and genuine outrage.

Without uttering a word, she pointed contemptuously at the naked body of a man who lay strapped face down on the Berkley Horse.

Since he obviously could not turn over, Jean moved to be within his field of vision.

'Are you the whore-mistress?' he asked, apparently unperturbed by his somewhat immodest situation.

He had made an entrance with the rest of the election clam-jamfry. She hadn't fancied the look of him then and liked it even less now.

'I own this establishment,' was her polite reply. 'I am responsible for the welfare of my girls, and for the measure of satisfaction provided to my clientele.'

'Good,' he responded, making no attempt to hide the sneer in his voice. 'Then you can tell the French bitch to do as I command.'

Jean stiffened at the words and tone.

'You're scarcely in a position to command anything,' she observed.

'I am a customer of your bawdy house. I pay my money. I demand my pleasure.'

Francine threw her hands up in a Gallic gesture of despair as Jean looked at her questioningly.

'He wants me to draw blood. It is against my skill of principle. I do *everything* but that. Look to see.'

The man's back, which was white and hairless, was indeed covered in a welter of stripes and weals, the flesh livid and ridged.

It was Francine's professional pride at stake here. She took her clients on many a painful journey to the Castle of Masochism, but the idea of blood horrified her.

'Blood is for *amateurs*. It crosses the fine line between pleasure and pain. For me, it is an insult!' she announced, hot with indignation.

Lily watched intently. She adored to see Francine in a bate, the aftermath was such sweet passion.

'I want it running down my back.' The man looked up at Jean. 'I want to feel it. Like a river. You are the chief procuress. You pimp. You pander. Arrange it.'

There was a cold contempt in his eyes. Of course he might be just trying to provoke her. If so, he had, only too well, succeeded.

Jean Brash had performed many strange acts in the course of her profession; one memorable time she and a colleague had stripped down to the bare scud and, while doing so, had wrung half a dozen pigeons' necks in front of a young man who expressed his gratitude most copiously.

She had felt sorry for the pigeons but business was business.

That and many other episodes possessed a curious innocence, however, compared with the feeling she now had as she looked into those pale-blue eyes and wondered what twisted thoughts fuelled these perverse desires.

Be that as it may, business was business. She turned abruptly away from the man and addressed Francine.

'The client's desires are paramount. Give him

what he wants. Here — I'll make a start for ye.'

So saying, she took a thin birch rod from where it had been soaking in water to keep it green and pliant, then brought it down with considerable force on the man's buttocks. There was an indrawn breath in response, and a thin smear of blood showed where the blow had landed.

She handed the rod to Francine who thought to protest then, catching the hard, stony glint in Jean's eyes, thought otherwise. The Frenchwoman shrugged, made a moue of sorts with her full red lips, then got on with it.

As Francine stepped up, Lily darted to be under the man where her manual dexterity might be called into play.

Because of the ingenuity of the structure of the horse, his private parade dangled within easy reach.

Just like milking a cow, Jean thought. And left them to it.

Outside the door, she took a deep, damp breath and glanced up to see Hannah Semple at the top of the stairs.

'I've been searching ye out everywhere, mistress,' she said. 'I have news tae relate.'

Hannah was dressed in her customary plain clothing, hair scraped back to expose the prominent forehead and stubby features.

She was no beauty, never had been, and now in her older years looked like the wreck of a ruin, but the keys round her waist proclaimed her keeper of the bawdy-hoose and she took that responsibility to heart.

One look at her face and Jean realised the news was not good.

'Tell me,' she said simply.

'Wee Tam Marrison knocked at the door. I payed him. But I'd wish for better tidings.'

Marrison was one of the street keelies who operated as an unofficial network of spies for Jean, to keep her privy to any of the rough happenings in Leith.

'There's another one been found. Like Sadie Gorman. Split tae buggery.' Hannah's face was grim.

'Do they know who the girl is?' murmured Jean.

'Not yet. McLevy was near hand, but the man got away in the fog. The inspector was bellowing like a bull.'

'He wouldn't be pleased,' said Jean.

The remark was inconsequential, mundane, but both these women had been on the streets in their time. A part of that death belonged to them. They could feel it in their bones.

They stood on the stairs as if frozen in space. Above them, the tinny music of the piano played and some voices sang . . . 'She was the belle of the ball, dear boys, she was the belle of the ball.'

Behind Jean, muffled through the door, came the faintest sound. As if someone had stood on an insect and the shell had cracked.

Francine, in the chamber, had just lifted the thin rod and brought it down like the hand of the Almighty. The blood began to criss-cross on the white body and trickle slowly this way and that as if searching for escape.

Lily squeezed for all she was worth. A grunt came in response from the spread-eagled form above.

She popped up her head and blew a kiss to Francine. The Frenchwoman wiped a bead of sweat from her brow, lifted the birch once more, and then let it whistle through the air.

Horace Prescott bit deep into his lip. It had been a hard campaign. This was the perfect end.

33

Other sins only speak; murder shrieks out:
The element of water moistens the earth,
But blood flies upwards, and bedews the
   heavens.

JOHN WEBSTER,
The Duchess of Malfi

The small axe was lifted and chopped down with an executioner's relish. William Gladstone had risen early, too restless to lie abed, and thought at once of the recently felled sycamore.

And there it was, still lying where he had brought it low, branches broken off willy-nilly. An untidy carcass, this would never do.

He had begun at the top of the tree. Always work down. Always start from the top. The smaller, younger shoots were to be found there and could be sheared with the one stroke.

It was a most satisfying process to reveal the white flesh of the wood in the action of a single gesture, like peeling off a skin.

Tomorrow, Monday, the Midlothian vote was to be cast.

Already he knew that he had been elected for Leeds (a fine twist of the political system being that the one candidate could stand in two constituencies), and because of the spread-out nature of the polling days, he also knew that the national result would be a Liberal victory.

Nothing could stop him now.

He would give thanks to the Lord later in church.

He had noticed a recent tendency towards fragmentary thought. This must be resisted.

Administration was the highest form of politics and he would ruthlessly pursue that end.

Now was not the time for an excess of empire.

Disraeli was lost in a dream. England, the Israel of his imagination.

The coming economic force was America. He had, during their Civil War, made the mistake of apparently espousing the cause of the South and had his knuckles rapped. No more of that. Now he was more than ready to embrace our American cousins. They may lack finesse, but they did not lack money or the energy to make such and he could see a day when they would have weapons to spare.

Such a mixture of races could not help but produce a desire to conquer and they were welcome to it, as long as they did not train their guns on Albion's shore.

No. Their countries would lie together. Like family.

A wild light came into Gladstone's eye. Now, were this tree Benjamin Disraeli, he would chop him down to size, limb from limb, the head, the arms, the legs, chop, chop!

He had been increasing his activity to almost that of a frenzy, lifting the axe as he spied a juicy fat branch, just ripe, just ripe for destruction.

A voice broke in on this singular and most pleasant pastime.

'You have a mark on you,' it said.

For a moment, Gladstone was completely disjointed, the axe hanging in the air like a broken wing.

A man stood watching him, the early morning light behind his stocky figure. Gladstone did not recognise the voice or shape.

The whole house would now only just be rising, he was alone, he loved the solitude, who would dare sneak up upon him and disturb his privacy, his Sabbath chopping of the limbs?

The figure was dark-clad, bareheaded, still as a pointing finger, an ominous silent finger.

He moved away from the tree, holding firmly to the axe lest this be an assassin. But the man did not give the impression of madness and William knew from experience that while most assassinations on the Continent were attempted for reasons of politics, in this country they were almost always committed by madmen.

Then the dark imaginings cleared. Yes, he was safe. He recognised the man now.

'You are the policeman,' he said. 'From last night. I saw you last night.'

'And I saw you,' the man replied with a peculiar emphasis to the words.

He moved at last, walking in slow deliberate steps past Gladstone to take in the grandeur of Dalmeny House and the estate.

Smoke was beginning to issue from the chimney pots of the house as the early morning fires were lit, and the raucous noise of a flock of hoodie crows, rising indignantly from a nearby field, signalled the onset of another day.

244

Legend had it that hoodie crows pecked the eyes out of the newborn spring lamb, it being a soft target. We all like a soft target.

Still facing away, the man spoke as if addressing the scene before him, as if he were pronouncing in a court of law.

'My name is James McLevy. I am an inspector of crime. My parish is Leith in the city of Edinburgh.'

'I believe you may have told me some of this in our previous exchange,' replied Gladstone dryly. 'I have an excellent memory.'

McLevy turned round. His face was sombre. It had been a hard long night which had slipped like a knife into the belly of this day. He had not washed or shaved, not had even a sniff of coffee, and now he was about to embark upon a line of questioning which had Roach been aware of same would have laid the good lieutenant prostrate on the putting green.

He stared blankly at the Great Man.

It was said families all over the country had Sweet William flowers on their table in his honour. Well, we'd see how sweet.

Gladstone for his part sensed a challenge, as one tiger will smell another in the jungle. But he forbore to ask the fellow why he was abroad, at this hour, in this place, for it has been often noted that he who asks the first question betrays a weakness.

'You have a mark on you,' repeated McLevy.

The inspector pointed at the right hand which held the axe and Gladstone let the implement fall on to the trunk of the dead sycamore. He then inched back his sleeve to reveal two livid scratches on the underside of his wrist which the inspector had espied.

'Nature's revenge.' The thin harsh mouth arranged itself in a smile of sorts as he gestured towards the tree. 'The first cut I made yesterday, one of the branches caught me. I was careless. One cannot afford that.'

He lifted the left hand to display its covering stock and was there an element of mockery in his tone?

'One must be alert. At all times. The world is full of menace. If you may observe . . . I have lost myself a finger.'

'Some lose more than that to menace,' replied McLevy. 'Some people lose their lives.'

A silence fell between them. Gladstone sat down on the tree, his back upright and his powerful dark eyes fixed on McLevy. He waited for the next move.

The inspector sniffed the morning air. It smelled clean enough, especially after the acrid smoke of the night before, but was it untainted? What other faint odour came wafting from Sweet William in the light morning breeze?

He began his interrogation. Place it under what guise you will, tiptoe around it as you may, he was about to put the future prime minister of this glorious country under the cosh of justice.

'The servants of your abode in George Street have confirmed to me that, at some point last night, they cannot remember exactly when, your absence was noted. It was assumed you had gone out for a walk. After your supper. A perambulation. Is that correct?'

'Indeed. I also cannot remember the exact time. But, it is my custom to do so after the exertion of addressing a large gathering such as we had at West Calder,' replied Gladstone almost placidly.

'Ye left by the side door?'

'Also my custom. The gentlemen of the press are wont to gather by the front. Their presence is not always welcome, I had been enough public that day.'

'Ye returned some time after midnight and then insisted on an immediate carriage to bring you back here. Is that correct as well?'

'It is. I realised that what I needed most of all was the soothing presence of my wife.'

'She wasn't with you, then?'

'She had remained at Dalmeny. The throng tires her.'

William shook out a large handkerchief and blew his nose vigorously.

Whatever benefits Mrs Gladstone uxoriously provided, it would seem unblocking the sinuses was not one of them.

'When ye walked, where did ye go?'

The Great Man blinked at such a direct question.

'I am afraid I cannot tell you,' was his concise reply.

'Why not?'

'The mist. The fog. It was so devilish thick. I was like a lost sheep. Sore perplexed. I wandered for what seemed like an eternity. It took me some hours even to retrace my steps home to recover from what I must confess was an error of judgement on my part. But the Lord saw me through; he often does to my enemy's discouragement and my own salvation.'

This had tripped off the tongue with an ease of practice. He then switched subject. Politicians do that.

'I am reading from Sir Walter Scott, these hectic days. The story of *Guy Mannering*.' A smile of sorts twisted the harsh mouth, but his eyes were watchful. 'I find it most . . . illuminating. Do you know the tale?'

'It is about treachery.'

'And *salvation*, sir. A man's salvation!'

'But not through God. Through human agency. An auld gypsy woman and a Lowland farmer.'

'God is behind every human act, sir.'

Gladstone laughed abruptly as if he had scored a debating point. He looked back towards Dalmeny House where a door opened and the figure of the skinny, hunched woman emerged, thick glasses pointing towards them. Gladstone, from his sitting position, waved vigorously and she lifted her hand a moment in reply before going back swiftly into the house.

'My personal secretary,' said Gladstone. 'I would be lost without her.'

He laughed again and clapped his hands together as a sign perhaps that the exchange was drawing to a close, but the inspector was not to be deflected.

'Ye say ye wandered in the mist?' he pursued.

'I did indeed. Sore perplexed.'

'Would your footsteps have led you as far as Leith?'

'As I have already informed you I knew not where I was,' rejoined Gladstone with a tinge of asperity. 'But I doubt I ventured as far as Leith. You seem to have, if I may say so, sir, an obsessive regard for the place.'

'A young lassie was murdered there, last night,' said McLevy flatly. 'Cut down in the streets. Not far from the church of St Thomas which your own father founded.'

The great man bowed his head as if in prayer or he may have been reflecting that the inspector's previous ignorance of the Gladstone family connections to Leith when they spoke at West Calder had been miraculously converted.

'How dreadful,' he murmured.

'A hazard of her profession.' McLevy's mouth had gone dry. He was near the edge and dying for a cup of coffee.

'Ah. A fallen woman.'

'Especially after she was battered,' replied McLevy, with savage black humour.

Gladstone's head came up sharply.

The inspector made no secret of his eye's journey to where the axe lay on the tree. 'Chopped tae buggery.'

William's mouth tightened at the brutal tone. He inclined his head questioningly as if to say, *and what is my part in all this?*

'A man of your favour was seen in the neighbourhood,' McLevy's mouth got even drier, 'and I was wondering . . .'

Now, as Mulholland's Aunt Katie would say,

249

ye're walking on the hen's eggs here, Jamie boy. Watch where ye put your big sclaffie feet.

'I was wondering if you might have seen something?'

'See? What could I see? I was nowhere near the place and blinded by the fog.'

McLevy persisted. 'Perhaps a man running. Glimpsed through the haar. Reflected in a shop window. Blood on his hands. Looking at you.'

'I saw nothing.'

'Thirty years ago, there was a similar crime. A divine punishment perhaps. A scourge of the unworthy. Did ye see nothing then?'

'Thirty years ago?'

'Aye. Ye walked the streets then. After the funeral of your daughter.'

There was a dreadful flash of anger in the Great Man's eyes, then he launched himself bolt upright.

'How dare you!'

'It is only a question.'

'It is an insult!'

'I am sorry you perceive it so.'

Gladstone looked into the cold, slate-grey eyes of the inspector and struggled to contain a mounting fury.

'I trust these insinuations are not what I perceive them to be, inspector. There is, however, a limit to my patience and you have gone far beyond it. Far beyond!'

As if in response to his outburst, there was a call from the house as the figure of Horace Prescott emerged followed by three other men.

McLevy knew he had but little time.

'That aroma from you, sir. Is it identifiable?'

'What? *What?*' The People's William almost jumped up and down in exasperation.

The inspector sniffed. 'It has a sort of tarry redolence. I was trying to place it.'

'It is carbolic soap. I use it every morning. For sanitary purposes!' Gladstone almost snarled.

'Very healthy,' agreed McLevy as Prescott, hastily dressed and moving it must be said somewhat stiffly, arrived with his bully boys.

One of them, a small podgy specimen, put his hand on the inspector's shoulder only to be shaken off, but any further confusion was stilled when William Gladstone raised a controlling hand aloft.

It was an orator's gesture but there was enough power in it to stop them all where they stood, including McLevy.

Horace was addressed in a voice which brooked nothing but complete obedience. Gladstone in command once more.

'I shall explain the circumstances later, Mr Prescott, but for the moment, be so good as to escort this man from the estate and make sure that he does not return. Good-day, Mr McLevy.'

Gladstone then spun on his heel and marched off without a backward glance, dismissing past events and exchanges out of hand.

The hoodie crows returned to the field, their squawks filling the silence.

'Well, well, inspector, it would seem as if you have strayed into the most severe reprimand it is within my power to arrange. Your stupidity

251

demands no less,' said Prescott, a cruel glint in his pale-blue eyes.

McLevy had fallen quiet, his eyes on the departing Gladstone as he walked rather jerkily towards the house.

'I shall make it my business to inform your superior officer, the fellow with the fishy name, Roach, that's the fellow, the Tory lickspittle, and then the man above him, and so on and so on as far up the chain of command as I can spread the word.

'I intend to make sure that you regret your blundering idiocy for as long as is humanly possible. How does that appeal to you?'

Again the inspector had nothing to say. The hunched woman came out of the house again and moved quickly down the path to meet Gladstone. They conversed for a moment then turned to go back inside, her strides matching his with some ease.

'Who is that woman?' McLevy asked as if trying to delay the inevitable.

'Jane Salter,' broke in the voice of little George Ballard who had been dying to join in the fun. 'Plain Jane, that's her name to all the boys. But, *your* name, inspector. Your name . . . is mud!'

He roared with laughter at his own joke and slapped Prescott hard on the back. The secretary's face whitened and, for a moment, he almost keeled over.

But then he recovered and pointed silently towards and beyond the iron gates of Dalmeny House where the crest of the Earl of Rosebery was wrought for all to see.

'Get back to where you belong,' he said.

McLevy was escorted to the gates and put out like a dog that had performed its business on the carpet.

They watched him walk down the carriage drive that led to the main road, the ground already chewed up by many wheels and sticky going.

Ballard glanced up at the sky darkening above and then at Prescott whose face was clenched and cold, an evil twist to the lips.

'With a bit of luck,' the little man pronounced with glee, 'it'll rain on the bastard all the way home.'

McLevy was thinking much the same thing as he saw the black clouds gather.

He supposed it was too much to hope that they might ask him back in for coffee and it was a long, long way to Leith.

He had begged a lift from a coachman he knew delivered in this area but he had no great hopes for the way back, and it was six long miles.

The first spits of rain started to fall and soon it would be a black downpour which would soak him to the skin.

He had much to ponder and the words of Horace Prescott echoed in his mind.

Back to where you belong, but where was that? All his life he had been outside the gates.

34

Alas! for the rarity,
Of Christian charity,
Under the sun!

THOMAS HOOD,
The Bridge of Sighs

The body in the cold room once belonged to a young woman called Jennie Duncan. She had worked as a chambermaid for a tobacco merchant and sought to augment her miserable wages by nightly forays on the streets. Such girls were known as dollymops. Amateur whores. Easy marks.

Mulholland looked down at her and sighed. This was a mess in all senses. Lieutenant Roach had arrived in the morning to discover a new corpse on the slab and his inspector, who had found the damned thing and had it lugged to the station, missing from the scene.

The police surgeon Dr Jarvis had come, whistling through his teeth. He had cut further open and found a foetus. A rough guess, from the size, would be two or three months. It would grow no more.

Jarvis informed Lieutenant Roach of such and the lieutenant bowed his head as if in prayer.

Jarvis left.

Roach raised his head.

'Where is McLevy?' he asked grimly.

The constable could not help the lieutenant find the inspector because the constable was none the wiser although he had an awful premonition that the inspector was up to absolutely no good at all.

Time passed. The tobacco merchant came in, identified the body but disclaimed the dollymop activity. He also disclaimed knowledge of the girl being pregnant.

The merchant left. Time passed.

Chief Constable Grant arrived as if he had a fire burning up his backside. He had been sitting peacefully at home contemplating the minister's Sabbath message when one of Prescott's men had barged over the threshold and delivered a very different communication. Grant took the lieutenant into his own room, the room with the only shiny door, and for a full hour all that could be heard was the sound of his voice, like a hand-saw cutting through a metal bar.

The chief constable left. The lieutenant emerged white with anger and humiliation. He looked around for someone to vent his spleen upon.

Mulholland had secreted himself in the water closet, snibbed the door shut and put faith in his bowel movements.

Sergeant Murdoch was in the Land of Nod and Ballantyne had pulled his head so far back into his shoulders that he resembled a turtle.

But then through the station door, a drowned man walking, leaving wet footprints with every step, came the drookit, sodden figure of James McLevy.

255

The crocodile jaws of Roach snapped shut. He crooked his finger, not trusting words in a public place, and the bedraggled inspector, looking neither left nor right, took up the invitation and followed him back into the office.

That had been a fair time ago. Mulholland had crept out of the closet into the cold room to rehearse his excuses and get used to the temperature, the anticipated icy blast.

He was implicated by proxy, guilty by association, all his sookin' up was to be in vain. Leave to attend the third wedding of his Aunt Katie would not be forthcoming. Indeed, he would be lucky to emerge with his testicles intact.

Pulling up the sheet, he covered the face of the corpse which appeared to be looking down in some dismay at its disarrayed rib cage.

The door opened and Ballantyne stuck his head in.

'The lieutenant wants tae see you.'

Ballantyne searched for something hopeful to say, he was a kind-hearted soul and wouldn't last long. A red tide showed just above the line of his collar, a birthmark about which he had been teased unmercifully by some of the other men at the station before McLevy announced one day that he had similar on his backside and would personally eviscerate the next person who mentioned same.

Mulholland had stood behind the inspector that day, as he now stood in front of Ballantyne.

'I think the lieutenant might be getting sore-throatit, he's been leathering his tonsils a decent time now. Don't worry what he says, ye cannae hear the words through the door and I'm not listening anyway.'

It was a somewhat confused benison but Mulholland nodded gratefully enough and crossed the greasy floor of the station to the office door which had been left ajar.

He knocked upon it anyway, just to be on the safe side, and entered.

The inspector was standing up against the wall as if pinned there by the force of Roach's invective. His hair was plastered flat to his head and he looked for all the world like a little boy who'd been caught out in the rain.

The lieutenant had his back to both of them and was staring up at the portrait of Queen Victoria as if seeking a source of strength.

McLevy drooped the one eyelid in a conspiratorial wink at Mulholland who rejected all reception of same and stood rigidly to attention. The constable knew there was a bucket of urine coming his way. From on high.

For his part, McLevy was not offended by the rejection and turned his attention back to Roach. You had to commend the stamina of the man. He been ranting for near thirty minutes and scarce repeated the same insult twice.

The inspector had been battered by authority ere now, and though his recitation of the salient facts had sent Roach into a fit of the vapours, he still felt he had a case to put forward.

But it was not much of a case and though McLevy had sailed his wee boat through the Storms of Reprimand before, this one was different. A great deal different.

Roach finally turned round and fixed his pitiless gaze upon the squirming constable.

'What have you got to say for yourself?' he asked.

Mulholland's mouth opened and closed but nothing much emerged except for a dry croak. All the rehearsed excuses had just dribbled out the back of his head.

'What did you think you were doing, if it's not too much to demand? I am intrigued as to your explanation. Just exactly what did you think you were doing?' enquired the lieutenant with enough ice in his voice to freeze an Aberdeen Angus where it stood munching.

'I . . . I . . . was keeping the inspector company,' came the stutter of a response.

'Company? *Company?*' Roach's voice rose in pitch and, with difficulty, he hauled it back to earth like a flag down a pole. 'You are not a chaperon, you are not some sort of Spanish duenna, you are a police constable! And as such, you are responsible to your station superior officer, none other, namely, than me!'

The lieutenant let out a baffled snarl and almost tore at his stiff collar as he once more addressed Mulholland.

'Why did you not tell me this madness, this . . . wild gallivant was in progress?'

McLevy judged it time to take a hand. 'It was my fault, sir,' he stated, face solemn, tone sober, as befits the repentant sinner.

Roach's head swivelled in his direction.

'*Everything* is your fault,' he muttered. 'Explain.'

258

'I prevailed upon the constable not to divulge the . . . direction of the investigation, until I had extended it to my complete satisfaction.'

'*Extended?*' Roach near howled. 'By God you extended it. Right up to one of the most important people in this country!'

But a dour nod from the lieutenant to Mulholland indicated some acceptance of his innocence in the affair.

Roach knew to his cost what a devious bugger his inspector could be. He turned a cold unforgiving eye back to McLevy. That which ye sow, so shall ye reap, and this was going to be a bitter harvest.

'Extended without a shred of proof,' he spat out the words like sour pips. 'A tissue of stories concocted by some female who sends you on a goose chase with madwomen, nurses, murders from thirty years ago, all tangled up like a whore's drawers!'

It was a measure of the heated indignation in Roach's breast that he had expressed himself so indelicately, but he wasn't done yet, not by a long chalk.

'And who is this woman? This . . . Joanna Lightfoot? Is she a figment of your imagination, McLevy?'

'She is real enough. And I shall find her out.'

'You have done enough damage,' said Roach. 'Acting on your own half-baked assumptions, you have tried to link these murders to William Gladstone. You have bothered and bearded the lion in its den and, as I could have warned you had you the decency to keep me up to scratch,

259

you have provoked the most implacable and punishing rebuttal.

'You are out of your league, inspector. I may not like the man's politics but he is one of the most powerful men in the country and a *beacon* of moral probity.

'Yet, you have sought to draw him in. Without a shred, an iota of proof. Not a shred!'

The lieutenant threw up his hands as if he had just seen a decent iron shot take a bad hop into a deep bunker.

He shook his head and fell silent. Righteous wrath was an exhausting process.

McLevy judged it time to try his luck.

'Did Dr Jarvis examine the fingernails of the corpse?' asked the inspector.

'He did, sir,' interposed Mulholland who thought he might make this remark without taking sides, 'and found remnants of human skin under the first and second digits.'

'No more than I noticed myself.'

'And what was your deduction, sir?'

Mulholland was trying to help, it was the least he could do after McLevy had rescued him from the bottomless pit; mind you, it was the inspector who had landed him there in the first place.

'William Gladstone had two deep scrapes upon his wrist. He claimed to have received them felling trees.'

'Are we to rove the streets arresting everyone who has a scrape upon them?' was Roach's flinty response.

'I followed him last night. Myself. I saw him.'

260

'You saw someone who looked like the man. In the fog. For a moment. And then disappeared. You saw nothing but your own desire to topple the statue of authority, and bring it crashing down.'

There was enough truth in that remark to stop McLevy in his tracks.

Roach spoke more in sorrow than anger, but not much more.

'You were following a trail of pure circumstance which has led you to a hellish pass, McLevy. *Why* did you not tell me, your superior officer, of all this?'

'I thought you might curtail the inquiry,' was the only answer.

'By God, I would have and am about to do so,' said Roach with cold anger. He moved to his desk and scribbled his name on a piece of official-looking paper which he then slid towards McLevy.

'You are now removed from the investigation. You will confine yourself to your domestic quarters for as much time as it takes this matter to blow over. Then and only then will you be allowed to return to the station with your tail between your legs. There will be, of course, an official reprimand put on your record. A *heavy* reprimand.'

As McLevy slowly picked up the paper and squinted at it, Mulholland felt a hot flush run through him, but what was the emotion?

'You can count yourself lucky,' added the lieutenant. 'Chief Grant wanted you reduced to the rank of third-class constable and banished to the dog patrol. I interceded on your behalf. Don't make me regret my decision. Now, you may take your leave. Pick up your bed and walk.'

McLevy seemed stunned by this turn of affairs.

'I will take command of the inquiry, and Constable Mulholland, as some measure of reparation, will assist me.'

The constable couldn't look at his inspector as he walked to the door. The flush was pleasure. A malicious pleasure that he took no pride in, yet could not disown.

McLevy usually had the last word, but not this time.

That seemed to be left to Roach. He spoke with some sincerity because, despite their differences, he respected the fact that his inspector had brought home cases that many another couldn't even begin to open the book on. But the man was a menace. An agent of chaos.

'I blame myself, James. I have indulged you too long. It is my misfortune to be of such trusting nature. And it is your nature and consequent misfortune to take advantage of that trust. Hell mend the two of us.'

He then reassumed a formal intonation.

'You will not approach William Gladstone, or anyone connected to him, in the immediate or foreseeable future. If you do so, you will be dismissed from the force.

'Go to your lodgings. Shut the portal. And stay there.'

McLevy stood stock still at the door as if a

thought had just struck him.

'Have you anything to say?' Roach asked in some desperation.

'Carbolic soap,' McLevy answered.

'What?'

'Frank Brennan said the man who paid him smelled of such an odour. So did William Gladstone, this very morning.'

Roach screwed his eyes tight hoping that when he opened them up again, everything would be different. But when he did, it was just the same.

'Carbolic soap?'

'The very odour.'

The lieutenant's jaw twitched.

'Anything else?'

'It's my birthday soon,' said McLevy.

'Many happy returns,' was the reply.

The door closed. The inspector was gone. Mulholland couldn't meet Roach's eyes. The lieutenant signalled him to leave the office and the constable slipped gratefully away.

Roach was left alone.

He sighed and looked up at Queen Victoria. She had it easy.

263

35

By a Knight of Ghosts and Shadows,
I summoned am to tourney.
Ten leagues beyond the wide World's end,
Methinks it is no journey.

ANONYMOUS BALLAD,
Tom o' Bedlam

Leith, 7 April 1848
Dear Jamie,

By the time you read this, I shall have gone to join my beloved husband, Hughie, in Rosebank cemetery.

After that, it is all in the mercy of God, although when I questioned the Reverend Strang about what was on my mind, he looked at me as if I had no right to ask and said, 'Your sins will find you out.'

He has aye been a miserable wee stick and never liked Hughie since the day somebody threw a Sabbath snowball at him and knocked his hat for sixpence. My husband came under suspicion for the act due to having a good eye and a merry disposition, but what harm is there in a ball of snow?

I fear that Hughie's sins may weigh more than mine. Besides the drinking, card playing and, I have to admit, occasional blasphemies under the influence, there was also the matter of various fancy women, one in particular, Olive the Gypsy.

On his bended knees, he begged me for pity and I was moved by his passion. The Prodigal Sinner is always worth more than the unco guid. But I was informed by the same nosey-parker neighbour who brought me the news in the first place, her man working the bar in a low dive, The Foul Anchor, in the Leith docks, that Hughie's knees were not to be trusted.

He had taken up with Olive once more, the charms of a Romany bangle I suppose.

I did not dare to ask him again because I knew I could not forgive him this time, so I took a mean revenge with Tam Imrie the cobbler. But I only did it the once, and Hughie did it all the time.

I hope, wherever we both end up, that I'm not looking down at him or vice versa, or we're both not looking at each other, level pegging, with the flames of hell spread out behind us.

That's what I was trying to ask the Reverend Strang. Without going into details, of course.

I have one other thing on my conscience which is the reason for this letter.

Not long ago you stood in front of me proud as punch because you had joined the police force. It's the first time I've seen any colour in your cheeks and I was glad I had asked Judge MacGregor to put in a word, mind you he owed me enough for keeping that crabbit-faced wife of his stuffed with cream crowdie and clootie dumplings.

Anyhow, I was glad for I know how much justice means to you, what with you not getting that much in your own life.

We never spoke of that day you found your mother lying in bed with a throat she stabbed for herself, and I was grateful because I had not the wisdom to puzzle it out.

But the one thing I lied to you about was your father. You often asked me when you were growing up about him and that your mother had always said that he was an Angel of the Lord.

I always answered that it was a mystery to me, but in fact it was not so. I knew more than I was telling. Not much. But a wee bit.

About the right time, by the calculation of the months which the Good Lord has set aside for the purposes of such, the number being nine before you made your appearance in the world, I met a young man in the hallway coming from your mother's door. It was Easter Monday.

The man was heavy set, white complexion, a sailor by his uniform. He nodded his way past me out the place and I never saw him again.

I believe he may have been a foreign body. The Italian Navy had a ship in the harbour that very week, but Italians are swarthy skinned are they not?

Anyway, Jamie. I think that might have

been your Angel of the Lord.

I have not the heart tae see your face when I break that news, you've had enough of a hammering.

You are about to start a new life and I have no wish to spoil it with such miserable tidings, so I will give you this letter, sealed, with the solemn admonition that you do not open it till your fiftieth birthday.

By that time, I will be long departed, and you will be of an age where you are able to bear pain as well as any other man. Which is to say, not much. But, enough.

I hope you can forgive me. I have loved you as best I could even when you spilled that beetroot all over my best tablecloth.

I hope that, by now, you are married with a tribe of children, but I doubt it.

Something in your heart closed that day. Love and trust will never come easy to you.

Except for me. You gave it all to me. And I have rewarded you by delaying the truth.

Forgive me again. Be good. Your loving Aunt.

Jean Scott

McLevy's hand trembled as he put aside the letter which he had now read many times since the opening of it.

Happy Birthday. Well, that was one mystery solved. Or was it? Best accept that he would never know.

Every Easter Maria McLevy had waited for a knock at the door. No one came to call. She looked down at her son and put the fault upon him. He could not help her so she took her own life. No justice.

To his astonishment, he found a trace of moisture in his eyes. But it was a trace only. Nothing a wipe with a hankie would not cure. See? All gone.

And if he shed a tear, though he was certain this was merely an optic irritation, it was not for himself or his mother, but for Jean. It must have killed her carrying that secret all these years.

He had to smile though at her having a wee dabble with Tam Imrie. Ye can never tell with women.

No, you never can tell.

An impatient scratch at the window took his attention elsewhere and he opened the frame to let Bathsheba slip past him into the room.

Since he had come back in disgrace the cat had not visited. Perhaps word had reached the rooftops, but here she had now arrived. Was this an omen of sorts, or was it more likely the cold snap following the mild wet weather which had driven her indoors?

As she made for her saucer of milk, he noticed that a subtle change had taken place. Usually the cat dived in, face down, not a care in the world, but now she seemed uneasy, the head coming up at any slight noise. That regal poise and grace of bearing, which Victoria to possess would have given her eye-teeth, had been disturbed. Her coat was a mite unkempt, the grooming perfunctory. What was going on?

He knelt beside the cat and ran his fingers

softly down the fur at the side of her neck.

A low growl came in response and she flinched slightly before hunger drove her back to the milk.

But he had felt the marks. She'd been pinned deep. Time would tell how deep it had gone.

He poured out some more milk then left the beast to her own devices and a measure of peace as he picked up the coffee pot from the hearth and replenished his cup at the table which was positioned by the open window.

McLevy sat back down and took a sip. It was black and bitter. Like his prospects.

That damned woman Lightfoot had jiggered up his cat's routine, chased Bathsheba out the window before her accustomed time so that she ran straight into a couple of big hairy toms, and had caused his own incarceration to boot. Happy Birthday.

Jean's letter was carefully replaced in its envelope and put inside his diary which, to be truthful, he had not had the energy to make an entry in these past few days.

It was late afternoon, the light still holding as he looked out into the streets below. The passers-by were muffled up against the cold, breath puffing out like a steam train, all was back to normal.

The Midlothian election result had been announced this very morning. Gladstone had won hands down. Sweet William.

A terrible lethargy had settled upon him. Each day that passed was like another layer of dust.

To keep his thoughts from shifting back to the

contents of Jean's letter and all the raw feelings it invoked, he replayed in his mind the last exchange of words between himself and Mulholland. Although that itself had not exactly been an ode to joy.

As he had walked away from the station up Charlotte Street, heading for the Leith Links where the rain could *really* get at him, a shout came from behind. He knew the voice but did not turn round.

He was filled with a terrible rage. He had never been taken off a case before; why had he not lifted up Roach's desk and hurled it at the man? But he had felt paralysed, quite paralysed, by the rain and cold and the long walk back, and the exchange with Gladstone, the instinct that something was not quite right, and something was equally very wrong.

His own desires, obsessions, played like a harp; something was behind it all, he knew it in his bones.

Roach was correct. Circumstances had led him by the nose. Yet something was behind it all and he was like a blind man, led by the nose. And so his anger was directed against himself. Who better to batter?

'Sir. Sir!' Mulholland swung in front and brought McLevy to a halt.

'How was the musical soirée?' demanded the inspector, a savage grin on his face. 'Did ye encounter anyone of interest? Any wee chookie birdies?'

'What? Yes. Yes, I did,' replied the nonplussed but slightly nettled constable. 'Emily Forbes is the young lady's name. And she is not a chookie birdie.'

'The daughter of Robert Forbes?' A reluctant nod from Mulholland who was wondering how he always ended up where he never intended to be when the inspector was in such a mood, like a matchstick boat in a raging gutter torrent.

'I know him well!' roared McLevy, oblivious to the rain pouring down his face. 'He was once, like me, an investigator. We broke a bonded whisky swindle one time. Danced on the tables of the Old Ship till we fell off on our faces. But he is respectable now.'

'He certainly seems to be,' was the careful response.

McLevy stuck his face close in to Mulholland, his eyes were bloodshot, face unshaven, the wild man of the forest.

'Well, you hang in with respectability,' he said with a mirthless smile. 'Because that's where ye belong. That's where your bread is buttered! Sook, sook!'

He brushed past Mulholland and headed up into the slanting downpour.

The constable was hurt and angry, his overture not even made, already rejected.

'It's not my fault things turned out to be so!' he shouted after.

The figure of McLevy carried on walking as if not having heard, then, as the street rose to a small crest, he turned and shouted back.

'I am sure yourself and Lieutenant Roach will solve these murders in two shakes of a lamb's tail. I look forward to that. Remember when you kiss his backside, it's to be right in the middle. Don't deviate. In the meantime I advise you to shun my presence lest you be contaminated by the desire for justice!'

Thus was the parting.

McLevy took another sip of his coffee and made a face. It was cold. So was his bond with Mulholland but better that way. Keep the young man out of trouble. Till the game was played through. He would wait for the next move. He knew it would come. Something was behind it all.

The cat had been nesting in one of the armchairs, treading the cushion to make herself comfortable, when she suddenly leaped from the chair and out of the window in two jumps, hair standing on end.

In his preoccupation, he had heard nothing, but now the creaking floorboards presaged a visit.

Rap-a-tap-tap on the door. His landlady this time for sure. He opened it a crack, foot poised to forestall Fergus if the dog smelled departed feline. It whined but nothing more. Mrs MacPherson peered in at him. He'd never known a more mis-doubting tribe than the Dundonians. Born wary.

She pushed an envelope through the narrow aperture which divided them.

'This was handit in for ye,' she announced. 'A wee street boy. Paid tae deliver. A *woman*, he said.'

She still held on to the envelope which he now had at least his fingers upon. Her face was dubious.

272

'Don't worry, Mrs MacPherson,' McLevy smiled as best he could, while he tugged the envelope out of her hand. 'It is not a love letter. The reputation of your house is yet above reproach.'

'Ye're getting a lot of visitors these days.'

'It's the weather,' he replied, closing the door gently on her then listening to her departing footsteps on the stairs before, he examined the missive.

It seemed to be his day for envelopes. He sniffed at the paper. The faintest touch of rose perfume, very delicate, no wonder Mrs MacPherson was suspicious.

He took the envelope to the window where the light was better, sliced open down the join with his thumb, and brought out two pieces of paper. One vellum with writing inscribed; the other, tissue, wrapping something within. He read as follows.

W.G. will celebrate his triumph tonight in the family house at Fasque. My friend has the secret diary and will meet you in the funeral vault on the hour of nine. The diary has all the proof you need in his own entries. You must bring this paper with you as evidence of identity. I cannot be there. I am otherwise engaged. J.L.

McLevy almost spat in disgust at these words. What did the woman think he was? Otherwise engaged? What the hell did that mean?

And yet his eye was drawn back to the words

273

. . . all the proof you need.

And then there was a postscript.

The other was found where the diary was hidden. I remembered your words, 'a silent witness'.

He slowly unravelled the tissue paper and found in its depths a fragment of white plume. The feather part was, to some extent, dried and shrivelled, but the spine was intact and showed where it had been snapped through.

McLevy moved quickly to the cupboard, brought out the mother-of-pearl box, opened it, and carefully, from its wrapping, teased out Sadie Gorman's broken and grubby panache.

He pulled out a drawer in the table, took out a magnifying glass and a piece of plain white paper. The two pieces were then slid together over the paper, his fingers trembling a little as this was accomplished.

He looked through the glass.

It could not be denied. A perfect match.

36

'Take the hand and say you do not know it.'
'I do not.'
'Lay your hand upon that face and say you
do not know it.'
'I do not.'
'Place your hand upon that bosom and say
you do not know it.'
'I do not.'

> Inverness. A murderer's testified denial,
> upon the body of his victim.

The castellated turrets of Fasque House had
withstood stronger blasts than this April wind.
Indeed it was a mere snipe of a breeze which
made no impression on the golden stones. The
lights were blazing, and there was a sound of
merriment and music from within which would
not quite carry to Balmoral Castle fifteen miles
away.

Even if the noise had and were the Queen in
residence, which she was not, being tucked away
safely in Baden-Baden, it is doubtful that she
would have joined in the joyful celebrations, her
worst fears realised, her champion unhorsed.

McLevy wasn't celebrating either as he
hunched his way up the long drive towards the
stately mansion. The coach journey to nearby
Laurencekirk had taken an eternity and then
he'd had to scrounge a lift to the outskirts of

Fettercairn and follow by tramping the rest of the way in this nagging wife of a wind.

The import of Roach's words kept circling in his mind.

If the inspector approached Gladstone, he would be dismissed from the force. Not an idle threat.

But he wasn't going to meet William head on, more . . . discover his way around. A glancing encounter.

Thus, falsely reassuring himself but feeling doom in the pit of his stomach nevertheless, he pressed onwards.

Luckily the main gates had been wide open and he'd already watched pass by two carriages of cheery gentlefolk who no doubt by this time were well inside, warm as toast, drinking a health to the Great Man and then each other. They had paid no heed to the dark figure skulking along the verge like a plague carrier to the feast.

An exposed huge swathe of grassland lay in front of the large doors of Fasque House, which opened and shut like a hungry mouth to gobble up the jovial visitors.

The houselights spilled on to this lawn with fine abandon and, in the darkness out of the circle of this artificial radiance, the eyes of nature glittered in the night as some curious deer gathered to witness the spectacle. But not too close lest they be seen and some celebrant lean out of the window to let loose a shot.

For that same reason, McLevy also skirted the edges of the light. He was searching for a building suited to darker purposes.

And there it was. Not far from the house but far enough that the music would not waken the dead and the dead not disenchant the living. The Gladstone family vault.

The stone glowed faintly in the surrounding gloom: four pillars with a flat slab of a roof and an iron railing placed around, of which the gate had been thoughtfully left, as he found when he tried it, unlocked and open to the touch.

Before he descended the worn stone stairs to the opening of the crypt, McLevy felt in his pocket for the comforting weight of an old black revolver. His lifesaver.

He cleaned it every month before replacing the weapon in its oilskin pocket. Aunt Jean had given it him on his twenty-first birthday, to protect him when she was gone.

She claimed her husband Hughie had gained it in a card game with some excise men who had confiscated it off a rum smuggler from Jamaica, but McLevy doubted that.

He had fired the gun twice in the line of duty. Once he'd missed, once he'd hit. But since it was at the same man, a blackmailing bastard who was shooting back at him, one cancelled out the other.

The wind whistled round his ears and McLevy realised he'd taken refuge in the past to avoid the present.

No more of that. This uneasy breeding of hesitation must be rectified. He took the revolver from his pocket and grasped it firmly in his hand as he walked down the slippery moss-coated steps. The entrance to the crypt was black as the

Earl of Hell's waistcoat. He poked his head inside.

'I am James McLevy, inspector of police,' he called softly. 'Whoever is there, make yourself known and let us parlay.'

Silence. The wind swithered above. He took a deep breath to calm himself and walked into the darkness of the tomb.

The air was cold and clammy but what else was to be expected from a congregation of long-dead bodies?

The inspector shuffled forward in the dark, all senses alert for danger. He might strike a lucifer but that would make a target of him and he felt his big backside was already sticking out quite far enough.

Then he saw a glimmer of light. It appeared to be coming from behind the defining edge of the sepulchre. He moved softly and, bending down so as not to be visible above the flat surface of the stone, sneaked a look around the corner.

A small candle flickered on the stone ledge of a bricked-up window.

It illuminated the shape of a book that lay beside, uneven pages protruding from the leather binding. On top of the book was a small bell.

Bell, book and candle. Were they not the auguries of excommunication?

'The dramatic in me,' said a voice behind him.

The man who had been lying perfectly still, arms crossed, on the top of the sepulchre, had swung silently off the stone surface hindward of the inspector. He reached forward, one hand to pull back the head, the other thumb and first finger to press hard just below the lobes of the ears before McLevy could swing round with the revolver.

Unconsciousness followed, like a lamb the shepherd.

37

Our torments may, in length of time,
Become our elements.

JOHN MILTON, *Paradise Lost*

The chapel of Maris Stella was empty, the
pungent odour of incense still hanging in the air
after the last service had been intoned and the
faithful departed.

The altar boys had taken off their gowns and
left, no doubt after trying the lock of the
cupboard where the holy wine was kept and
finding it, as usual, made fast.

Father Callan did not begrudge them the
exploration. Boys will be boys, and when holy
robes are removed, animal nature often reasserts
itself.

The young are entitled to their wild ways, the
heavy duties of adulthood come soon enough.

The bishop, of course, might have quite
another view. He clove to a most severe
authority, but then it was rumoured he had once
whispered in Pope Pius's ear not long before His
Holiness departed this mortal coil.

Or was it that Pope Pius had whispered in the
bishop's ear?

Whatever. They were in whispering distance
and the little priest had never got closer to the
Universal Father than a large portrait of Pius on
the wall in the bishop's study, when he delivered

to his superior a monthly report on the comings and goings of the Leith congregation.

It was said the recently ascended pontiff, Leo XIII, was a forward thinker. Hard to tell from his portrait which had been stuck up opposite Pius, but Father Callan hoped so. God knows the Church needed such.

There were many of the cloth who would not agree, but then he had always regarded himself as a secret radical.

He had arrived a young man from Ulster at the height of the Great Famine to find the congregation, a large part composed of recently emigrated Irish Catholics, driven hard in on themselves by a hostile society and clinging to the skirts of Mother Mary for spiritual consolation.

Callan was supposed to be a small cog in the holy machine of this fine new building who would make way for bigger wheels, but somehow he had got stuck in the works and now, thirty years later, he was still on hand.

He lived amongst the poor. He blessed them, visited the sick, comforted and buried them. As best he could.

His superiors wafted past, rings glittering in the candlelight, and looked down from a great distance at this worker ant who, when he gave service, wore his robes like a blacksmith wears his apron.

He was regarded with benign condescension, but they left him alone and that was all he asked.

To be left alone. To labour. To do God's will.

That was not always an easy task.

His eye fell upon the Stations of the Cross, which ranged around the inside of the chapel, high on the walls. He knew their particular depiction now as well as he knew his congregation and indeed, at times, intrigued himself by superimposing the faces of the poor on the actors in the drama. Not upon Jesus Christ of course. That would have been blasphemous; but Saint Veronica for instance.

Many women who knelt before him to worship could have wiped the sweat of death from the Saviour's countenance.

'*Adoramus te, Christe, et benedicimus tibi.*

'*Quia per sanctum Crucem tuam redemisti mundum.*'

He murmured his own priestly words and their response as he walked slowly down the side of the church.

He had worked hard to build some bridges between the Protestant and Catholic poor of his parish, with some success, but now the Home Rule movement had reawakened tensions between them.

Many of the Catholic clergy were in favour and spoke accordingly at meetings for the repeal of the Act of Union and a parliament in Dublin, but Callan steered a middle course. Church and the State. A bad mix. He was no great prophet but he could sense the most hellish upheaval.

The Liberal party was apparently sympathetic, but so was the serpent when it offered Eve the apple.

Ireland would be a battleground. Lives would be lost. The Irish were good at killing each other.

Like dogs in a pit they'd been set so many times past, face against face, to snarl and draw blood. They had a taste for it now.

His footsteps echoed in the silent chapel and then stopped. His mind shifted.

He had gone to that meeting in West Calder out of a mild curiosity. But when he heard Gladstone speak on the platform it sent a shiver down his spine.

Something in the voice, the harsh, sonorous tone, awakened memories, drifting memories that were brought back into focus. But it was all so long ago, and who was to say that his mind wasn't playing tricks?

Then amongst all the faces of the crowd, he saw the one staring back. His gaze had met McLevy's and he had left abruptly, much disquieted at the coincidence of these events being drawn back together.

Thirty years ago. The same implacable gaze. A young constable, asking questions that Callan would not, could not answer. The constable must have sensed something because he kept pressing hard and it had taken all of Callan's training in the art of priestly blankness to keep him from betraying what he had witnessed.

During his years at the chapel of Maris Stella, he had heard many confessions, many souls had poured out their pain, some small and even tawdry, some fierce in agony.

But, the one. That night. It had never left him. He looked back towards the confession box and it was as if a floodgate suddenly opened and the images seared through his mind.

He had been sitting alone and enclosed, the hour late, to commune with his Maker, but heard footsteps echo in the empty chapel and then a thud shook the other part of the box as if a wild animal had blundered inside.

He tried to invoke the formal beginnings of the confessional exchange but the man had paid no heed. Either he did not know the responses or did not care.

The voice was low and rumbling as if being wrenched out of the man's very soul; the words ugly, disjointed.

From where Callan looked down through the grille, all he could see was the top of the head, the hair thick, a few stray shafts of light running across like spiders.

'Blood. Blood is the cure. Stinking wombs, they chain my soul. To Satan.'

The priest took a deep breath.

'You must calm yourself, the way to forgiveness is not to be found in violence of word or action. The humble penitent is beloved of our Lord Jesus.'

A harsh cough of laughter was the response as if the very devil himself was squatting on the bench.

'I will cut them down. Out of their body I will cut my salvation. Out of their stinking wombs!'

Then, astonishingly, the voice changed to that of an educated tone, as if the mind was split. The tone was deep and powerful.

'For what says Proverbs?' asked the man. 'Do not hearken to a wicked woman; for though the lips of a harlot are like drops from a honeycomb which for a while are smooth in thy throat, yet afterwards you will find them more bitter than gall, and sharper than a two-edged sword!'

Then the man scrabbled up the side of the partition and put his mouth against the small opening of the grille.

All that the horrified priest could see was the orifice, mouth opening and closing, the red tongue flickering, teeth bared like a beast and flecks of spittle covering the metal grille and dripping down slowly like some sort of obscene Satanic fluid.

'For her past sins, St Thais was walled up in a convent cell in which there was but one small opening through which she received a little bread and water. Her cell filled with her own excrement until, at the end of three years, she was finally cleansed. Of her sins!'

The mouth laughed then dropped out of sight and the man once more squatted like a beast below.

Father Callan tried to still the trembling in his voice. He felt as if surrounded by a miasma, an unholy exhalation which seeped into his very pores. To breathe was to be infected.

'What is it you have done?' he managed to whisper.

'I cleansed her,' came the chilling response. 'And I rescued her. Out of the stinking womb.'

'How? How did you do this?' the priest asked.

For the very first time, the man fell silent. Father Callan could finally bear it no longer.

'If you do not say, I cannot help you. What have you done?'

285

A howl of pain, as if from a wounded tortured soul, and then there was a gleam as a sharp steel blade swung up against the grille, denting the metal.

The blade stuck for a moment and the horrified priest could see the smears of blood on the edge.

The blade whipped out of sight and a pair of eyes glared into his, burning with hate.

Then the man was gone. Footsteps. Crash of the outside door, Silence, once more.

If it had not been for the patch of blood where the man had leant against the partition wall, blood that the priest had carefully cleansed away from it and the lattice-work of the grille that very night, Father Callan might have wondered if he had not suffered a demonic visitation, a rupture in the fabric of reality.

But all that was dispelled when he heard the terrible tidings next morning. And then, some days later, looked into the eyes of Constable James McLevy and denied all knowledge of murder, the faint smell of paint and linseed oil mixing with the incense inside the bright new building.

He had no option. He did not know whether the man was Catholic or no, or what perverse demons had driven him into the chapel, but the sanctity of confession must be protected no matter how crude and incomplete the process.

He would carry the burden for the rest of his life. It was a matter of faith.

Father Callan shivered as he came out of these thoughts. For a second he thought someone was behind him and startled, but it was his own shadow on the chapel wall.

All these years ago, he had made his own confession to his bishop and been told to dismiss the matter from his mind. The Catholic Church did not welcome such scandal.

That should have been the end of the matter but now he felt strangely unshriven, as if a feeling of guilt he had carried all these years had been stirred into a raw hunger to confess his suspicions. But that would be wrong. Against his creed.

And if he did, what could he tell? A memory, shifting like sand, compromised by time. Nothing more. What use would that be to McLevy and his like?

Father Callan found himself looking up at the last and fourteenth station.

Jesus is laid in the tomb.

38

For those who have been defeated, good
becomes bad, and bad becomes even worse.
      MIGUEL DE CERVANTES, *Don Quixote*

When McLevy opened his eyes it was to discover
himself tied up, as Aunt Katie would have put it,
like a turkey on the Christmas table.

His hands had been pinioned behind and his
feet, which stuck straight out in front due to the
fact that he had been propped up against one of
the stones, were also bound together with a thick
strong cord.

'I do apologise,' said a voice. 'I shall unloose
you in due time but I am afraid you will gain
little benefit from the action because of a certain
insensibility. Namely, that of death. This, from
your point of view, is undoubtedly unfortunate
but needs must when the devil drives, eh?'

A dry chuckle and then his own revolver was
levelled at the inspector's head. It appeared to be
aiming straight between the eyes, the muzzle
steady as a rock.

A finger tightened on the trigger which drew
back under the pressure. McLevy's magnified
focus was centred on this sight. He watched the
hammer pull away from the striking pad, then
farther back and farther to the limit when it
would snap forward like a deadly snake.

For some reason, Jean Brash came into his

mind, roses in bloom, high summer, red hair, green eyes, lips smiling as she reached towards him with the sacred pot.

'I don't suppose,' he croaked, 'you have such a thing as a cup of coffee on your person? I would like to satisfy my thirst before you shoot me with my own gun.'

A sardonic laugh came in response and the revolver was lowered to the side.

For the first time, McLevy was able to take stock of the man in front of him.

Dressed for the evening, a black silk scarf wrapped around his neck, part covering the bow tie and white shirt.

Both men were revealed by the glimmering candlelight though that was as far as equality went. The inspector was cramped like a rag doll on the flagstones, while the man sat on the top of the tomb opposite, one leg swinging in a carefree gentle arc.

A definite elegance, tall, slim, stage-door Johnnie silver hair, strands of which fell negligently over the one eyebrow and occasioned a flick of the head to keep all in place. Face smooth, features small, not for a moment memorable, like that of a baby, unformed almost, until you got to the eyes. Everything stopped when you got to the eyes. Ice-blue. Cold. A killer's eyes.

The man had suffered McLevy's scrutiny patiently enough then, on bringing out a pocket-watch to check the time and nodding acceptance of a reasonably tight schedule, spoke in a brisk fashion with traces of an upper-class drawl.

Though that might well be a disguise, like everything else about him.

'I'm afraid, old chap, there is no coffee to hand and your demise will not involve anything so neat as a bullet hole.'

He relaxed his finger from the trigger, laid the revolver down on the surface beside him and delved into the recess of his jacket.

'This is the fellow for the job. A bit messy. I do hope you don't spout. One can never tell with people.'

He produced a small axe, the like of which McLevy had seen Gladstone use on the tree. The edge of the blade shone murderously keen in the light.

'I sharpened the little beauty this very morning, with my own fair hands. You've a bit of heft to you but it should cut through the blubber.'

McLevy was perfectly still. It was his habit in extremity of danger. You may have only one move to make.

The man raised an eyebrow at the lack of response, perhaps even a little nettled by it.

'I shall render you unconscious first, of course. It's the decent thing.'

'Like ye did Frank Brennan?'

A moment. Then, a charming smile. All of McLevy's senses were fixed on that smiling face. Perhaps the man wanted to toy with him, as a cat will a mouse. That was fine by the inspector, he would encourage such a cruel pleasure.

Anything but the axe. Anything that might provide the smallest chance of surviving this hellish predicament.

'Ye did a fine job: lockpicks, the pillow, in and out like a ghost, but what was the necessity, sir?'

McLevy let humble admiration creep into his voice and watched the man nod acceptance before replying.

'Over-elaboration. Fault of mine. My reconnaissance had led me to believe that money would keep him in the tavern and removed from his pimping ground. But then, inevitably, he saw me in the doorway, and there was always the prospect that sometime, somewhere in the future, there might be another recognition. I don't like loose ends.'

That took care of that and anyway Frank Brennan wasn't worth the breath. The inspector had other things on his mind. Play for time. Act the innocent.

'Ye said, *render* me unconscious? But, ye've already done that, sir. I was out like a light. Ye could have finished me off there and then. Why bring me back to life?'

'I felt the least I could do, old boy, was thank you. Face to face, as it were. After all, you've done a tremendous amount of work on my behalf.'

He smiled again. McLevy's face was like a mask. The fellow had to see himself in someone else's eyes to behold his own genius. That might be a weakness.

'Alas, I am forgetting my manners in this heathen country. Allow me to introduce myself.'

The man levered himself off the tomb and bowed as if meeting a stately dowager.

'Graham. Sir Edward Graham. I have an official position. Security. But I also run and provide a service, most secret, to those in highest authority. Those who kiss the Queen's hand. When split from my official guise, I become another person. And I call myself the Serpent. A silly name but it satiates a melodramatic streak.

He bowed once more.

'At your service. The Serpent.'

'*An adder in the path that biteth the horse's heels so that his rider shall fall backward,*' the inspector quoted, in apparent acquiescence of the man's function.

'Genesis. Exactly! But what says Matthew? *Be ye therefore wise as serpents and harmless as doves.*'

'Harmless? But, ye've murdered three people.'

'Oh, more than that. In my time.'

McLevy closed his eyes as if the full extent of his dreadful plight was beginning to dawn.

Keep the bugger talking, words don't kill.

'All this . . . all that has happened . . . was your planning. Was it not?'

'Indeed. Start to finish, old boy.'

'But why? For God's sake, why?'

McLevy blinked like a bewildered child and the Serpent almost laughed at the look on the face opposite.

He assumed the manner of someone delivering a lecture, a dissertation, an anatomy of events.

'Let us suppose that the advent of William Gladstone was not welcome; indeed a foul, *unacceptable* prospect to someone in the highest reaches, exalted almost.'

'Like a Majesty, maybe?'

A sharp look came into the Serpent's eye and McLevy schooled his features back to bovine.

'A messenger approached me, a most high messenger, and a remark was made. Implication more than command, but to be *hard* reckoned and in no way ignored.

'The import of it being . . . *who will rid me of this turbulent priest? . . .* that sort of thing, eh?'

McLevy nodded as if his dull brain was managing to follow it all so far, and the Serpent carried on.

'So it became my task to put these, as it were, unspoken words into practice. This is what I have done, To the best of my modest ability.'

'And what is your reward?' McLevy asked most humbly.

'I shall sit on the right hand of power. Together we shall play the long game. Though to tell you the truth, old boy, a great reward also comes from the strategy and the act itself.'

He laughed lightly and flipped the axe up into the air so that it described a circle before the handle landed back in his hand. McLevy eyed the sharp blade and kept talking.

'How will you effect this purpose? What is your strategy, Sir Edward?'

'To the point. Good. It is as follows. William Gladstone will be found here, a little dazed in his wits, holding the bloody implement of murder, your body at his feet. Some torn pages from his most private diary, genuine enough, which detail his covert meetings with prostitutes and self-scourging, will be found in your pocket.'

He hoisted himself off the tomb and McLevy noticed the man's shoes were highly polished. Good-quality leather.

'Your part in all this is already a matter of record. Your colleagues and even Gladstone's own men can attest to the fact that you pursued him for these murders. It will be assumed that you taxed him with the further proof in your pocket and that he gave in to the evil influences which had set you on his trail in the first place.

'A witness will also swear that she saw him rise from the corpse, axe in hand, covered in your blood, etcetera, etcetera.

'Bravo, inspector! The case is solved. Pity you had to die, but we shall all travel that road, sooner or later.

'In your instance, however, *sooner* carries the day.'

The man skipped happily across the flagstones in a way that reminded McLevy of the night he trailed the supposed figure of Gladstone through the fog.

Unbeknownst to the inspector, what was causing an excess of spirits in the Serpent's breast was the thought that soon he would be reunited with the little fleshly beast. Would lie in her arms once more, and feel the naked pulse of pleasure.

'Of course, I, in my official capacity, can make sure that the whole thing is hushed up. But Gladstone will be finished. He will never assume office. In any capacity. A toothless and disgraced old man.'

'What about his party? They can take office, can they not?'

'Without his backbone they will collapse. A whiff of the scandal will encourage the rot. There will be another election, and no mistake on this occasion.'

A look of detached cruelty came in his eye. Almost time to render. And chop.

McLevy wasn't quite ready for that.

'How did you know about . . . thirty years ago?'

'Records. We keep records on everything that might be useful. Including your good self. Thirty years ago, William Gladstone was in emotional crisis. He had lost his daughter. He was in Edinburgh, on the streets that night. The very night a brutal crime was committed that set the headlines all aflame. *A Lamb to the Slaughter*.'

The quote set the Serpent into a fit of laughter but McLevy could smell the blood lust underneath.

'It caught the public imagination, old boy. I'm always keen on anything that catches the public imagination.'

McLevy creased his brow as if following all this had sorely strained his mental resources and the Serpent, with a certain contempt, spelled out his strategy.

'It could all be woven in, you see. I knew if I could link that past crime with a present likeness, you would not be able to resist. I play the long game, but you? You are a predictable type, inspector. A servant of the Crown, who deeply resents authority. I knew if I laid a trail of tasty enough morsels, you would gobble them up. Gobble, gobble.'

'So, everything . . . was a lie?'

'Who knows? All these years ago, that murder, someone had to do it. Who knows?'

A look came over the Serpent's face as if some strange thought had surfaced, but then he was back on course.

'The nurse was genuine enough. And the deaths of the daughter and sister. I always like to mix fact with fiction. Oh, and by the way,' out of his top pocket he took the piece of paper with the writing which McLevy had received earlier that day. 'I went through your pockets, I hope you don't mind. Thank you for bringing it. As I have said. I don't enjoy loose ends.'

'Joanna Lightfoot,' McLevy heaved a regretful sigh. 'What is her part in all this?'

The Serpent had been about to move in on the inspector and bring the curtain down, but this query brought a flush of pride to his smooth face.

'She is my best operative! It is she who will lead Gladstone here, stun him, lay him down beside you, put the axe in his hand, and then let rip. She has a healthy pair of lungs, believe me.'

'I am sorry I will not see her.'

'You might be disappointed.'

The Serpent suddenly went into peals of laughter at a hidden notion. The fellow was undoubtedly insane, McLevy surmised. Too many secrets can do that to a person.

A gleeful look came into the man's eyes.

'There is a particular talent we both share.

Like the Eucharist. Transubstantiation. Allow me to demonstrate.'

McLevy didn't give a damn what he did so long as the axe steered clear of his breastbone.

The Serpent stood like a little boy about to do his party piece, fanned out the fingers of his hand and passed it slowly over his countenance like a sun over the horizon.

McLevy's jaw dropped. The face left, when the hand passed, was that of William Gladstone.

The mouth especially, and eyes, more than individual features; it was an *impression* of another being. Even the Serpent's physicality had changed.

He then reversed his hand and became, for what it was worth, himself. And laughed to see such fun.

'A gift from childhood. Helped one no end at Harrow.'

He dropped the heavy blade into his jacket pocket so that the handle jutted out awkwardly, flexed his fingers, and moved towards McLevy.

'So when you thought to follow Gladstone in the fog. You weren't far wrong. It was me. Being him. Doppelgänger. The Germans have a word for it. They always do.'

'But Gladstone went out that night. What if he came before you?'

'I knew his routine old boy, a spy in the house and all that. I could beat him to it. The fog was a great help. I sneaked up the side, and made myself visible.'

'How did you know I'd be there?'

'You are predictable. Not unlike death.'

He reached out and took McLevy by the throat just under the jaw-line.

The inspector swallowed hard.

'What about the carbolic?' he suddenly demanded.

The Serpent giggled.

'Part of the character. I'm very thorough, old chap. I *became* the man.'

'And in his name, you killed that wee girl?'

Somehow it seemed as if the positions had changed. As if the Serpent was being interrogated. He didn't appreciate it, and his fingers tightened.

McLevy's mouth was dry but he persevered. All his thinking had led but to the one conclusion. His only hope was fear. The pretence of fear.

'In the fog. The dollymop, was she by chance?'

'Not at all. I had paid her earlier to be on hand at her appointed place, she was pathetically grateful.'

'And poor auld Sadie, you broke her plume.'

'I did indeed. An unfortunate adjunct to a necessary act. Came in useful on this very day. Improvisation. A card to play. To hook you in.'

'Why did you choose Sadie?'

'I admired her style. She reminded me of someone I once knew long ago.'

But a shadow of sorts crossed his face. The memory of long ago had its own sharp hooks.

'And to gratify those high above, ye killed those who had done you no harm?'

'*Exitus acta probat*,' murmured the Serpent. 'The outcome justifies the deeds.'

His fingers had now found perfect purchase and he began to squeeze.

'Say your prayers, inspector. If you know them.'

McLevy let out a sudden roar of terror and hurled himself to the floor where he writhed helplessly like an insect on its back.

The Serpent shook his head in sorrow.

'I had thought better of you, sir. Are not the Scots famed for enduring all things? A hardy breed? Think on the concept of predestination; you were born to die here.'

Another roar came in reply as McLevy wriggled, his legs sticking straight out from the reluctant trunk.

'There is no point in making all this commotion, dear sir, we are underground, the living dead. No one at the house will hear. Now, take your medicine like a man.'

One more bellow like an animal protesting its slaughter brought a wince of distaste in response.

'I had hoped for a little more dignity. Now, come along, old chap, act the brave soldier. I grant you a favour. I could chop you up with your eyes open. Think of the pain.'

Saying so, he straddled McLevy's bound legs and leant down, fingers splayed, to administer the *coup de grâce*.

There is a violent movement from the hanged man as his legs thrash in the air just before death. The fraternity have named it Kicking the Clouds.

It had been adapted and utilised by many a street keelie. One of them, a wee lover of Sadie

299

Gorman, had bruised McLevy sore by the knack of it.

Now, it was his turn. He kicked the clouds.

The bound feet, propelled by two powerful legs that had seen more than thirty years on the saunter even if they didn't like to run, cracked up into the Serpent's groin with the most terrible force.

The crunching impact produced a high-pitched squeal as the man reeled away and hunched over, paralysed by a most profound agony.

McLevy rolled over to one of the tombs and inched himself up until he regained his feet. It seemed to take for ever. He began to scrape the rope that tied his hands behind him against the edge of the stone, but then observed the Serpent beginning slowly to unfold upright.

There was only a matter of yards between them and, as the fellow said, needs must when the devil drives.

The inspector hopped forward and butted the man full in the chin as his head came up. The Serpent fell like a sack of potatoes and McLevy lurched back to get on with his sawing.

He felt some of the strands beginning to fray, and thanked God the Gladstone family had used granite and not some ignoble alternative, because the edge was still sharp.

McLevy had already noted the names on the tombstone, *Jessy and Helen Gladstone, R.I.P.*

Come on, girls, don't just lie there . . . more strands parted but bugger me it was a thick rope . . . *release me from my bondage and I will bless your name evermore.*

They answered with a vengeance and he let out an exultant howl as the last twist parted and his hands were free.

As McLevy bent down to untie his feet, there was a scuffling noise. He glanced up to see the killer limping towards him, hand bringing the axe out of his pocket.

His revolver was on the other side, behind the Serpent. No time for niceties. The inspector jumped forward on his tethered feet and threw himself round the man to pinion his arms by his sides.

They were face to face like lovers. Save for the murderous glint in the Serpent's eyes and his mouth parted in a snarl.

He spat full into McLevy's countenance but the inspector did not flinch, jerked his head to the side and butted the man again, just to keep him honest.

The Serpent wriggled and kicked but McLevy hugged him all the tighter and wedged his forehead into the side of the man's face.

They spun around in a grotesque dance, the only music their gasps for air.

'I didnae realise,' grunted McLevy, 'ye had grown so fond. I would have washed my oxters.'

The response was a slither to the side which enabled the man to bring up the axe so that it was caught between them. He turned the handle so that the sharp edge cut into the inspector's belly and McLevy cursed the fact of his excess flesh; this was no way to lose his avoirdupois.

A savage grin spread across the Serpent's face

and he twisted the blade cruelly so that it cut in again.

'I'm going to have such fun with you, old chap,' he breathed. He twisted his head round to try to bite into McLevy's ear but the inspector spun out of the way and, repeating the move he had made with Frank Brennan, whirled them both round in frenzied spinning circles.

The Serpent yelped as the agony in his groin was brought once more to his attention, and he jerked the axe up so that the edge dug firmly into McLevy's guts.

An insane gleam in the light-blue eyes. Death was coming, death was coming. Spin the wheel.

McLevy gasped in anguish. He lost control of his footing and like two gargoyles falling from a cathedral roof, they toppled over and crashed to earth.

For a long moment they were still and then the Serpent rolled away. McLevy looked down at his tunic. A dark red stain and spreading. Good red blood. The pain would soon follow. It was a deid strake. Death wound.

The inspector crawled into a dark corner like a wounded animal, levered himself up against the wall and looked over to where the man was resting on all fours, in front of Jessy and Helen's tomb.

The Serpent rose to his feet. He smiled down at the inspector where he lay in the darkness, and walked slowly out of the crypt.

McLevy leant back and waited for death.

39

The old order changeth, yielding place to new,
And God fulfils himself in many ways,
Lest one good custom should corrupt the world.
ALFRED, LORD TENNYSON,
'The Passing of Arthur', *Idylls of the King*

Benjamin Disraeli sat in the darkened room and stared defeat in the face.

He had found himself, by some strange chance, ensconced in Lord Salisbury's home at Hatfield, the master being conveniently abroad.

A few servants, like sly spectres, drifted in and out, but mostly it was silent.

Like the grave.

He lit a cigar and blew the smoke over a tray of liver and bacon which added ignorance to insult. A last supper.

The inventory was bleak and inescapable. It was a bloodbath.

Only two years ago, all had been set fair. Disraeli had been chief minister of state and lord of all he surveyed.

The fleet set for Constantinople to put the Russians in their place and Gladstone's windows broken by the outraged populace because of his opposition to that very action.

William had thundered against an unjust war, a fleet of iron-clads that were a waste of public money, sending troops out to die without

303

necessity in foreign climes and thereby upsetting the probity of the budget.

It was a deeply unpopular position and Disraeli had been delighted to see the Liberal party bear the brunt of the people's anger.

The mob had chanted a trite, belligerent little music-hall ditty outside Gladstone's London home, before they stoned his windows.

'*We don't want to fight but by Jingo if we do,*
We've got the ships, we've got the men,
we've got the money too.'

Jingoism. Ugly word. Heart in the right place though.

Disraeli blew a thoughtful smoke ring from lips that had tasted many strange fruits. A succession of intense relationships with young men, mostly his secretaries, had given rise to salacious innuendo but only Benjamin Disraeli knew the truth, and Benjamin was not telling.

Only two years ago. And look at him now.

In Scotland the Tories had fallen from nineteen to seven. Only two survived in Wales. Even England had a non-Conservative majority.

Only in Ireland was there a surplus of Conservatives but that was more than balanced by the number of Home Rulers most of them firmly affiliated to Charles Stewart Parnell. A man who, with a bit of luck, would be a gadfly to Gladstone for the rest of his life.

Already three confidential cipherograms of an increasingly hysterical nature had arrived from a stunned Victoria who, unlike himself, had not contemplated the electorate's rejection.

Despite Gladstone's avowed intention, when he had served her last as prime minister, to 'tranquillise' the Irish, Victoria could not rid herself of the illogical fear that somewhere Gladstone was a secret Fenian and would impose Home Rule and democracy willy-nilly.

As for the loss of Beaconsfield himself, it was like a death in the family. The only minister since Melbourne to become her friend had been snatched from her by . . . *that half-mad firebrand who would soon ruin everything and be a dictator.*

I would sooner *abdicate* than have any communication with this man!

Disraeli sighed. That was the ultimate threat and nothing might stand against it because the position of a minister who forced it on would be untenable. It would bring chaos to the state and the country would not stand for it. Whoever did so would be politically annihilated.

But in that terrible victory would also be the seeds of the Queen's own destruction.

It would take time. But, inexorably, her ruin and that of the constitution would follow as the night follows day.

The monarch must accept the electoral will of the people. Break that compact, and she would fall like a stone.

That was unfortunately unthinkable and though Disraeli might gain a certain warped pleasure in delaying the inevitable . . . *inevitable* it most certainly was.

He might advise her to send for Hartington, the present leader of the Liberals who had been completely eclipsed by the Messianic return of Sweet William and bore a healthy grudge, perhaps even bring in Puss Granville at a pinch.

But . . . no. Harty Tarty and Puss. Compared to Gladstone, they were shadows on the wall.

Victoria would have to accept the proposal and there's an end to it. Even the Queen must walk to the altar.

He would advise her so. She would survive. She was a tough old bird.

He smiled wryly at that thought and looked down at his green velvet trousers. Then another thought struck, not nearly so pleasant.

What of him? Would he survive? He was too old to come back and form another government unless by miracle.

He would become a desiccated creature of society, moving from one soirée to another like some sort of Egyptian mummy.

He had few real friends; what politician does? Even Salisbury within whose house he was now immured, wrote formerly of Dizzy in his letters as a 'Hebrew varlet', and a 'mere political gangster'.

Hebrew varlet, eh? A little rich considering his ancestors had attained a high level of civilisation at a time when the inhabitants of England were going half-naked and eating acorns in the woods.

Disraeli walked over to the window, twitched back the curtain and looked out into a black night.

In the glass, his reflection stared at him like a

ghost being slowly but surely drawn back into the darkness. He puffed on the cigar and though the ghost did the same, the other did not seem to enjoy it as much.

Dignified imperturbability. That was what he presented when they brought him the news.

But inside, his world had collapsed. He had lost everything, his Faerie Queen, his power, his very title, prime minister. He had lost it all to a humourless fiscal puritan. A roundhead to his cavalier.

Indeed his hatred of William Gladstone was the only thing to sustain him at this precise moment. Otherwise he was an empty shell. Thank God for malice.

Only a miracle could save him now. An act of God or someone who confused himself with the deity.

His mind returned to the conversation in the private room of the club. The fellow had offered him a very decent brand of cigar. That was surely a good sign.

Disraeli had not made his desires plain. That would never do. He left the interpretation to others.

Perhaps nothing would occur.

Still . . . hope springs eternal, does it not?

Who knows what was happening out there in the night?

He pulled shut the curtains and noticed, as he turned, a brandy decanter that stood on one of the small tables.

He would puff on his cigar and raise a glass to his beloved Queen.

Who knows?
There might be one last roll of the dice.
Hope springs eternal.

40

Nievie, nievie, nick-nack,
Which hand will ye tak?
The right or the wrang,
I'll beguile ye if I can.

CHILD'S RHYME

She stood in the corner, fingers grasped
awkwardly round a glass of champagne,
watching the Great Man receive due tribute
from admirers who would melt like snowflakes
should the result ever emerge otherwise.

From the huge population of Midlothian, only
3,620 electors were franchised to vote, but a
comfortable majority had voted for Sweet
William.

Gladstone's cheeks were unwontedly flushed:
red wine and the press of bodies. He would have
a headache in the morning, deranged liver and
bowels, castor oil prescribed; oh yes, he would
have a *dreadful* headache.

She hid her smile behind the fluted glass and
watched as, around his ungainly figure, some quite
beautiful women fluttered like butterflies, drawn
to the fire, the source of power. Butterflies.

Or was it moths? They burnt in ecstasy at the
flame. She had once viewed them die in a hotel
room in Venice, the window open on a hot airless
night, a single candle in the lamp to lure the prey
to death.

They had wagered on the number. She had lost. The forfeit had been deliciously degrading.

Soon, she would be back in his arms. Safe and damned. But not yet, there was much yet to do.

She checked the French windows through which they had agreed he would enter, their being left a little open despite the chill of the evening to let the smoke of best-quality cigars escape into the night.

He had not yet appeared.

To still the tremor of anxiety she turned back and surveyed the magnificent drawing room and double cantilevered staircase, thronged with elegant figures, gowned and suited, laughing and gay, mouths open, eyes sparkling. And yet, despite it all, there was an animalistic quality to the crowd she found . . . quite repugnant.

A realisation that she was looking at it through his eyes. So be it. Who better?

Fasque had been inherited by Tom Gladstone, the eldest brother, who had always lived in William's shadow and was doing so once more, somewhere in the happy gathering. There was coolness between him and the Great Man; little wonder since Tom was a staunch Tory and she wondered if William had demanded the reception here, just to spite his brother.

Through the library doors she glimpsed the figure of Lord Rosebery, his doughy complexion and pale hazel eyes more pronounced than usual.

After victory was announced, a torchlight procession had arrived at the George Street house to be addressed by first Gladstone, and

310

then Rosebery. But that was as near as his lordship would get for a while. He did not have the common touch, mostly because he detested the masses. He was a misanthrope. He detested everyone. Except himself.

Horace Prescott leaned forward to murmur something in his master's ear and was rewarded with a pale smile. Both men stared at Gladstone and somewhere else, she was sure, no doubt guzzling champagne and stuffing his face from the trays of food proffered by an ill-qualified retinue of local girls and tradesmen masquerading as servants, was little George Ballard.

She liked George, he was a treacherous soul but he had some value. He spent much of his time trying to insult her in various ways or shock with lewd insinuations, but she had enjoyed the tale of him sneaking down the cellar steps of a rampant bawdy house to spy Horace being soundly flagellated.

He had slapped Prescott hard on the back, next day.

Dear George.

He, too, would have his eye on Gladstone and she was reminded of a painting she had once viewed. The leader of a pack of lions. Isolated in his own pride. Only surviving so long as he had the strength to keep the claws of others at bay.

For a moment she felt obscurely sorry for the old man and almost regretted the part she would play in his downfall but then Gladstone turned to smile at her.

Ah yes. A strange bond. She would have no difficulty persuading him to the family vault that they might both pray and give thanks for victory at Jessy's tomb.

She would kneel at his feet and look up with adoring eyes. Sweet William liked that. He would put his hand upon her shoulder and she would shake as if moved by a secret desire she could not name. He liked that even more.

An obsequious sexuality, charged and hidden, under the cloak of worship. Not a word said, not a carnal touch, but he relished her submissive adulation.

As the Serpent had once remarked, she was an artist in erotic transference.

Catherine Gladstone, noticing the direction of her husband's gaze, also smiled over. The woman had borne his various obsessions with beautiful creatures of low and high degree, being assured for herself that he would be incapable of the act of infidelity to the marriage bed.

But did she consider *delectatio morosa*, adultery of the heart, the insidious delight in contemplating the evils of lechery without actually committing same?

The good wife saw no danger here and thus smiled over. A mistake on her part, as she would soon discover.

Another look to the window. Nothing. Damnation. Run through the strategy again.

She would move back as if to allow Gladstone a time of private prayer with his daughter, then render him a moment unconscious. She had been taught well in that particular skill. Drag out the body of McLevy from its hiding place, God grant it wasn't too bloody and she didn't see the face. Then press the axe into Gladstone's hand, wait for him to show signs of recovery, run back to the top of the steps and scream back into the house till people arrived.

The story would be simple. Gladstone had used her as cover for a rendezvous, knowing her to be a simple and obedient soul. He had instructed her to wait outside the crypt but she heard shouts and then a single scream and, taking her courage in both hands, crept timidly down the steps to find a hideous carnage.

Sir Edward Graham, an honoured guest and high official in Her Majesty's security forces, would lead the pack and take command.

And there he was! Out of the corner of her eye she observed him stroll elegantly through the French windows. Her lover. The Serpent.

The timing was perfect. Gladstone, for a moment, had separated from the crowd. Perhaps he sought adoration from a different source and she would supply that.

She waited for the signal. The Serpent would take out a cigar, light it up, then move into the throng.

But he did not. Instead he *looked* at her. This broke the rules. Direct contact was to be avoided until the task was completed, and then the most strenuous consummation might be enjoyed but not till then!

She had to meet his gaze. The intensity brought her eyes round to lock with his. He smiled. A clumsy servant jostled him, and the black silk scarf parted to reveal a spreading patch of blood on the white shirt.

This time, the death she saw in the Serpent's eyes was his own.

He fell to his knees and sprawled out his length upon the floor.

One of the maids screamed and dropped a tray of glasses. The sharp noise cut through the babble to produce a most profound silence.

And in that silence, to fill the Serpent's place in the opening to the outside world, as if by magic, stepped the figure of James McLevy.

A bloody axe in hand which he laid upon a silver tray and, noticing a cup nearby, availed himself of a jolt of coffee before turning to stare, slate-grey eyes in the white face, straight at her.

The inspector *knew*. The game was up. Her lover was dead. What did it matter?

She had stood there paralysed but now she slowly removed the thick glasses from the bridge of her nose and dropped them on the floor. She reached up for the wig, pulled it from her head and shook the golden hair free.

Then, like the Serpent, she spread her fingers and passed them deliberately over her face.

The pinched features spread and relaxed.

Then the stooped hunched figure of Jane Salter straightened to become Joanna Lightfoot. And stayed that way. Transformed unto herself.

McLevy did not seem surprised.

The silence was broken by the voice of William Gladstone.

'God preserve us!' he announced.

314

41

That was all! And yet through the gloom
and the light,
The fate of a nation was riding that night.
HENRY LONGFELLOW,
Tales of a Wayside Inn

When Lieutenant Roach, in his hours-of-darkness sleep, dreamed about golf, the route to the hole consisted of inaccessible staircases and weird conduits which became more and more difficult with each nightmarish twist.

But once, only once, he had dreamt of a verdant fairway sloping gently upwards and had then hit a drive which soared a bisecting arc to the most perfect lie.

When he reached the ball, however, he noticed with a sinking heart that the green which lay fairy-bower-like on a small plateau, was just as far from him now as it had been when he first struck the shot.

Progress is an illusion.

For some reason this had come into his mind as he looked across the desk at James McLevy.

The inspector stood at attention, freshly shaved and pomaded, hair for once in some kind of order. He had even pressed, or someone had, his uniform, trousers and tunic all shipshape and made ready.

He looked like a man you could trust, a man

for an emergency, a man who also knew his place in the great grand scheme of things.

It was a truly sinister sight.

Mulholland stood a little behind him to the side, which is where the young man belonged. How could he hope to match this resplendent vision?

'I don't know how you did it, McLevy,' said Roach. 'But you have somehow redeemed your stupidity. If I had been where you found yourself, against instruction and flouting every rule in the book, I would have had a cardiac seizure and had to lie down in the long grass.

'You must have a guardian angel, that's all I can say, because your ignorance of common sense is matched only by a complete inability to recognise danger when it is full in your face and ready to strike home!'

The inspector could have said much but he averted his eyes modestly. Besides, he sensed that Roach's heart wasn't fully committed to further reprimand.

Chief Constable Grant had been summoned before the even higher heid-yins to be told that a crisis of state had been averted by the prompt action of a humble inspector from Leith station.

The precise detail had not been released and never would be, but Leith was now the toast of the Edinburgh force and its gallant leader, Lieutenant Roach, to be commended.

Through gritted teeth, the chief constable had done so, and the lieutenant had enjoyed every moment of watching his bullying superior crawl up his own backside.

Mason or no mason, Brother Grant owed Brother Roach an apology and it would get round the lodge in no time.

Brother Roach would see to that.

For a second there was something that almost approached a smile on Roach's face, then, catching McLevy's eye, he reached into his bag of frowns and stuck one on.

'You redeemed yourself. By the skin of your teeth. The next time, you may not be so lucky. And let there not *be* a next time, because if there is, then, as I have already just remarked, you may not be so lucky, and that is undeniable and a fact!'

The lieutenant had got himself in a fankle. Not for a moment did McLevy's face register this.

'I'll bear all that in mind, sir,' he replied. 'How did your own investigation proceed?'

This innocent-sounding query provoked some tension between Roach and the constable.

'It got nowhere!' Roach's jaws snapped together. 'The constable spent most of his time shaking his head over my suggested lines of enquiry.'

McLevy turned to look in seeming astonishment at Mulholland whose mouth had set in stubborn lines.

'Diagrams. With all due respect, sir. Lines going from one spot to another. On a piece of paper.'

Roach's lips thinned. 'I was applying scientific theory.'

'In my experience,' Mulholland thought *to hell*

with it, I'll never get that leave anyhow, 'the only place to solve a crime is where it was committed. On the street.'

'In your experience?'

Roach was near apoplectic and this was obviously a sore point between them that, in normal times, McLevy would have enjoyed witnessing till the cows came home.

But he had an appointment to keep.

'I'm sure the lieutenant would have led you in the right direction, constable,' he ventured with an emollience which took Mulholland's breath away, 'as he has done with my good self, so many times.'

He inclined his head gravely towards the lieutenant who responded in kind. McLevy tried for another.

At times like these ye cannae have too many nods, was his thought.

'And I must ask you, sir, if I may resume my activities in the parish? Crime never sleeps.'

Roach pondered. 'How are your scrapes healing up?' he enquired of the injuries McLevy had so recently incurred in the line of duty.

'On the mend, sir. On the mend.'

'Then, you may resume,' said Roach. 'And take Mulholland with you; he is of no further use to me.'

Then, as they moved to the door, Roach surprised himself.

'You have my thanks, James,' he said. 'Only you could have brought this off. Therein lies your strength and your potential downfall.'

Then the dark Presbyterian fear of being too

effusive seized him, and he added a footnote to his thanks.

'You don't deserve them, but you have them anyway.'

'In that case I may ask a favour of ye, sir?'

'Ask away.'

'I know Constable Mulholland desires a small leave of absence to attend the betrothal of a close relative. I wonder, might we spare him for a few days?'

'I shall try to notice his absence,' muttered Roach, which was his way of responding in the positive.

As McLevy and a dazed Mulholland were about to pass through the door, Roach could not resist a last dig.

'And Mulholland? Mrs Roach still has her eye on you for a tenor voice. Let us hope you survive the scrutiny. She the blackbird, you the worm!'

They closed the door on the snort of his laughter and McLevy hummed contentedly under his breath as the two surveyed the station.

The morning shift had just left, Sergeant Murdoch was contemplating a tin mug of sweet tea and Ballantyne, as befitted the youngest and most recently recruited, was at a table laboriously copying out reports.

He looked up, smiled shyly, and bowed his head in grave acknowledgement of a shared triumph.

McLevy smiled back but there was an element of worry in his eyes. The boy had a gentle and trusting nature, a bad combination for a policeman.

Whereas Mulholland now . . . a different kettle.

The inspector turned to regard the wary face of his constable.

Beat him to the punch. Just for mischief.

'What was all that about diagrams?'

Mulholland moved them away from Roach's door just in case the lieutenant had his ear against the panelling.

'The man is all theory,' he muttered. 'Good enough behind the desk and a fine superior officer, don't mistake me now — '

'I wouldn't dream of such a thing.'

'But — he thinks everything can be solved with a pen! Names here, times there, arrows pointing, lines running like a chicken with its head chopped off. It got us nowhere. I mean . . .'

Mulholland looked down at McLevy from a great height.

' . . . at least you think you know what you're doing, sir.'

'Thank you, Mulholland.' McLevy rubbed at his eyes as if to hold back a well of appreciation. 'I shall treasure that remark till the end of my days.'

He made to turn away but the constable had more to say.

Here it comes, thought the inspector.

'How did you know I needed time away, and the reason for it, if I may so ask?'

'You may.'

McLevy assumed an air of gravity, as if examining a witness in court.

'Your Aunt Katie sent you a card, did she not?'

'She did indeed.'

'On that card were the precise details of the wedding and your requested presence, were they not?'

'They were so.'

'That card was sticking out of your coat pocket as it lay on the hook, was it not?'

'It might have been.'

'Some careless person, Sergeant Murdoch possibly, must have brushed against the coat and dislodged the card. I found it on the floor, and, returning same, could not fail to notice what was writ thereupon.'

'Thereupon?'

'In a nutshell.'

McLevy looked innocently into the hard suspicious eyes of his constable, then decided to take the offensive.

'Therefore when you were sookin' up tae the lieutenant I knew exactly your motive. Why did ye not confide in me?'

Mulholland stepped back a little.

'I . . . I . . . didn't think you'd have an interest.'

'Ye mean ye thought you'd find a sleekit way to avoid me altogether. Never mind, let that be and answer me the following question, but come up honest this time!'

How is it, when dealing with McLevy, you always ended up, no matter where you started from, at the back of the position you had formerly occupied?

'Go ahead,' Mulholland said glumly.

'Ye had a chance to redeem yourself, like me. Ye could have kissed his backside over these diagrams, why did ye not so?'

'Because it was a murder investigation,' came the reply. 'And some things cannot be passed.'

Not for a moment did McLevy indicate the pleasure he derived from that rejoinder. But he was glad he had pressed the favour out of Roach. Very glad.

'I'll make a policeman out of you yet, Mulholland.'

'I look forward to that, sir.'

For a moment they shared an ironic appreciation of each other's faults and virtues, then McLevy moved abruptly away towards the station door.

'Ye can thank me for my intercession by the purchase of a hooker o' whisky at the Old Ship the morrow night, but for the moment I have an appointment to keep.'

'Not another secret mission?'

The question brought McLevy round. His face sombre.

'Not exactly. But it is something I must do. In common with the man whose life I took, I do not enjoy loose ends.'

Then he was gone.

Mulholland had come out of it smelling of roses. He had got his leave and the lieutenant would soon forget his chagrin. One decent putt would see to that.

He was due some time off the following day and though the morrow night was now taken up with McLevy at the Old Ship, the constable still maintained an afternoon assignation with a certain young lady.

There was a touch of spring in the air. He would lift his voice in song.

42

We lay, my love and I,
Beneath the Weeping Willow.
But now alone I lie,
And weep beside the tree.

ENGLISH BALLAD

'How did you know?'

The golden hair had been pinned back from her face and she wore a drab grey dress whose coarse material fell to the floor like a dead weight.

Joanna Lightfoot had the brand of an institution already laid upon her, but her face was clear, the eyes calm. She had nothing left to lose now except her liberty and, from her demeanour, it would seem she placed little value upon that.

McLevy spoke quietly. A female warder of sorts sat in the corner, apparently paying no heed, but the inspector was not naïve enough to think that because the authorities, in their gratitude, had granted him this one favour, they were to be trusted in any other business.

They were going to sweep the whole thing under the carpet and needed his silence.

But that was all they needed.

'Ye walk like a soldier,' he said. 'A person can disguise many things but the walk often gives them away.'

In his mind's eye, he replayed the moment when he watched her, as Jane Salter, stride up the path with Gladstone and registered a thin slice of intuition.

She smiled at the irony. Throughout the years, the Serpent had often taken her to task for her gait.

'As if I had just dismounted a horse?'

'Ye might say that.' He scratched his ear, oddly discomfited. 'I wasn't exactly sure. It was just a moment.'

'And you follow such moments?'

'Most of the time.'

She fell silent. McLevy was at a loss. There was an ending to be made between them, but he was damned if he knew what form it might take.

'But other than that, ye made a fine stab at deception. Led me a merry dance. Twisted me like a fool.'

'Not at the end,' she said. 'At the final reckoning, you had your revenge.'

He remembered in the tomb looking down at his tunic to discover that most of the blood came from another source. As they had fallen to earth the axe blade must have turned so that the Serpent had impaled himself.

McLevy had been underneath. A man on the ground is not necessarily a man defeated.

He was gouged some, but not mortally wounded, so he untied his legs, retrieved his revolver and followed the fellow out to watch him die.

'Did you have no qualms of conscience?' he asked. 'You would ruin a man's life?'

Though Gladstone was a politician, he was still a human being. Somewhere.

'No regrets?'

She looked at him in surprise.

'Not at all. It was a job of work.'

'A job?'

'Yes. I joined Sweet William's staff and made myself indispensable. It was easy to become his little pet because we had researched his . . . predilections.'

It all seemed logical to Joanna.

'Then I waited for my instructions.'

'Which you followed to the letter?'

'Of course.'

McLevy shook his head. This was worse than being in the fog. She witnessed his confusion and smiled.

'There is no hatred, or love. Only instruction. It is like a game. The long game, we used to call it.'

She tugged at the neckline of her prison dress. The rough material obviously chafed.

'Gladstone was just part of the game. It never ends.'

'But what about the deaths? These poor women?'

'I did not perform them. He . . . ' for the first time her voice faltered, not for the committed act but for the lost lover . . . 'He provided.'

'But was not that evil?'

'I am the operative. As I have said. Good or bad means nothing to me.'

'That is where we differ.'

It was like being in a fairy tale, lost in a deep

forest which made perfect sense unto itself yet for the traveller led nowhere and folded into darkness.

'Have ye ever killed?' he asked.

'That is not my function. I seduce. I entice. I . . . create illusion.'

'How long have ye been so?'

'As long as I can remember.'

She laughed suddenly and, as before, he sensed the bitter pain behind that sound.

'I have always been in the field. The only difference this time was that . . . He was with me. A pity. A great loss.'

Another silence. Her gaze had fallen inwards.

'Was everything you told me about yourself a lie?'

She was jolted out of her introspection by this question and her lips, still that bit on the thin side, screwed into a bitter smile.

'Not at all. My mother was indeed a whore, a game and brazen one. She had no shame, she loved life and dressed to kill.'

McLevy was put in mind of Sadie Gorman.

Again Joanna spoke in those formal tones which were so much part of her character.

'She became the mistress of a young man with some measure of nobility, and had a child by him. He provided in some way for her. When she died, he removed the daughter. He lifted her from the slums she and the mother had inhabited, and took on the role of the child's guardian.'

She stopped.

McLevy now knew why he was here. A twist to

327

the blood he sensed from the moment they had first met.

'The girl grew up. She had everything money could buy. A good education, pretty clothes. And then one night, at the age of eighteen, she came to him.

'That night, they broke the law. And thereafter.'

The inspector licked his dry lips. She smiled and passed her hand almost playfully over her face.

For a moment he was looking at the Serpent and then, another pass, and the features had rearranged to Joanna Lightfoot.

'A trait we both shared. Father and daughter.'

One of McLevy's legs set off in an uncontrollable shaking as he gazed into the dark blue eyes.

'I am a damned soul,' she said. 'If there is perdition, a future punishment as Mr Gladstone would term it, if there is a hell, I shall meet my lover there.

'We will burn together.'

She reached deliberately forward, took up McLevy's hand and kissed it. The imprint of her lips stayed on his skin.

A long silence. Most terrible to bear.

Then he leant forward and blurted out a mundane thought, but anything to break that silence. 'Why did ye dress up for me?'

'In case I was described, there would be nothing to connect the woman with Jane Salter. In any case, you were a hard nut to crack, inspector. I needed every weapon at my disposal.'

She smiled. He did not respond.

'And I bear you no grudge for his death.'

'He deserved it.'

McLevy's eyes were hard and without pity.

She was glad of that. She whispered close, her own eyes mocking.

'But does not one thing puzzle you, inspector?'

'What is that?'

'The scrap of material found on Mae Donnachie's body. I thought it a great stroke of luck that I could weave it into the story. But what if the story of long ago was true?

'What if the man we led you towards was in fact the man you sought? What if we were God's agents instead of Satan's helpers?'

McLevy felt the barbs going into his flesh.

'Just a scrap. The rest was conjecture and lies.'

'But what if some of it were true? Now, you will never know. You've cut your own throat.'

She laughed softly.

'You have lost as well, inspector.'

'I have lost many times in life,' said McLevy. 'The feeling is not unknown.'

He stood abruptly and walked to the door where he turned to look back at her. The quality of his gaze was measured and dispassionate. It took Joanna by surprise but she managed a crooked smile lest he sense the emptiness and pain that twisted in her heart.

'You will never hear of me again. I shall disappear. As if I had never been. *Burnt at the stake, old boy.*'

The tones of the Serpent.

McLevy left without goodbye.

329

Though, outside the door, he gazed back through the judas hole.

The woman in the corner stood. She walked over and laid her hand on Joanna's shoulder. The seated woman shivered a little at the contact.

He closed the grille. Joanna Lightfoot was gone.

43

The warlock men and the weird women,
And the fays of the wood and the steep,
And the phantom hunters all were there,
And the mermaids of the deep.

BORDER BALLAD

McLevy sat by his window and watched as dusk
fell on his beloved city.

Behind every window was a potential crime.
He would rest content with that observation.

The events of the last few days filtered through
his mind like flakes of quartz which float for a
while in the stream then fall to join the sediment
of the river.

A strange thing but it was mostly dead faces
that swam in his mind always.

Sadie Gorman, Mae Donnachie, the wee
dollymop, Frank Brennan and, of course, George
Cameron, waiting eternally in that hospital bed
for the solving of a murder.

Last but not least, Sir Edward Graham, to give
the murderous bastard his proper name, also had
his place in the parade. The father.

And Joanna Lightfoot? The first moment met,
he had looked at her bosom instead of her face.
Mis-direction. And it had never changed. Yet,
those dark-blue eyes would live with him. Empty
and damned. The daughter.

He pulled his diary towards him, opened it at

a blank page and took a slug of coffee. It was bitter as a tinker's curse. Where the hell did Mrs MacPherson get the stuff?

He must ask Jean Brash for her supplier, though it was probably some Levantine smuggler with an eye-patch and gold tooth to boot. Snaggled no doubt, the tooth.

He began to write.

The Diary of James McLevy

I feel a lowering of spirits which is customary at the conclusion of a case.

I have found much to surprise me, especially about myself.

In the personal, to wit . . . my father is apparently an Italian sailor. If alive, he'd be a good age now, but Tarry Breeks are soaked in brine, he may well yet survive.

Perhaps he lives in a wee village beside the sea where his grandchildren gather round his knees to hear of his adventures in far-off lands.

Every Easter I can remember, my mother would take me down to watch the ships come in and then we would go home and she would wait for the knock at the door.

She told me often enough it was my fault the angel never came and I was too young then to question her, like a proper policeman should, as to how she arrived at that conclusion.

My real father and mother are wrapped up in the one body. Jeannie Scott. I will

332

admire that woman till the day I die. I regret spilling that beetroot on her best tablecloth. I was overcome by greed, my eyes on the black pudding. I am glad she found it in her heart to grant me absolution.

In the general, to wit . . . politics is a dirty business and attracts the lowest type. Now and again an honest man may appear but he will be one light shining in eternal darkness.

They are addicted to power. It is their opium. Hell mend them. I have lost interest.

McLevy closed the page. Brevity becomes the soul.

Darkness had fallen on the streets below. On the coping of the roof, some part to the side, he saw the silhouette of a cat outlined by a stray beam of light.

It was Bathsheba, he was sure of it, and was not her belly hanging lower than previous?

He whistled but the cat paid no heed and disappeared into the dark. Never mind. With a bit of luck, she would return.

With women, you always need a bit of luck.

And what of the Gladstone affair?

The mother-of-pearl box lay on the table before him. He laid his hand upon it gently and, in his mind's eye, he could once more see George Cameron shaking his big Highland head in severe disappointment. *What a snowflake*, he would be thinking and McLevy had to accept that judgement. One day he would take up the trail again but for now he must accept his

333

impotence, like a dull pain that never leaves the body and irritates the soul.

A noise brought his attention to the street below. Some kind of torchlit procession, Home Rulers perhaps, part encouraged by the noises the Liberal party was making, but we'd see if they came up trumps.

Every time the Irish trust the English it ends in grief.

McLevy finished the dregs of his coffee and looked downwards once more.

The procession. Another parade of power.

It was led by one bright torch and the lesser lights snaked out behind it.

Like a serpent.

44

On with the dance! Let joy be unconfined;
No sleep till morn, when Youth and Pleasure
   meet
To chase the glowing Hours with flying feet.

LORD BYRON,
Childe Harold's Pilgrimage

Constable Mulholland and Miss Emily Forbes walked down the hill with a decent enough distance between them. Not hand in hand by any means and if there were a brushing contact of sleeve upon sleeve, the uneven quality of the paving stone would surely stand count for that.

They had made rendezvous at a teahouse where he watched indulgently as she, a trifle greedily it must be said, munched her way through two large slices of Dundee cake, followed by a marzipan concoction. That was fine by Mulholland; he disliked marzipan intensely.

After that, their footsteps had led them, as they wandered at random, to the high reaches of Leith, where they were both enjoying the light April breeze and pale spring sunshine. A perfect day to be young and, if not at once in love, Cupid might yet be lurking in the rhododendron bushes, arrow sighted.

Emily cast a sidelong glance at the tall figure of Martin Mulholland, for such was his Christian name.

The constable was a fine height, his feet were big which was always a good sign, and his voice was true.

They were considering a duet, a song of Burns, to wit 'My love is like a red, red rose' ... not an easy melody but Mrs Roach thought that since Mulholland already had some acquaintance with the tune, it might encourage the young man to rise above himself.

Emily was all for that.

She wondered what her father would make of the constable. There was no doubt of his serious mind and steady disposition but policemen were often in contact with the lowest part of humanity, and might this not somewhere, in some osmotic fashion, cause a degree of corruption?

Mulholland, for his part, had suddenly recognised (his mind wandering with his feet) that the road down which they so happily perambulated, though respectable enough in itself, had within and upon it one house which he hoped to slide past without incident. Gently does it.

Emily's young bosom trembled in appreciation of the fresh air and Mulholland was put in mind of a saying of his Aunt Katie's.

Never confuse the jam with the jelly.

'I have my eye on you, Mulholland!'

The constable sighed, his worst fears realised as a harsh, derisive, and most vulgar shout rent the air and Emily grasped on to his arm for protection.

They both witnessed, through the gates of one

of the houses, a large white face leering most inappropriately. The man's stubby teeth were bared, more than a few gaps visible, and his hair seemed to be standing up on end.

'You owe me a drink this night in the tavern and don't you forget it!' the fellow bawled.

'Who is that awful man? He seems to know you, Martin!' gasped Emily. 'Is he insane?'

'No. He is my inspector,' replied Mulholland grimly. 'This is his idea of a prank.'

'A *prank*?'

'Haggghh!' with this last roar the man then turned and ambled back to where a red-headed woman sat at a table in the middle of a rather splendid rose garden.

Mulholland knew the house behind that garden only too well and prayed that Emily did not.

'But surely?' her eyes narrowed. 'Is that not . . . a house of ill repute? I have heard it said. A blot on this nice neighbourhood. Is that not so, Martin?'

'There is the odd rumour,' said Mulholland steering her rapidly down the street, though she would glance back.

Emily, like many of her sex and breeding, was both fascinated and repelled by the prospect of depravity.

'But what is your inspector *doing* there?' she cried.

'It'll be some sort of official visit,' muttered the constable. 'Now let us leave this scene, Emily, for there is nothing to be gained at this juncture.'

337

However, she was like a dog with a bone.

'But what goes on in that house, Martin?'

'I wouldn't know,' he replied. 'I've never set foot in the place myself.'

This was not strictly true but now was not the time for explanation.

He swept her round the corner, pausing only to shoot a vicious look rearwards to where the man in the garden, now seated, waved cheerily in farewell.

Thus the young couple departed to search out a better world and James McLevy turned to watch contentedly as Jean Brash poured him out his first and freshly brewed cup of best-quality coffee that day.

'You're an awfy man,' she observed.

'I like tae keep him on his toes,' was the blithe response.

He sniffed the aroma of the coffee and frowned in concentration. 'I can smell palm trees,' he said gravely.

'Lebanese. A dark grinding.'

He lifted his cup. 'The mysterious East.'

She raised her cup in reply to his toast. They drank.

McLevy sighed. This was as near heaven as he would ever get.

Jean watched him through lowered lids, she did not cleave to direct scrutiny. Although he had leapt up quick enough when he spotted Mulholland on the street, he was looking tired. His eyes were sunken, and that animal ferocity, never far away and so much part of his nature, seemed at a low ebb.

She remembered the moment so long ago when he lay on the tavern floor, with Henry Preger about to kick his face into pieces. She had winked at the spreadeagled young constable, in provocation or in sympathy who knows, but McLevy came off that dirty planking like a madman.

Jean often wondered if that beating had not contributed to Preger's death some years later. Along with the arsenic the man had unwittingly ingested.

No matter. Preger had been an evil vicious swine. He had put her out on the streets scarcely a bairn, and abused her as pimp, lover and partner.

That night he had met his match in McLevy, and, in Jean, his nemesis.

As the inspector slurped his coffee, she further considered.

Indeed there was a madness to McLevy which the fraternity recognised and respected. He was mortal enemy, but he also shared a wild spirit. Hers, in particular.

Though if she ever broke the law to achieve a wicked end, he would have her in the cells quicker than a judge's spurt.

But he'd have to catch her first. He knew it. And she knew it. This moment, though, they could appreciate each other for what they were. Coffee hounds.

The whores were giving the bawdy-hoose a springtime clean, their shouts and laughter echoing from inside. A series of thwacks shook the air where Francine, heavy cane to hand, knocked hell out of a dusty carpet laid across the washing line while Lily knelt at her feet, making a crown of daisies.

'Strong arm, that girl,' the inspector noted.

'Years of practice,' Jean replied.

The giant Angus, scythe to hand, was lopping through a thicket of tall thistles. All grist to the mill.

His daughters, the Dalrymple twins, each to a window, shook out some white sheets. It was a sight to behold.

A quite different vision emerged from the side door as Hannah Semple peered out into the light.

'Do we have any call for bananas?' she cried.

'What did you say, Hannah?' Jean shouted back; she surely had not heard the woman correctly.

'*Bananas!*' Hannah bawled out impatiently, holding the fruit aloft. 'I found a bunch under one o' the beds.'

'Are they ripe?'

'It would appear so.'

Jean considered.

'I think the best thing,' she pronounced, 'is to throw them into the scaffie cart. Skins or not, you wouldn't want to trust their previous employment.'

'Aye. Right enough,' said Hannah. She scowled when she saw who was sitting with her mistress at the table. 'You behave yourself, McLevy. Ye're not in the station, now!'

The door slammed shut.

Another cup was poured, the aroma of the

coffee mixing with the faint sweet scent of the early blooms. Amongst her other attributes, Jean Brash had green fingers.

She indicated a newly planted shrub which had yet to show its wares. 'Maiden's blush,' she murmured. 'It will flower in summer. Blue-grey.'

McLevy took a deep breath and marvelled at his experience of life.

Not long ago he had stared death in the face and now he was looking at a beautiful, if morally flawed, specimen of femininity.

But whatever Jean's faults, at least she wouldn't be trying to lure him into a situation where he got his guts chopped up by an axe. He winced.

The lacerations on his stomach sustained from the encounter, despite his disclamations to Lieutenant Roach, still pained him. It had been touch and go.

'I have it on good account, you were the hero of the hour,' remarked Jean, who heard everything, eventually.

'That's the tale,' said McLevy. 'But one thing I may tell you for true. Sadie Gorman's death has been avenged. And the wee dollymop as well.'

'So all has ended in a blaze of glory,' Jean murmured.

His face clouded over.

'No. There is still one mystery. And I am still bound to a promise.'

They sat quietly together while a few insects took precarious flight and Lily laid her circlet of white daisies on Francine's black hair.

Innocence can be found everywhere but the

341

opposite is also readily available.

Good and evil. Entwined together. In the dance.

We do hope that you have enjoyed reading
this large print book.

Did you know that all of our titles
are available for purchase?

We publish a wide range of high quality
large print books including:
Romances, Mysteries, Classics
General Fiction
Non Fiction and Westerns

Special interest titles available in
large print are:
The Little Oxford Dictionary
Music Book
Song Book
Hymn Book
Service Book

Also available from us courtesy of
Oxford University Press:
Young Readers' Dictionary
(large print edition)
Young Readers' Thesaurus
(large print edition)

For further information or a free
brochure, please contact us at:
Ulverscroft Large Print Books Ltd.,
The Green, Bradgate Road, Anstey,
Leicester, LE7 7FU, England.
Tel: (00 44) 0116 236 4325
Fax: (00 44) 0116 234 0205

Other titles published by Ulverscroft:

THE RIVIERA EXPRESS

T. P. Fielden

Gerald Hennessey, silver screen star and much-loved heart-throb, never quite makes it to Temple Regis, the quaint seaside town on the English Riviera. Murdered on the 4.30 from Paddington, the loss of this great man throws Temple Regis's community into disarray. Not least Miss Judy Dimont, corkscrew-haired reporter for the local rag, the *Riviera Express*. Investigating Gerald's death, she's soon called to the scene of a second death, and, setting off on her moped, finds Arthur Shrimsley in an apparent suicide on the clifftops above the town beach. Miss Dimont must prevail, for why was a man like Gerald coming to Temple Regis anyway? What is the connection between him and Arthur? And just how will she get any answers whilst under the watchful and mocking eyes of her infamously cantankerous editor, Rudyard Rhys?